A MATE NEGLECTED:
SHADOW MOON SERIES – BOOK I

by

Cassie Smilez

DORRANCE
PUBLISHING CO
EST. 1920
PITTSBURGH, PENNSYLVANIA 15238

Dorrance Publishing Co
585 Alpha Drive
Pittsburgh, PA 15238
Visit our website at *www.dorrancebookstore.com*

ISBN: 978-1-6386-7266-1
eISBN: 978-1-6386-7617-1

DEDICATION

This book is dedicated to my unique support system, husband Andre, children Hayden Mckenzie, and Josiah Noel, who have lit my life with the brightest light one could ever ask for in one lifetime. I could never forget to mention my mother, Cassandra, who's critiqued, read, and never failed to amaze me with her imaginative insight while personally falling in love with the characters in my books. Because of her tenacity, my imagination held no limits. It was always a great time discussing characters with her as if it was the hottest gossip in the tabloids. Last but not least, my best friend, Alicia Dionne, my rock, lacks imagination but is plentiful in encouragement, love, and optimism. She may not have understood the supernatural world of werewolves, vampires, and witches, but she indulged in my writing, easily being captured by the real-life scenarios each character faced. John, you are aware of your value, or at least I hope you do! It's because of you that I ever completed that query letter in the first place. I could never thank you all enough!

ACKNOWLEDGEMENTS

Never in a million years would I have thought I would have written a book, let alone multiple. Yet, none of this would be possible if my mother, Cassandra Smith, sister, Letitia Signater, and best friend, Alicia Cannon, hadn't encouraged me to continue pushing forward. Each of them stood alongside me through every struggle and all my successes even outside of this book.

What can I say about my good friend, John Kremer, who has been a true force behind the interest of the opposite sex and as an unbiased reader. His input, encouragement, and consistency further energized the purpose of my writing. It meant so much to me because I always knew it wasn't his genre of choice, but he made it a priority because he's just that amazing, even if he never acknowledged it.

To my few social media readers who faithfully continue to stand by me through this process, know that you all are truly appreciated and always welcome to have an inside scoop into my imagination. Their attention to the text was valuable in this writing journey. You all are forever appreciated!

PREFACE

Nova is the daughter of the Beta for the Shadow Moon Pack. She is often misunderstood, so she is beaten, betrayed by those she once called family and friends and blamed for a horrible accident that has shaken the fate of her very existence. She is relentlessly harassed because of an accident that seemed to be her fault, leading to her best friend and mother betraying her.

Nova seeks refuge in the hopes of finding her mate to release her from the daily hell she endures. When she discovers who the Moon Goddess has fated her mate to become, she is terrified and disappointed, yet hopeful! With the help of some unforeseen allies, will she ever get an opportunity to redeem herself? Will her road of self-discovery end in tragedy? Will the past reveal a promising future for Nova and her allies?

CHAPTER 1: I AM WHO I AM

Shadow Moon Pack has a reputation of being powerful, ruthless, and loyal in all accounts. There's not many who have allied with us know us as a strong bond worth keeping. Besides the tough exterior, Shadow Moon is absolutely gorgeous and its leadership is fair and just.

My name is Nova Arabella Ryan. I am the daughter of the Shadow Moon Pack's Beta, Malachi Ryan and his wife, Naomi Ryan. I have a brother, Malik, and a sister Melody. Yes, I am the black sheep, ugly duckling, or dust mat, whichever is more fitting according to my pack. My pack HATES me! I have been silently and openly abused and tortured. I know what you are thinking, I should tell someone, right? I DID! Not only did they not believe me but gave me a beating and emotional abuse to top it off.

On top of that, I am permanently labeled as the pack's snitch. I have learned to cope in silence. I am not allowed to train with the rest of the pack because they cannot stand the sight of me. They think I am weak, pathetic, and a nerd (this part is true). I have tried fitting in only to be rejected in more ways than necessary. There have been rumors that the Moon Goddess has fated me to have a rogue as a mate after what happened. I mean, how else would you explain it?

I wear hand-me-down clothing and I am not afforded the opportunity to get a job or experience pack activities. I am literally the pack's slave. The Luna has tried investigating what was going on but I wouldn't know if it was genuine or not. She of all people has a good reason to hate me.

I prepare just about every meal, stack and fold the pack's laundry, and any odds and ends thing they could think of to torture me. My mom says that I have to do something other than lay on my back for the pack's Omegas. Boy, does she think highly of me. She looks at me in such disgust! I mean, I thought I was pretty long ago. In fact, I was told how I am blossoming into such a lovely lady but that changed after the incident.

I stand at about 5'6", long black curls that fall to the small of my back. My glowing tanned skin was flawless when it wasn't covered with dirt. My firefly green and hazel eyes and pouty lips used to make a statement when I was a kid. My dimples used to steal the attention of both the mated and unmated wolves. Yet, my mom looks at me as a mistake. I do not favor my mom as much as my older sister, Melody.

Even my father could not figure out why she could not stand the sight of me at times. He would die behind the love for her though so he began to search for flaws in me as well. My brother and sister definitely were no better! Sadly, I have heard my brother, Malik trying to sell my virginity to a few of his friends. This broke my already shattered heart along with the respect I had for him.

My brother does not refer to me as if I am not a person at all. And do not get me started with my sister. She has convinced all the other she-wolves not to talk to me or I would spread some infectious disease that I had acquired from sleeping with the rogues found on our territory just a few weeks ago.

No one will speak to me out of fear of being guilty by association. To even think that my mother is the main conspirator drives me nuts. I truly feel as if I have never done anything to make them treat me this way. Many thoughts of ending it all have crossed my mind. I was almost successful if it was not for a sweet girl, I am proud to call my dearest friend.

My ONE and only friend have been there for me through the good and the bad. Her name is Willow Lancaster. She is a petite girl that stands about 5'5" with dirty blonde hair with green eyes. She is beautiful if you asked me, but she is very modest about it. Willow is the daughter of the pack's Gamma, Emmitt. He was appointed after his brother Nathan's death. He and his wife Elena are really kind to me too.

There are these pretty cool guys named Matt and his best friend Jonah that have always been nice to me. At least they speak to me and occasionally sneak me goodies from town. It did not hurt that they were physically flawless. It was scary because they could pass for twins. Their perfectly chiseled tanned muscular bodies glistened even through their shirts. There was never a time they were not showing all thirty-two teeth. One had short wavy light brown hair with green eyes and the other had long curly light brown hair that was a tad bit higher than a fade with blue eyes. I love the fact that they are not big on hopping on the "Hate Nova" bandwagon.

I prayed to the Moon Goddess for one of them to be my mate. I had no preference because they are equally fine in my eyes. If I could not have either of them, I prayed that my mate would not be a part of this wretched pack.

Things were not always bad for me, in fact, I had a lot of friends and me and my family were close for the most part. I had to try twice as hard to please my mother because she was a bit standoffish from me.

There are rumors that she acts this way because she did not plan to have any more pups but ended up pregnant with me. The walking accident was my household name as me and my siblings grew older. Well, how do I begin to explain my super awesome life (note the sarcasm).

FLASHBACK
One day my best friend, Joy (Alpha's daughter), and I were playing in the fields of the pack territory when a rogue attack happened. Joy was the light of the pack. She could do no wrong in anyone's eyes, heck, not even mine. We were just pups then and were told to run. We did what we were told but we did not succeed.

A rogue grabbed Joy and slung her as if she were a rag doll into a huge boulder, knocking her completely unconscious. It was so much blood! My heart ached to see her in that state even if it was for a brief moment before I too was tackled by this horrible smelling ROGUE! I felt helpless, petrified, and lie there in complete shock. The rogue stood over me as he prepared to devour my flesh and spirit but he stood there as if he could not move. I could sense he was sniffing me as if I were familiar, but how? Before I could process what was happening, I blacked out completely shaken by my nerves.

When I finally woke from my slumber, I was told that I had been in a comatose state for three days by our pack doctor, Denise. I was later informed that Joy was not awake, in fact, they were afraid that she never would regain consciousness.

I was immediately discharged and sent home. I was expecting to be welcomed by my family's warm embrace. Boy, was I wrong! I was knocked to the floor by what I could only imagine was cast iron skillet. Mind you, I have yet to get my wolf (no fast healing for me). I should have known better because no one was at my bedside when I woke and apparently, I didn't have any visitors. Unfortunately for me, it was too late to reach that realization.

I felt every last blow to the head, stomach, and legs as I yelled for the beating to halt. I was choked until I blacked out AGAIN. Honestly, I tried fighting back, I really did. I was small, but I could not give up until I was hit from behind knocking me to my knees. I turn my eyes my father who had just walked through the door barely witnessing what had just transpired.

At this time, my feet were no longer on the ground. I was being carried to my bedroom with spouts of dry blood on my father's shirt. I heard echoes of an argument from a distance. My father was angry with my mother for the first time that I could remember. I blacked out again from the excruciating pain in my head.

I was woken up by a pail of ice-cold water being dumped over my head. To be honest, I could not wrap my mind on why my brother and his friend, Neko would do this. Where is my mother and sister while this happens? Turns out, my mother ordered that I be punished for embarrassing the family's name. This broke my heart. I knew she resented me, or I suspected it but I never wanted to admit it. Yeah, she was fairly nice to me in front of people, but my elder sister and brother were her heart and we all knew it. Yes, I am the baby of the family, but it is as if she did not want me here that part for sure.

When I got the news about two weeks post my hospital release that my so-called best friend had awoken. I was so elated! There would be at least one person I could be around that did not blame me for what happened. I run as fast as I can to the pack hospital only to be met by intense looks and to be physically thrown out on my ass. I had the opportunity to spot Joy who greeted me with a look of pure disgust and hatred! It HURT like hell because I didn't understand.

I found out later that she was the cause of too much of my pain but not all. Turns out when she was recovered from by the bolder, she was conscious.

Our Alpha and Luna were furious! She panicked and told them it was me who led the rogue to our lands and that I provoked the attack by calling out to them.

Oh, that is not all. She claims that I orchestrated it! That horrible lie spread through the pack like wildfire. I was only 12! No one cared if I were telling the truth because they adored Joy so much. She would never create such a lie, right?

Honestly, I genuinely believe our Alpha and Luna did not buy it because they never mistreated me even after that LIE! It was Joy's idea to play in that particular spot that day. I found it odd because we never played there before but I obliged anyway because she was my friend. It was all just coincidental, but I was blamed either way.

The last conversation I held with Joy was to ask her why she lied. She spit in my face and lunged at me to take her nails and dig them in the skin of my face. I proceeded to tackle her to the ground and punched her at least seven times before locking my hands around her throat. Even though nearby pack members witnessed the whole thing, they still sided with her. I was severely punished by a few pack members. I was cuffed with silver links and I was forced to smell of my own burning flesh until I passed out from the pain. So yeah, that is another reason why I am such an outcast. I nearly killed the Alpha's daughter in their eyes. It began to look as if I did orchestrate that rogue attack.

How could my own family and friends be so cruel to me? I had no one in my corner to protect me, to believe me, and no one to tell me this too shall pass.

To add insult to injury, Joy has not uttered many words to me since she attacked me. Instead of her telling the truth of what happened, she decided to jump on the bandwagon with everyone else. How could my best friend betray me like this? Was she afraid I would expose her secret?

I guess it is easier to discredit the person that could blow up your life. At this point, no one would even believe me. I know this because I tried pleading with my parents on what really happened that day and the events leading up to it. My mother threatened my life if I were to ever mention this again to anyone else. My father, the pack's Beta agreed like I knew he would. It was unlike him to go against my mother, his mate. He worshipped the ground she walked on.

Why on earth was I chosen to be the scapegoat? This was so unfair and I could not do much about it.

Eventually, I was banned from enjoying pack festivities and shunned by what felt like the entire pack. My father just assumed that I did not want to participate or I was afraid to. He did not push the issue either. My mother thought it would be a good idea to try and earn the pack's respect back by preparing all the meals and picking up extra duties for a little while. I was told to avoid the Luna at every cost. I was made to believe that the Luna could not stand the sight of me after losing her best friend, Nathan during the rogue attack and it was all my fault. It was not my fault and no one believed me. I was just as terrified of the happenings as well.

This extra duty idea was only supposed to be temporary, which turned into four years of slaving over a stove and carrying dirty laundry up and down five flights of stairs.

Our packhouse was huge! It was actually a mansion surrounded by beautiful gardens and obstacle courses. It sat just a few miles away from one of the largest water sources in our area. When you enter its gorgeous walls of the pack mansion it is decorated in modern coloring based off the time of year with furniture that seemed to be picked out of a magazine. The Alpha's family lived on the fifth floor and my father being the Beta, we lived on the fourth. I was always nestled off into a room a third of the size as my siblings'. It has been this way as long as I remember.

The pack's guest home alone was ten bedrooms that slept at least forty people. It was off-white in color with a wrap-around porch with porch swings to complement it. Both houses had their own personal pool and hot tub proponents accompanied by two huge outdoor kitchens. The rest of our pack lived lavishly on the pack grounds too. Everyone had to pull their weight around here but in the Alpha's mansion I pulled the weight of five people. It was really beginning to diminish my spirit watching everyone else over the years enjoying each other's company and partaking in the mansion's movie room, off-premises parties, and hooking up. I was not sure if I could take this much longer.

ALPHA KADE's POV

I have been the Alpha to this pack for over sixteen years and have never witnessed a rogue attack like this one. I lost one of my fiercest warriors and nearly lost my Luna and two of our pups. I am not really certain as to what happened but I am being told that we have a young pack member that's befriended rogues. I'm not sure I believe this to be entirely true.

If she were not the Beta's daughter, I would have banished her along with her rogue buddies if it were. My Beta has been my best friend for over 23 years, and he pleaded with me not to send Nova off packing. I just could not find it in my heart to do that to a child either. So, I agreed under the condition she was to stay on pack grounds until she could gain the trust of the pack again as we further investigate. It was never proven that she was the cause of the attack and my intuition was telling me otherwise as well. I hate to say it but I feel that my daughter, Joy knows more than she has led on. How do you force your daughter who had just experienced a traumatic event to tell you the truth? She would most likely assume I was blaming her. My Luna would never let me off the hook for that.

LUNA LEAH's POV

My husband, Kade and I both were afraid for our pup's safety and mine when that attack happened. I am the pack's Luna and I was carrying the soon to be youngest of the pack within my womb. When I was warned about the rogue attack in the courtyard my first instinct was not about my unborn pup but about protecting my pack, my family. Sometimes you just do not have time to think, you just react.

As I ran outside to find the commotion I shifted and strode into war. The rogue's eyes were greedy and they had an objective. I look over to see one of them towering over a young, scared Nova. It lifted her limp body off of the ground to begin carrying her away when I intervened causing him to drop her on the ground. A rock broke her fall when it smashed into her head.

As the fight progressed, I noticed the rogues were beginning to retreat. A rogue took me by surprise as it crashed into me. I sunk my teeth into the its neck almost immediately ripping its throat out.

My attention was redirected when I spotted a bloody and unconscious Joy lying next to the perimeter boulder. I saw RED! I went after every rogue that hadn't retreated that stood in my way to get to her. I attacked almost never taking my eyes off of Joy.

Witnessing my little girl lie lifeless in the field as I made my way to her felt like an eternity. I was distracted as I began to get attacked by three rogues at one time. Because I am a Luna, I have been gifted with the strength of two werewolves. I fought as long as I could until a fourth one joined the party.

Nathan, our Gamma at the time felt my exhaustion and came to my rescue. He was successful in freeing me from the pile. He fought with everything in him.

Nathan died that day at the hands of dark magic. One of the rogues shifted and doused him with wolfsbane and Mercury he had tied to his ankle. It was not meant for Nathan but for someone else. At least that's what we assumed.

ALPHA KADE's POV

We rushed Nathan, Leah, Joy, and her best friend, Nova to the pack hospital after killing the bold rogues that stayed behind. We kept one rogue from the attack in the dungeons. He could rot there for all I cared.

Then came the accusations of Nova's possible involvement from none other than her own mother. A young Malik and Melody sided with their mother out of fear of the repercussions. I wasn't completely buying it but I had no other witnesses.

Once the pack doctor cleared Leah, we received the news on Nathan's passing and his body was out away by some of our trusted warriors. We couldn't bear to see Nathan's lifeless body again. The wolfsbane and Mercury had moved twice as quickly through his bloodstream than normal. It caused him to have a heart attack.

Joy was knocked into a coma with the uncertainty of her ever-gaining consciousness again. I was furiously overwhelmed with guilt for not protecting my daughter.

Malachi asked about his daughter's current state and was relieved that she was expected to wake any day now and overall, she was fine. I would occasionally see him sneak away to pay her a visit as she slept. My Luna did the same.

LUNA LEAH's POV

As the Luna, it is my responsibility to nurture and care for those within my pack regardless of age or gender. I would often sit at both Joy and Nova's bedside in hopes that at least one of them would open their eyes. I would sit and have whole conversations with the two of them as I crocheted tiny items for my new baby boy still in my womb as I sat next to their bedside.

I was gentler with Nova. She was expected to wake before Joy and I knew she would blame herself for what happened to Joy. And to think her mother is the one who orchestrated the hate that was brewing against her daughter within the pack.

From this day forward, I vowed to keep a close eye on little Nova. On the fourth day, I went in to visit Nova, but was told she had gone home. I was happy to hear that she was okay, but a bit concerned that I had never seen any of her family here at her bedside other than Malachi who looked terrified. I decided to pay periodic visits to Malachi and Naomi's home. I made an excuse for teatime just to have a look inside to check on Nova.

That poor girl avoided me like the plague. On many attempts I have tried telling her that none of this is her fault but she is terrified of me. I have thought about ordering her to come to my office as the Luna, but I felt this would scare her into running away. I have just been a spectator in her life, always watching from a distance.

CHAPTER 2: SEVERAL REASONS WHY

NOVA's POV

There is so much more to the story. We lost our Gamma Nathan that day and nearly lost our Luna who was also pregnant. I was blamed because Joy would not wake up, our Luna nearly lost her pup, and to top it off, our Gamma died all trying to protect ME.

My pack members claim it is because the rogue was after something that I must have taken from them. You see, I have been chased by rogues at least twice before. I thought I was helping by venturing off to help my pack find the location of the rogues' hideout. Believe it or not (of course they did not) I found it! I warned my father and mother that I overheard the rogue leader mention attacking our border.

They were after something or someone but I could not quite make it out but they were desperate. Lady Luck was always on my side because each time I manage to be rescued by one of our pack warriors. I was already labeled as mischievous and irresponsible by the time I was six. The last attack happened when I was twelve. I used to be given praise by the male pack members and sometimes resented by the females but all in all, they loved to hear about my escapades until that horrible day. It is all my fault!

So, we have discussed the top two reasons why. Well, for the third, after the excruciating beatings started it became harder to keep up with the pack during training, my limbs just ached! I was labeled as weak, lazy, and a cry baby but I somehow knew my family knew I was a fighter. I was not used to this. Then there is the fourth reason. So, I began to cut myself because I felt I deserved to be punished. The scars on my wrist were very visible which caused me to be labeled as the pack's psycho. It was a cry for help!

I could not cope with the new nickname. So, I became very discreet when I made cuts in my flesh. I was a pro at concealing my scars. Eventually, Willow convinced me to seek help and I did. The pack's psychiatrist recommended a healthier outlet like running. Because I was not allowed to train with the pack, I basically trained myself before I began to train with Willow's father, Gamma Emit. The abuse became worst over the passing months but I never set there and took it.

"NOVA! Get your sorry ass down here and make our breakfast, now!" yelled my brother who easily towers over me standing at 6'3" with a muscular build.

Before I could turn the corner to the kitchen, my hair was pulled simply hard enough by the pack's real SLUT, Meyonna that I fell backward hitting the base of my neck. For a second I felt paralyzed and feared that I would never walk again. Why is she even in our house so early? Probably sucking Malik off I bet.

"You're so weak, NOVA!" Meyonna hissed at me.

"You are such an embarrassment to our family!" yells my sister, Melody.

Where did that come from? I wondered.

"There are days I cannot even look at you," Melody says staring directly at me. "When Kylo returns and I am his Luna, I will banish you! He is already aware!" Melody yells.

I muster up the strength to sit up and launch an attack for both Melody and Meyonna only to be kicked in the chest by my brothers' close friend Neko. The air leaves my chest as tears convulse uncontrollably from my eyes. "What is wrong with you people!" I yell.

The following day I wake around 5 A.M. to sneak in my seven-mile run then off to make the pack's breakfast and sneak and hide food later for my lunch. I am not allowed to eat until everyone is done and often times there is nothing left. If I am caught eating while cooking, I am held under scolding hot water for what feels like an eternity by one of my brother's friends. NEVER will I do that again! It was awful!

It has been times that his absolutely sick friend, Derek would smell my breath to ensure I have not taken a bite. I'm snapped out of my thoughts as my best friend joins me in the kitchen.

"What's for breakfast, No-No?" asks Willow with a smile.

"Food," I joked smiling back at her.

"Would you like some help?" Willow asked.

"I'm fine. Do you not remember the last time you helped me?" I asked arching an eyebrow.

"I am not afraid of him, Nova," Willow states confidently.

"You should be," I murmured.

"No one will mess with the Gamma's daughter because they understand the repercussions," Willow replied shrugging her shoulders.

"True," I agree chuckling.

"We will be sixteen in a few days and we may find our mates and maybe leave this place!" Willows says excitingly.

"Fat chance! I don't want anyone from this damn pack," I mumbled.

We both laughed at my comment. Willow knew what I was experiencing but I begged her not to tell her parents. I couldn't chance it getting back to Luna and my parents. They may kill me.

"Why is your sister so hung up on the idea that's she's Kylo's mate?" she asks.

"She feels that could be the only reason she has not found her mate yet," I sarcastically state.

"Ugh! That would be tragic for us all," Willow scoffed.

"Tell me about it. I would leave and never look back," I replied.

"Amen, sister, Amen!" Willow chanted.

"I wonder who my mate would be," I said a little above a whisper.

"Me too. Do you have your eyes on anyone?" Willow asked with a smirk.

"No!" I whisper shout.

"You're lying!" Willow replied.

"Look, let's just talk about how my bitchy sister may end up being our Luna," I giggled.

"Stop saying that! Kylo would be a dumb ass if his wolf chose her," Willow said making me laugh.

Honestly, I would not be surprised if my sister is the soon to be Alpha's mate, she is gorgeous. My sister stood at 5'5", hazel eyes, perfectly tanned skin, full lips, and slim build but curves in just the right places. She has golden locks that stretched right odd her shoulders. Not to mention, she is a badass fighter.

Melody walks with confidence and the other she-wolves are intimidated by the mere mention of her name. There is one big problem, Luna's duty is to take care of her pack members and be merciful, caring, and sympathetic when necessary. Melody was the exact opposite! She was vain, arrogant, and her tongue was lethal!

My mom praises her, though. She is legit a mini-Naomi in training. So, as for the fifth reason, no matter how hard she strives to, Melody does not intimidate me.

"Who knows, Nova, Kylo just maybe your mate!" she says giving me the side-eye.

"Have you lost your got damned mind, Willow?" I scream at her. "Do you not remember everything that he has done to me or stood by and let happen?" I say breaking down in tears just from the memory of Willow's family found me on the brink of death.

"I'm so sorry, Nova, but he's been gone for a couple of years and he could've changed," she keeps pressing.

"I don't care! If he's my mate I will run away and never come back. If they catch me, I'll beg for death. That would be doing me a favor," I added.

"It could save you, Nova! A mate will love and respect you, especially an Alpha's mate. The bond is much stronger than you imagine, I heard. Just don't freak out. Who knows, you could be destined to another in a different pack," Willow said grabbing my hand.

"Let's hope so," I replied with a sad smile.

Willow continued to remind me of how Kylo tried multiple attempts to apologize to me before he left, and I was not trying to hear it. I avoided him like the pestilence he was. He cornered me one day as I entered his room to grab his laundry. No one knows but Kylo tried to kiss me after I listened to his spill about how sorry he was. I smacked his face so hard and ran away as fast as I could. It was at that moment I could not even get Kylo to acknowledge my existence. He was so cold and shut off from me.

Kylo decided to congregate with his small crowd until his dad reminded him of his duty as the future Alpha. He was then shipped off to Alpha training prematurely. No one knows what transpired with us that day and I don't plan on them figuring it out either. They all just assumed he hated my guts along with the rest of the pack. *Go figure.*

"What are you looking at?" hissed Meyonna.

I just look down and finished my duties of cleaning the kitchen. To be honest, she has this weird stench to her this morning. Of course, if I mention it, I will have to tear up the kitchen I just worked so hard to clean from trying to kill her. Welp, looks like it is going to be a bad day for her. She was probably having a quickie with someone else's mate after a patrol.

"Such a slut," I mumbled not realizing I said it aloud until I felt a stinging sensation across my face from my very own MOTHER! "What was that for?" I managed to croak out.

"Someone as low as you should never speak to anyone in the pack that way," my mother spat.

"I'm your daughter and you're making up for that cunt?" I asked furiously.

"Watch your mouth!" my mother yelled.

"Seriously?" I asked storming outside of our house.

I was pissed! I was close to attacking my own mother. She would probably kill me but I didn't give a shit. She would be doing me a favor.

Meyonna's parents were awfully close to mine, seeing that her perverted father was one of our top warriors. The way he looks at his daughter is enough to know that something can't be right in their household.

Basically, the sixth reason being that my sinister mouth and thoughts are not always the greatest. I have no issues with getting reckless with my mouth. I'm never one to cower away from much. It doesn't stop them from wanting to break my spirit, though.

PRESENT DAY...

CHAPTER 3: MY PERSONAL HELL

NOVA's POV

After my intense training session with Willow and Gamma Emit, I can barely lift my arms and legs. I scurry back to pack mansion and start preparing breakfast for the pack. I easily prepare eggs, bacon, sausage, pancakes, biscuits, yogurt, fruit assortment, and oatmeal in bulk.

Oh, yes, I have to provide options according to my devilish mother. I swear she is worse even though she does not physically abuse me. Her manipulative ways begin to eat at your soul which is way worse. I will rather be punched in the face. Sometimes I watch how loving she is with my father and siblings and cannot help but wonder how she became so soulless when it came to me even before the attack all those years ago. My father never voiced it but I could tell he was suspicious as well. I didn't bother to give him the details as I felt my mother would just side with him either way.

Anyway, off to school. I throw my hair up in a messy bun, slip on my gray joggers and a graphic tee that said "Be a Kind Human," with my three-year-old black Vans. Because no one ever offers to give me a ride, and Willow walks our daily 5 miles to school. Willow could easily get a ride but she knew no one would want me to ride. Her parents were always busy with pack duties to notice.

We convinced each other that it will help us with our secretly improving fitness. We both laughed at the thought. Honestly, our once average bodies begin to slowly chisel themselves.

"Willow, what will you do if your mate is in another pack?" I ask a little above a whisper.

"I'm not sure. I don't want to leave the pack," she replied sadly.

"Will you reject him?" I asked.

"ARE YOU FREAKING KIDDING ME, NOVA?" she yells nearly startling me. "A mate is sacred and I would never dream of rejecting what the Moon Goddess blesses me with," she says in a tone of disbelief. "You?" she asked.

"I don't know. I hope he wants and adores everything about me honestly but I fear he would reject me." I sighed.

"Don't be silly, No-No, you are gorgeous, funny, and super nerdy smart. Not only that, you are brave and secretly a badass," she snarls as she nudges me.

It was then she noticed tears were falling from my eyes.

"What's wrong, No-No?" she asked worriedly.

"No one has ever called me pretty let alone gorgeous in the last almost four years," I respond.

Those compliments were reserved for my sister even as a young lady. Any attempt I ever made to look halfway decent always ended up in a scolding from our mother. She accused me of sleeping around many times when in all actuality it was one of Malik's friends, Neko sneaking in my bedroom trying to have his way. That jackass never succeeded and he never will.

"Thank you, Will," I responded embracing her in a bone-crushing hug.

"You're my best friend and I'm sick of you bringing yourself down. Don't ever dim your light so that others can shine brighter. You are a gift from the Moon Goddess herself. Don't you ever forget that, my badass friend," Willow said staring into my eyes.

"I won't and I promise whoever my mate will be I will be willing to try. I really do hope it's Matt or Jonah, though," I chuckled.

"YES! I'll take Jonah and you get Matt. That would be epic!" Willow exclaimed.

We finally make it to school, dang near running. We enter only to be scolded by Meyonna and her trolls, I mean her friends. Willow was never phased by their antics as she knew what she was capable of and the punishment they would receive if she ever came home with a scratch on her.

They tried bullying me because I had no one to come to my rescue. I shook off their nasty stares and went on about my day. I ran to grab my algebra book from my locker only to have my entire arm be slammed in my locker door which caused me to scream out in agonizing pain. Although I am hurt, no one saw what happened so they started chanting, "PSYCHO, PSYCHO, PSYCHO," all led by my dear brother and his dumb-ass friends. I can't believe Malik just slammed my arm in the locker.

I scurry to class trying to pretend that I wasn't hurt. I would be placing itching powder in his underwear drawer at the first opportunity. *Asshole.*

I will be graduating a year ahead of my peers and that makes a lot of my family more upset because I am now in the same grade as Melody. I outperform her by A LOT which is embarrassing. She's smart but doesn't apply herself as she feels as if she doesn't have to. What a dumb Luna she would be, I thought to myself.

Classes moved slower than usual. Lunchtime came and all I wanted to do is close myself in the janitor's closet and go to sleep. Instead, I walked to the cafeteria to have lunch. I always tucked myself in the back where most humans hung out. They were so oblivious to werewolf kind so I had no issues fitting in with them. I looked around and found a vacant table. It wasn't long before Willow spotted from across the room.

"I got you something!" Willow shouted embarrassing me.

"Are you crazy or do you just like to bring attention to yourself?" I laughed launching a piece of broccoli at her.

"Of course, I love attention. Can't get enough of it," Willow said sarcastically.

"Anyway, what did you get me?" I asked excitedly.

"It's a surprise for your birthday. I'll let you see it when it's time," she giggled.

"Come on, Will! You know I had a rough morning," I whined.

"Fine! Here you go," she said smiling.

"It's so pretty! Where did you get this?" I asked staring at the gold half-moon necklace.

"Put it on!" she exclaimed clapping her hands.

Willow helped me clamp it around my neck. I knew I should remember to hide it when I got home.

"So, you love it, huh?" she asked cheesing.

"Of course, I do! Thank you so much," I replied giving her a hug.

Malik, Derek, Neko, and Sloan were all walking by when we hugged. Why the hell are they even back here?

"I knew you two were bumping coochies," Neko said loud enough to embarrass us.

"You're just pissed because you can't find a coochie that wants you to bump with it," Willow replied with an attitude.

"You're lucky you're Gamma Emit's daughter or I would have ended your ass a long time ago," Neko said seething.

"Fuck you! Go find someone else to harass! You wouldn't want people knowing what you like to do on your lonely nights, now would you?" Willow asked hinting at his late-night trips trying to get me to sleep with him.

Just like she knew Neko would, he pulled everybody away with him. They were all busy laughing at his embarrassment but I knew it would further fuel his rage toward me. Why is he so obsessed with me?

"Let's go. I lost my appetite," Willow said rolling her eyes.

"I'm done anyway," I said looking down at my empty tray.

We walk out into the school courtyard after we dump our trays. You see all sorts of cliques coming to this school on a daily basis. Even human females are talking about Kylo as if they actually have a shot with our Alpha. They don't know there are werewolves amongst them but there have been some pretty close encounters.

"Hello? Earth to Nova!" Willow shouted snapping her fingers in front of my eyes.

"What's wrong?" I asked looking dumbfounded.

"I was asking about our birthday. What do you want to do? My father said he will take us off the territory to wherever we like. He's already gotten clearance from Alpha Kade and your father," Willow said.

"That's amazing but you do remember the Alpha Ball is coming up. I have to help the omegas with the plans." I sighed.

"You shouldn't have to. You're a freaking Beta Female. Like it or not you have a rank. It's your birthright," Willow replied.

"I know but I really enjoy the wine gas company. Our head omega, Mrs. Walker is like an actual mother to me. She ensures I'm fed and that I don't end up working too hard in the kitchen," I confessed.

"Fine, but I'm helping you guys." Willow smiled.

The bell rang for our next period. Willow and I parted ways and I headed to the gym. I hated this class simply because I shared it with my sister.

"Hey, loser! I thought you were getting your class switched," Melody said with a quizzical look on her face.

"I never said that," I simply replied looking down as I tied my shoes.

"You should," she retorted still hovering over me.

"Can I help you with something?" I asked annoyed.

Melody laughed and walked away. She didn't waste any time slamming the door behind her.

"You're lucky it was Melody you were talking to. If it were me, I would've flattened your skull," Meyonna said flaunting her too-little gym shorts.

"Sure, you would," I snicker.

"Don't test me, bitch," she said getting dangerously close to me.

"Why would I do that? You'd do what you always did with the test, fail it," I replied fighting back my own lighter.

She tried to smack me across my face but I caught her hand mid-swing.

"If you ever lay another finger on me, I will fucking kill you in your sleep," I threatened.

"Everybody is right. You are a psycho!" she echoed stepping away from me.

She looked horrified for whatever reason. It didn't take long for her to exit the locker room and leave me in my thoughts. She-wolves rarely tried putting their hands on me.

SHIT seems to always roll downhill...

CHAPTER 4: FUTURE ALPHA

NOVA's POV

Today is the day! Our future Alpha, Kylo returns. These last two years he has been in Alpha training preparing himself to take over from his father, Alpha Kade. Everyone is all excited but I am hoping to avoid him at all costs.

Kylo is probably a bigger douche bag than he was before he left, I think as I roll my eyes. He is expected to assume some of his Alpha duties from his father within the next few months.

I have not seen or spoken to him since he left, not like he would find himself associated with me either way. Okay, so yeah, I have had a crush on him since we were pups but once the abuse started, I developed a strong sense of hate for him. I used to low-key burn a hole through the back of his head from my lingering stare. No judging!

All that changed the years ago. I was probably the only she-wolf that was no longer attracted to him in that way in the pack. I have no intentions of greeting him when he makes it home either but they will most likely make it mandatory. I am sure the witch, Melody, and that cunt, Meyonna will be there damn near dropping their panties for him. Good for them, I think out loud.

Melody had already declared herself as our next Luna and promises to get rid of me will as her first declaration. If Kylo listens to her and decides to banish me then so be it. I will pack my bags ahead of time and head for the bus station with no regrets other than leaving Willow and her family since they've been so kind to me.

KYLO's POV

I am really happy to see my pack after these last two years of Alpha training. I must have been acquainted with every Alpha and soon-to-be Alpha across this entire continent by now. It was exhausting, to say the least.

My mentor and I have hoped through our many packs visit I would have found my mate by now. An Alpha needs a Luna to properly lead a pack and tap into those fiercely gifted Alpha genes. No such luck on my end. My last hope is maybe she's in Shadow Moon already. Many would jump at the opportunity but I'm very selective. Leadership is my primary task and I can't have a bimbo leading at my side.

Yeah, I have had my fun with the local she-wolves but I feel nothing remotely close to how the mate bonds are explained to be. Our Beta's daughter, Melody is convinced she is my mate and I would not mind that one bit but her attitude sort of sucks. She is beautiful though but that may not be enough. We would work on that if she is in fact, my mate.

Anyhow, I cannot wait to hang out with my boys once I make it back. I need to have a serious conversation with them about the rumors I hear about them torturing one of the pack members. It is not what I want my pack to be about. Clearly, a lot has changed while I was away.

"You don't say, dumb ass," my wolf Jax interrupted.

"I liked it better when you were quiet asshat," I reply.

"If you don't find our mate soon, you'll be alone, dick!" he retorted.

"You're nothing without me," I laugh.

"Neither are you, dumb ass," Jax growled.

"I know that but if I don't find my mate I may as well not be an Alpha," I said stating facts.

"I'm not arguing with that. It's your own fault, though! If you wouldn't have been sticking your sausage in every bun you came across, we would have found her by now!" Jax growled again.

"I slept with three people and now I'm a man whore. Funny coming from a horn dog," I retorted.

"I quit," Jax said cutting off our link.

He was such a drama queen. It's best when he's quiet instead of giving me a damn headache.

NOVA's POV

After finishing breakfast, well, after the pack finished breakfast, we were mind-linked by Alpha Kade to meet for assembly.

"As you all know my son will be returning home in a few days. We must ensure his arrival is without disappointment," he all but yells.

"Then shove Nova in the fire pit!" yelled my brother's dim-witted friend, Neko.

If looks could kill, Neko would have died right there where he stood. Our Alpha did not tolerate ignorance of any sort. He quickly shut the hell up.

With that being said, the planning for the Alpha Ball preparations was underway. For just one night and one night only I could be like all the other she-wolves. I am sure they will be locked in on Kylo and too busy to torment me. I am low-key excited! I asked Willow's mom to help me find a dress.

My mother was displeased by this and I couldn't care less. So, she threatened me to look presentable and begged me to not embarrass the family with my silly antics. After all, I am the daughter of our pack's Beta (rolls eyes). I strategically planned our trip to town around the time Kylo is expected to return. I don't want to be in the crowd when he arrives. Kylo would probably make an example of me in front of the pack.

NEXT DAY

Willow came to my room squealing like a young schoolgirl as I was hopping out of the shower.

"WHAT THE F—" I yell before realizing it was her.

"I'm sorry, Nova! I am just so excited Kylo is coming home!" she squealed.

"Ugh, not you too," I say as I roll my eyes.

"Look, what he did to you was a long time ago, No-No. I'm sure he regrets it. I could see it in his eyes before he left," she says with her lips in a straight line.

"Whatever! I'm not mad anymore," I say nonchalantly.

In all honesty, I plan to avoid him at all costs, BUT I should still look presentable, right? RIGHT! I throw on my only pair of decent blue jeans, a white t-shirt, and my princess flats. Sounds plain but I have to work with what I have. I threw on some mascara and rosy pink lip gloss. I cannot do the powdery or liquify face mud as I call it. I let my big bouncy black curls free for the first time in months as I throw my rosy pink cross body bag across my shoulder. Yeah, I will explain that later. With that, we were out of the door for school.

Willow decided to sport her navy blue wedge heels with a ballerina-style sundress that had the most beautiful colors in it. She went all out with the eyeshadow too with just enough tint to her eyes to accent her entire ensemble.

"You pinned your hair up like you're preparing for a ballet showcase," I chuckle.

"Really, NOVA!" she grimaces.

"What I meant to say is, DAYUM, BARBIE!" Willow shouted.

We both laugh uncontrollably at this. My best friend always knew how to lighten the mood.

"Nova, I like seeing you happy like this," Willow says as tears swell in her eyes.

"Me too, girl, me too," I say as I give her a bone-crushing hug.

Did I forget to mention that Willow and I share a birthday? That day happens to be today! Because today is such a special day her dad gave us a ride to school before handling an issue for the Alpha.

So, the story behind the curls, I used to wear my hair out A LOT. I did not used to dress like a bag lady either. One day while sitting in the courtyard socializing with the school's outcast as they call them, I was caught off guard by a negative vibe from across the yard. I was completely minding my own business. I noticed this guy staring at me for a while but I ignored it. His girlfriend got mad at me and attacked me. She claimed that I seduced her mate. After spewing curse words at me and saying that I am an ugly witch whose head should be shaved, she hit me. I was shocked at what I was hearing because her mate was the one staring at me. I grabbed on to her hair for dear life not realizing I was nearly digging into her skull. I left her nearly bald out of an act of desperation. No matter who tried to pry us apart it didn't work. I was angry and there was no way I would walk away disrespected by the likes of her. It is funny now but it was not then. I just did not want to take the chance that someone would do that to me. So, messy bun or braid days it has been since. I actually earned the respect of a lot of people that day because that skank was flat out mean and nasty!

I keep my eyes low at school to avoid anything like that from happening again. Did I mention the guy staring at me was one of my brother's torturous friends, Neko? Since then, he has done everything in his power to make my life a living hell because of his sick crush on me and his jealous mates' insecurities. Did I mention that she's not even his fated mate?

So, why do I further want to avoid us soon to be Alpha? He lied and told everyone I offered him my virginity in exchange for popularity. He apologized in private, of course, but I was too devastated to forgive him. I knew he did it just to cover for himself. Up until he left, I have never spoken to him since not that he seemed to mind anyway. The bad thing about it all, we were actual friends when we were younger. Let us set the record straight, I am a virgin and I am saving myself for my mate which of whom I pray will save me from my personal hell.

CHAPTER 5: NIGHT OF THE BALL

NOVA's POV

As the preparations for the ball continue, I find myself scrummaging through Willow's mom's closet for a dress that fits me instead of going to town. Unfortunately, no such luck. Why did I wait so last minute? Well, in between slaving to clean the whole packhouse, secretly training, school, and setting up Kylo's room for his arrival I have not had much free time for myself.

Willow's mom thought it would be a good idea to visit the town's thrift store as we originally planned. Hey, beggars cannot be choosers and I was DESPERATE. We left the pack premises right as what looked to be Kylo's caravan pulling in. It was three large Denali SUVs with blacked-out windows. I rolled my eyes at this.

After driving for about 25 minutes, we arrive outside the thrift store's parking lot. I noticed its sign said "HELPING HANDS." That is cute, I thought, because I needed all the help I could get. We walk in the store as the bell rang as it closed behind us alerting the store clerk of our arrival.

"Yes, can I help you?" she asks with a Cheshire cat smile on her face.

"We are looking for a formal gown for a ball," Willow interrupted.

"That's exciting!" she exclaimed.

She could tell I had doubt written all over my face after 45 minutes of searching. The only dresses I managed to come across made me look like a church elder, no offense. BUT there it was! It was a silver yet white dress with sparkles filling its appearance from the top down. Nearly the whole back was revealed with a single cubic zirconium chain-link leading to the very top of the buttocks. The front revealed just enough cleavage to keep ogling eyes guessing. It is separated my breast just enough to have the straps hug my shoulders. I was happy about this since it would hide my horrible scar thanks Neko. Yeah, I'll explain that later.

Anyway, the dress bypassed my feet in a small flare while the rest of the dress fit every curve, I did not know I had. The only problem is the cubic zirconium link was missing a few stones and there was a hole in the hip area. No wonder it was sent here. Either way, we can patch the hole and hope no one recognizes the missing stones.

I cannot wait to see the looks on the pack's face when they realize I am not that same scrawny she-wolf they have known for so long. My arm, leg, and stomach muscles were definitely present! OKURRR! Hell, I was impressed and I do not even think I am that pretty.

"It's gorgeous!" I whimper.

FLASHBACK

So, about that scar... right after the incident happened with Joy and I being attacked by rogues, the pack began its emotional abuse. At first, I tried to ignore them but that just provoked them to graduate to physical abuse. I was pretty much alone those days, no one wanted to be associated with such a disgrace. One evening as I sat alone on the packhouse steps I was dragged off by my brother, his friend, Neko, Kylo, and a few other stooges. They called me names, spit at me until I could not ignore it anymore! I lunged at Neko (the one that spits in my hair) and nearly dug his eyes out of the socket before I was dragged off by none other than my brother and Kylo. I yanked away and Kylo let my arm go as my brother held tighter and later pushed me to the ground. Neko could not get over the embarrassment so he pulled out a SILVER envelope opener. Malik and Neko gave each other the most heart-wrenching grin I have ever seen to this day.

Before I knew it, I was hobbled over from the slit on my neck where they cut me as I began to ooze blood. I listened to my brother say, "You will never find your mate and we will make sure of that. What makes you think your mate would want damaged goods like you?" as he grimaced with such evil present in his eyes.

Yes, he gashed my neck deeply where my MARK from my MATE will one day be. I highly doubt this would be possible now. Just a little fact, your mate marks you on a very specific spot on your neck signifying you are THEIRS. I could hear Kylo and the others yelling.

"Werewolves don't heal from silver, you idiots. What were you two thinking?" Kylo shouted.

I remember seeing Kylo yanking the tool away and launching it in the woods before I passed out. I just saw blackness before I woke to the most beautiful woman which so happened to be Willow's mother.

This is where I first met Willow and her mother as she held me tight as our Gamma treated my scar. They asked me who did this to me but I refused to say anything because no one would believe me anyway, this so much was proven. This much is even true today but I know I have true allies in Willow's family now. The Gamma was outraged! He wanted to make a public announcement of whoever did it would be severely punished by 50 wolf-bane lashes which they would most likely not survive. I hated them but I did not feel they needed to DIE!

That was the day I felt I could love. I wouldn't want to face rejection as I feared I would experience when the time came. I'm bruised, beaten, and nearly broken. I HATE my brother! I HATE them all!

How could you not protect your little sister? Our Gamma did inform the Alpha of what happened which led to the announcement being made anyway and completely out casting me even further. Like I stated earlier, I was already labeled the pack's snitch! They didn't lash them with wolfsbane but they were in solitary for three weeks. They were a hot mess by the time they were set free. The abuse stopped for months only to start up worse. It's like they grew bored or something. Neko was the ringleader this time, though. I think he's convinced I'm his mate. Oh, Moon Goddess, say it isn't so.

PRESENT DAY
My hair was in knots from the constant messy bun routine but Willow was all over it!

"Don't you worry, No-No. I got you covered!" she said was so much excitement.

"You always do." I smiled.

"My day was shitty," she blurted out.

"How so?" I asked surprised.

"Don't worry about it. Tonight, is your premiere," she chuckled sadly.

"Will, what's wrong?" I pushed.

"Nothing, I promise! My day was crappy because I didn't do so well on my chemistry test," she replied.

"You're lying," I simply said.

"I don't like you right now. You know me too well," she chuckled.

"Tell me," I demanded.

"I promise I will tomorrow," she replied.

"Okay," I replied dropping the subject.

Because it is our 16th birthday today, we were hoping to discover our mates. Well, Willow was excited. Werewolves were summoned from all over the continent to attend this ball. It would be at least seven different pack Alphas, Betas, Gammas, Lunas, and at least six of their best warriors in attendance to the Alpha Ball tonight. It has to be nearly 2000 guests invited. Tonight will be the best chance of finding our mate tonight than we will ever have. A small part of me is really hoping if I did find my mate, he's in a different pack.

I decided to head back to my room for an hour nap. I was awakened by a small voice in my head.

"Hello, Nova," the serene voice said.

I thought someone was trying to torment me through our werewolf mind link. Honestly, they blocked me off the link quite often so that thought left me quick. I did not respond because I thought I was losing my damn mind at this point. Until it came back.

"I'm Amethyst. I'm your wolf," it said.

"What, how, huh?" I asked with confusion.

No one ever explained to me what it would be like to get your WOLF. So, you could imagine that I think I'm going batshit crazy.

"Don't worry, Nova. We will meet soon enough," it said with a little arrogance and joy in her voice.

"What do you mean?" I asked quizzically.

"I am you and you are me and we will be one when the moon is at its highest peak tonight when we meet our MATE," she said with so much excitement.

"Well, it's nice to meet you, Amethyst, and I can't wait to meet either of you," I say as I fall into a deep slumber.

I may have lied about meeting my mate but gaining my wolf and hearing how excited she almost gave me hope.

AGAIN, I am woken up. This time it was my devilish mother and sister trying to make sure I did not embarrass them tonight. They claimed to have come and help me get myself together for the ball. FINE TIME!

"I am okay, Mom, dear sister. I will not embarrass you," I stated sarcastically.

"Where's your dress?" my mom asks.

"I will not be getting dressed here, Mother," I replied.

I have people that actually care for me helping me, is what I wanted to say but instead, I respond by shrugging my shoulders. She launches a dull blue dress at me that was at least two sizes bigger than my actual size 4; however, the shoes fit perfectly. She offered to quickly take in my dress but I told her I had it covered.

"Promise me, Nova, you will look presentable?" she asked with almost concerning eyes.

"I promise, Mother, I will do my best not to embarrass the family any further. Who knows, I could possibly meet my mate tonight," I say with fake joy and confidence.

With that came two loud giggles followed by tears from both of their evil faces.

"Hun, you can't meet your mate until you're sixteen," my mother states clearly unaware that my birthday is today.

"Don't you know anything?" Melody asked.

I am genuinely HURT but not at all surprised. When they left, I fell to the floor as I sobbed while saying, "I'm weak, I don't matter, I'm ugly, I'm pathetic, and no one will ever truly love me!" It is like a constant reminder that I am an outsider. I rush to the bathroom to begin to CUT when that voice came back.

"NOVA, please don't do this to US. We are beautiful, we are loved, we do matter, and we will be free tonight because MATE is here!" Amethyst yelled making me nearly stumble over in the tub nearly hitting my head.

Luckily, I caught myself between the sink and the toilet. "Well, that was embarrassing even though it was just me," I said with a smirk.

NAOMI's POV

Everything came together for our young Alpha's celebration. Luna Leah and I spent countless hours to ensure EVERYTHING was what it should be. From table settings to the menu was all coordinated by us. I had to put on a united front and place Nova at our table even though I knew she would not be happy about it. I still feel there is a part of her that desires our acceptance. I'm snapped out of my daze when I see Melody's jaw drop, figuratively.

When I notice Melody's reaction looking toward the door, I follow her eyes nearly choking on my wine as I see a scared-shitless Nova dressed in an exquisite dress. It was fitting every curve she was born with thanks to me. For the first time in a while, I noticed she elected to wear her curls down. I nod in approval at her.

"She is a spitting image of...," I stopped realizing I said it out loud.

"YES, NAOMI, she looks so much like you when you were her age," Meyonna's mother Terri said nudging me with a cackle.

I feel that Nova has brought so much shame to our family name it is hard for me not to be hard on her. I would have assumed that she would have accepted my idea to ship her off to this school I have heard so much about in the countryside. My husband Malachi was against it. He said it would make us look like a family divided and we needed to figure it out on our own. Besides, he would miss her too much. He didn't understand why I needed her to stay hidden.

Malachi is never here because he is so preoccupied with Beta business, especially rogue attacks have increased recently and peace treaty renewals were on the rise. I'm sure that's how I get away with my behavior.

Nova is a constant reminder of heartbreak and a dark time in my life. I did not want any more children. I was devastated when I found I was pregnant with her. I guess I somehow blamed her.

Malachi adored her and he hoped I would grow to love her as well. Do not get me wrong, I love Nova. I am always agitated or angry at her because she was me at one time in my life.

In some cases, she does remind me of a younger version of me but she was not supposed to be here constantly reminding me where I went wrong. The thought alone irritates me. I need to shift my focus to something that matters right now, such as helping Melody lockdown Kylo before it is too late.

Melody deserved to be the next Luna of this pack. If she could bear Kylo's pups before he finds his mate, she is a shoo-in. I had to call on one of my old friends that dabbled in a little black magic. I wanted to create a mate bond between Kylo and Melody. Because it is sacred, the fake bond would be temporary and destroyed once Kylo's fated mate surfaces. I am willing to get rid of his fated mate if I ever find out who she is. My plan is already in motion and I will not fail.

CHAPTER 6: LET'S DO THIS

Before the ball...
KYLO's POV

Shadow Moon us always been my home and I had every intention of making it even better when I took over as Alpha. My fellow pack members were celebrating me tonight. I was grateful but a simple quiet dinner would have sufficed. I'm a simple werewolf.

I arrived at the packhouse about six hours before the main event. I am excited because my wolf, Jax told me my mate is here. We pull up in three blacked-out Denalis and before I could get out of the car good Jax was losing his mind!

"MATE is here,"' he kept repeating.

I catch the scent of pure vanilla and caramel whisk past my nostrils. It is the sweetest smell I have ever encountered in my entire life. It smelled like a bakery when they first rake their fresh batch of banana nut muffins from the oven. I was hypnotized by my mate's scent and she didn't even know it yet, or does she?

As my wolf continues to lose his mind as we try to follow that delicious smell, I am bombarded by these overly zealous she-wolves. It was clear what they all had on their mind other than becoming the next Shadow Moon's Luna. Unfortunately, I had no interest in anyone other than the one the Moon Goddess promised me.

"Welcome home, Kylo!" they all seem to say in unison.

"Hey, babe, long time no see. I'm looking forward to RIDING you for a LONG time like the old days," said the pack slut, Meyonna.

"Yeah and no," I simply replied as I strode past her.

I am not even sure why I ever slept with her. She was honestly something to do back then. We were friends hanging out one night until we turned into her buddies. If I had known I would be her first I would have never crossed that line. She has been chasing me ever since. It is not my fault she wanted to do something strange for a piece of change. I was young and dumb. If I could undo it I really would.

"Hi, honey! I'm so excited to have you home, sweetheart!" my mom says embracing me in a tight hug.

"I'm happy to be home too. You and Dad look younger." I laugh.

"Laugh all you want but I sense some truth in that," my father replied.

"I really mean it, though. You guys look happy," I added.

"Nice save," my mother said roping her arm within mine.

I have missed my mother the most. I will go to hell and back behind that woman.

"Young Alpha, are you ready?" my dad asked.

"I am as ready as I'm going to be! I have so many ideas for the pack!" I nearly yell in excitement.

"I can't wait to hear about them all. Your instructors kept us updated on your progress while you were away. You graduated top of your class. We are proud of you, son," my father replied.

My father gave me an approving pat on the back before pushing past onlookers. It was good seeing how happy everyone was and how well our territory had been kept up. I shook hands, gave kisses, and hugged a lot of my pack. When I approached my best friend, Malik he was standing next to his sister. She quickly became bashful.

"Hey, Kylo, how was your ride up?" Melody asks completely ignoring the moment I am having with my parents.

"It was peaceful," I replied.

"Ignore her. Welcome back, buddy!" Malik said giving me a half-hug you give a brother.

"Thanks, man. Stop being mean to your sister," I replied shoving his chest.

"She's used to it," he says shrugging his shoulders.

"How was the Alpha Academy? I heard it's brutal," Melody said still trying to create a conversation.

"I'll catch up with you later. I'm sure my dad will want to discuss our duties as Alpha and Beta," I replied sending them a wave goodbye.

Could Melody be my mate? But her scent is of citrus and lavender. It is nice but it is not her. My wolf would've probably jumped her if it were her. Too bad because I think she is stunning, but a bit rude. I just had to laugh to myself before realizing I never responded to her question.

"It wasn't too bad," I finally respond locking eyes with her as I walked further away. I could see the disappointment and disgust in her face as I walked away with my parents taking four of the pack members with us.

"So much has changed," I said in awe.

"All for the better." My mother smiled.

I didn't suddenly forget our pack was feared among many. We have one of the largest and lethal packs in our region.

We trained hard, took our studies seriously, and placed emphasis on pack loyalty. This brings me to the realization that I have some apologizing to do to my best friend, Malik's little sister, Nova. I was so mean to her sometimes or I just ignored her. Maybe my pride couldn't get over her rejection after I kissed her that day. While I was gone, I asked of her often and I was met with horrible truths. They would say she was whoring around, refused to train, and preferred slumming it with the omegas in the kitchen. My intuition told me otherwise. Now that I think about it, was she at my welcome home greetings? If so, I must have looked over her.

I should have intervened when she was being bullied by her own brother and my cousin, Neko. I was young and I did not want to interfere in family matters. I wonder if she is around here these days. I did not want to ask about her and my parents make it a big thing.

"Have you given any thoughts of finding your Luna, son?" my father asked as he stopped in his tracks. "An Alpha can tap into his full power when he has his Luna by his side providing guidance, love, and balance in his life and for the pack," he went on to explain.

I decided not to announce that my Luna is already here and I planned to make her MINE tonight.

"I've given it a lot of thought," I simply replied.

"You know there's always match-making that could create solid treaties among other packs if you agree," my father said looking between me and my mother.

"No! I want who I was promised by the Goddess herself even if it means I have to delay taken over as Alpha," I replied confidently.

"Okay, son. Just promise me that you would consider it if you haven't found her by your 20th birthday," my father pushed.

"Let me think about it," I said trying to drop the conversation.

Now to get ready for tonight. I made it up to my room only to be met with nothing but a warm welcome. There were so many scents in my room that I couldn't focus but one scent was familiar vanilla and caramel. I looked around the room at the four she-wolves and indiscreetly tried to sniff them. This was going to be a long night.

MELODY'S POV

There he stood at a 6'4", muscular build, sapphire blue eyes, chiseled jaw line, perfectly tanned skin, jet-black curly hair, and that GOT DAMN pearly white smile and those dimples! JESUS, this man looks delicious just as he did when I last saw him! I want to put him on a plate of syrup and eat him like a biscuit! The things I have imagined letting him do to me over the years is enough to make me repent. I would not mind tasting every part of his infrastructure! Anyway, I did not sense that he was my mate which was disappointing. When I told my mother, she was highly disappointed.

"Sahara, why isn't he our mate?" I ask my wolf.

"He is NOT our mate. His wolf, Jax told me that his mate is here but it isn't us," she added.

Who could this mystery mate be? I wonder too aloud to myself. Well, she better watch out because I am pulling out all the tricks tonight. He will be swimming in my juices tonight, PERIOD!

MEYONNA'S POV

All those feelings came rushing back at once. MAN, Kylo used to give me the business three years ago as a young she-wolf. I could only imagine what that mouth would do now that he's fully grown. I swear that man has had his way with every hole on my body. I am not going to lie; I was more than sprung behind him. He got the gift that makes you want to say, "Stick it in my stomach, my ear, my ass, my forehead," anywhere you want to, baby! Not to mention, his stroke was unmatched. He also made my throwback game what it is today. I miss that so much and I want it.

Too damn bad that he is not my mate, but it is not going to stop me from sitting on his face later, BET! The way he used to spread my ass cheeks to go deeper while he pulled my hair toward him simultaneously smacking me on my ass made me feel like he had eight freaking arms. Oh, do not get me started on how tight he hugged my small waist as his strokes became brutally satisfying. No one satisfies me the way he did. I am talking tears involuntarily falling from my eye's kind of sex. He taught me how to ride the waves of orgasms too. Had a bitch being obedient, "Yes, Daddy!" Just the thought of old times has my core crying oceans right now. Ugh, he is MINE! Melody is one of my best friends but I wasn't going to share him with her. I don't care what I would have to do.

CHAPTER 7: TONIGHT, IS THE NIGHT

NOVA'S POV

As I sit in front of the mirror watching Willow perform a miracle on my hair, I cannot help but think that I may find my mate tonight.

"Willow, can you make it perfect?" I ask.

"You're already perfect, Nova." She smiles. "You have to wear that confidence, your outer appearance may seem flawless, but if you're battling internally it doesn't matter, do you understand?" she asks while telling me.

"How did my little friend get so wise?" I asked while judging her with my elbow.

Welp, after about an hour doing hair and makeup we slide into our dresses and take one last look before walking out of the door. I decided to let my long black locks stay down. I had Willow pin my bundled curls to the left side of my face flow down the front to my shoulder, completely leaving one side of my neck exposed. We arrive about thirty minutes into the ball. Willow changed her dress last minute to a strapless emerald mermaid-type dress that exposed her obliques all while also complemented her eyes. She had her entire neck and shoulders exposed and she added her sparkly moon and star necklace to draw attention to her flawless neckline. When we walked in, it did just that. I cannot lie, we were killing it but so were the other she-wolves. There were dress types of all sorts and colors. Everyone looked amazing! My face immediately turned to one of disgust as I noticed Neko with his mouth wide open as he eyed me, clearing dry-humping me with his stare.

"UGH," I said before I realized it seeped out.

"What's wrong?" Willow asked.

"Neko," I hissed.

"Ignore that pervert," she replied and I agreed.

After disregarding Neko's revolting stare, I realized that Willow and I had the attention of nearly the entire ballroom. I must have been beet red if that were possible, but Willow took this opportunity to strut in like "I look good and I know it" attitude. Me on the other hand, I could not get my feet to move. I stood there looking like a statue because of my level of comfortability.

My mother, Melody, and Meyonna, and her parents were huddled around their table enjoying each other's company. As I stood there glued to the floor, I saw Meyonna nearly trip over her chair trying to whisper something in Melody's ear that caused her to shoot angry eyes over at me. When my mother saw her reaction, she too turned in my direction, clearly impressed with my choice of attire. She would never applaud me for it, though, because she is just a hateful person. I have to admit, it felt good to be noticed and feel the jealousy that radiated off that entire table.

"NOVA! You ready break some necks tonight or not?" Willow interrupted apparently ready to make her way through the crowd.

"Break necks, huh," I laughed as I proceeded in her direction. "I just have one thing I need to do first," I tell Willow.

She watched as I strutted to the table where my family's seats were reserved and removed my name from it. I wasn't in the mood to pretend with my horrible family.

"Nova," my mother greeted me.

"Mother," I nodded returning pleasantries and walked away.

I could feel their eyes burning in the back of my head as they watched as I placed my name on Willow's family's table. I had no regrets about it either.

"You go, girl!" Willow exclaimed hardly containing her excitement.

I turned and gave her a wink before walking back in her direction. Before we departed for the ball, our Gamma Emit and his wife Elena agreed to let me move with them. I am hoping I can get my father, Beta Malachi to agree. I can't take the abuse anymore. I just cannot.

After I made my power moves that I am sure I will have to pay for later, Willow and I were on our way to the dance floor. We walked past so many others. Willow did not exaggerate when she said we would break necks tonight. Some looks were of pure jealousy and others were silent kudos on our hair, makeup, and dress choices. I was so distracted that I accidentally bumped into Joy and Malik on the dance floor. Malik shot Willow a guilty glance and she dropped her head and tried pulling me away.

"Are you blind, you dumb broad?" Malik yelled loud enough for me to hear over the music.

"My apologies, I did not notice you standing there, ass clown," I said with a huge smile on my face.

"Ignore him. He's a promiscuous jerk!" Willow shouted over the music and we kept walking.

"Did he do something to you, Will?" I turned and asked.

"NO! Trust me, it is I he should hate. All positive, I promise."

"I'll drop it for now," I said pouting.

I was ready to fight at any moment at this point. I am sick of being a push-over. It was either they fight me or leave me the hell alone. Willow stood next to me with her arms folded like "I dare you!" as we stood across the room. Joy just stood there with a nasty look on her face followed by her rolling her eyes and pulling Malik deeper into the crowd.

"She's such a brat," I said to Willow.

"You're being much too nice. She's a bitch," Willow calmly replied making us both laughs.

Willow hated Joy before we were friends and even more so after she found out what she had done to me. Willow mentioned why the two of them had a falling out. In unison, we both rolled our eyes and walked away as I flicked my hair unbothered. I swear if Joy's biggity ass would have uttered just one word, I would have delivered her a top-grade skar drag all around his ballroom. I have been waiting to tighten her up for a while now.

Once we made it to the center of the ballroom floor, we joined the crowd in proceeding to dance. After about ten minutes of letting go on the dance floor, I was approached by this tall, dark, and handsome specimen named Devyn from Redstone Moon Pack. He was mad cool! After he danced with both Willow and me, he introduced us to some of his pack members.

Then I heard Willow say "MATE," followed by "MINE," as she stormed toward the crowd. We all kind of watched until she was lost in the crowd. We must have laughed until tears filled our eyes. I bid farewell to my newly found friends and proceeded to grab a bite to eat. I had not eaten all day with the fear of my bloat showing through my dress. I laugh at the thought of this and now I was starving and planning to make up for it now! I found myself looking for Willow wondering who the lucky wolf was.

As I walk to the serving bar there was the most intoxicating smell I have ever encountered. It was like fresh laundry and cinnamon buns. Weird combination, I know! I followed it until I realized that I was being dang near dragged by my elbow to the corridor. I look around in horror realizing where the scent was seeping from. I wanted to stab him.

"NO, there is no way that you are my mate!" I yell at him.

The smell led me to one of my very worst nightmares. I wanted to cry, run away, and pass out all at the same time. Instead of running away from who the Moon Goddess fated me to be with, I decided to figure it out and make it work. After all, he is my mate. Something unexpected happened that knocked the air out of my brief optimism.

"I, Kylo Gabriel Stone...," he trailed off making my heart pound in my chest.

"Please don't...," I murmured as I trembled.

"I, Kylo Gabriel Stone...," he started again.

"Think about what you're about to do," I interjected trying to sound confident.

"I, Kylo Gabriel Stone, reject you as my mate and my Luna. You cannot be my Luna. The pack doesn't respect you and you've proven that this is not what you want," he says without any regret.

"What are you talking about?" I asked incredulously.

"I think it's best you find a second-chance mate in another pack, if that's even possible," he said almost sounding disgusted.

I fell to the ground as I felt this heart-wrenching pain burn throughout my body as tears fell from my eyes.

"Wh... why?" I asked.

Then it hit me, Willow's words of wearing my confidence both internally and externally manifested within me. I confidently stood up and recited what I needed to.

"I, Nova Arabella Ryan, accept your rejection," I said clearly and with confidence.

I felt like I was being hammered by boulders that crushed my soul. I saw the darkening of his eyes. It was odd, it was like I BROKE him. Kylo's jaw clenched tightly and his intense stare cut into me even while suddenly being dragged off by horny she-wolves. I just stood there feeling like an abandoned idiot. He gave a little straight-line smirk while shaking his head and went on with his night like nothing ever happened. It was like I was nothing to him! It HURT but I refuse to let him ruin my night.

"I'm so sorry, Amethyst," I say to try to calm my now whimpering wolf.

"Mate doesn't want us," she says in between moans of disparity.

That night I promised myself that I would enjoy my time on this earth as I planned my escape. This pack has made my life miserable. Once I fixed my makeup I headed back to the ballroom where I found Melody all over my mate, I mean ex-mate.

"She's touching our mate, rip her throat out NOW! "Amethyst said without hesitation.

"He's not ours anymore. He thinks we are weak and therefore not good enough to be his Luna," I respond but I cannot help but have this desire to snatch her bald at this very moment.

As if I would want to be the Luna of this hateful pack in the first place. I guess I should be counting my lucky stars. I would not feel safe to bare pups without the constant worry of someone trying to bring them harm.

Anyway, I grab Willow by her arm and drag her to the dance floor since I catch her near the snack bar. We felt eyes all over us and for the first time, it was welcomed! I could feel the steam coming off of Kylo's body as he watched me dance with other males. He looked PISSED and I did not care! Hell, he was not giving me the attention I wanted, the attention I NEEDED from him as my mate. I wanted him to feel the hurt I felt.

He even grabbed me a few times and actually danced in between the circle Willow and I created. It was hilarious I admit. "Let's Make

Love" by Silk came on over the loudspeakers and I was escorted to the dance floor by the most handsome 6'2" muscular specimen with chocolate brown eyes. His name was Liam from the Opal moon Pack. As we danced, I was intoxicated by his smile and conversation. There were no sparks just grinding and laughs. And there it was.

"May I dance with my mate?" Kylo interrupted.

"Oh, I apologize, Alpha. I did not know she was your mate. She's all yours," he said as he smiled and waved goodbye to me.

"I'm not his mate," I added earning a death glare from Kylo and a worried one from Liam.

Before I knew it, I had stormed out of the ballroom headed straight for my bedroom. I just could not bring myself to dance with him. He rejected us, DAMNIT! He broke our hearts!

I hate that this bond has me fanning over this man, his scent, his body, his wolf, and his everything! It is infectious! The mate bond is too strong for me to hate him. UGH! Before I could exit the ballroom good enough, I was grabbed by Willow who had the most joyous look on her face.

"NOVA! I found my MATE!" she yelled nearly drowning out the music. "I assumed that much. Congratulations, love," I said giving her a hug.

No lie, that multiplied those feelings of rejection I just experienced. At the same time, I was so happy for her.

"That's so AMAZING, Willow!" I shout. "So, where...who is he?" I asked excitedly.

"His name is Zion from the Redstone Moon Pack," she said while blushing.

As she finishes her statement, this sexy 6'0" tall caramel-skinned, muscular warrior with light brown eyes walks up and grabs her by the waist. He looks in my direction and offers me a warm smile.

"You must be Nova?" he asked.

"And you must be Zion?" I asked.

We give each other a bow of approval and turned to try to exit once more. I was not so lucky yet again.

"NOVA! This is our jam! Can you please stay for this last song?" she asked excitedly.

She could tell I was not in a good place and this was her attempt to cheer me up.

"Fine," I say giving in.

It was "Killing Me Softly" by the Fugues. Well, that does not help! As they grind against each other, I am there dancing with my invincible mate until some random guy names Zane came to join me. He was cool as a fan too, no lie. I just decided to enjoy what attention I could get even if it is just for one night. I think we danced to just about every song that came on for like an hour. I could tell that he was his pack's good guy and funny wolf. You know, the one that cheers everyone up and handsome but not arrogant with it. It is exactly what I wanted and needed.

CHAPTER 8: I NEED IT

KYLO'S POV

"KILL HIM NOW! He is touching our MATE," says my wolf Jax.

"EX-MATE," I snarl.

"Yeah, ex-mate thanks to you, jack ass," he grimaced cutting the link off between him and I.

My wolf hated me at this very moment. Even though I was dragged off by some badass she-wolves, none of them held a light to Nova. Against my better wishes, I was drawn to her. I mean I felt like a legit stalker. My eyes were burning a hole in her back as I intensely stared at the way her body swayed to the music.

"Yeah, swaying with another WOLF," Jax interrupted.

"DAMNIT, Jax, I thought you were done!" I let out an involuntary growl scaring those around me.

Something came over me I could not control, before I know it, I was cutting in their dance. As he walked off so did Nova. That caught me by surprise, but I did not think that it would physically feel as if my heart were breaking and waiting for it to drip out of my ass later. This is awful, I think to myself. What have I done? I NEED her and I WANT her! She is MINE! I look up out of my trance only to see her hugging the Gamma's daughter Willow while meeting who I am guessing her newfound mate.

There it was again, that sting in my stomach that had me hobbling over. At one point I thought I was going to pass out.

"Are you okay, honey?" my mom asks with one overly concerned furrowed eyebrow.

"I'm fine, Mom, maybe too much to drink," I lie.

"Son, she's here, I can just feel it, don't let it bother you too much," she says with almost a smirk.

How does she know? Damnit, does she know I found her and rejected her all within 30 seconds of seeing her? With this, I am determined to get her back. She is radiant but I am afraid the pack will not respect her and may try to bring her harm. I am snapped out of my trance once more by the one and only Jax, of course.

"We are the pack and the pack is us. If they hurt MATE, we will be fucking rip open their insides and expose their soul!" he said angrily.

No lie, he made my flesh crawl with that but I agreed as he was spot on as usual. I would do anything for her at this point. I could teach her to be a badass Luna and dare anyone to lay a finger on her or our future pups.

"I see you're planning to plant your seed already, huh?" Jax says sarcastically.

"You're such a horn dog," I chuckled.

"We are one and the same," he added.

"Indeed," I say possessively.

NOVA's POV

I have not had this much fun in like NEVER! Zane and I exchanged numbers before we parted ways. He introduced me to his crew, and they welcomed me like I was one of their own. One of my friends would not stop hitting on me, it was cute. I think his name was Maxwell of Matthew or something like that. I did not focus mouth on pleasantries, I just enjoyed my time around my newfound comrades. More than what I had with my own pack. "When A Man Loves A Woman" by a Percy Sledge came on, my eyes were damn near pulled from the floor which I was staring at to my mate, I mean, ex-mate. We had an intense stare at one another as his eyes suddenly went dark. This happens when your wolf surfaces and is ready to mate, if you know what I mean.

"Damnit, Amethyst, fight it!" I yell at my wolf.

She wanted it and she wanted it bad, hell, I wanted it. I am a virgin, so I am not even sure if I want a man that rejected US to be our first and last.

"You're thinking too much, the Moon Goddess made him our mate whether you like it or not," Amethyst snaps at me.

"I don't care. He doesn't want us. So, you're willing to just give my body to him so freely?" I asked.

"You're so negative," she replied.

She was right, no matter how much you try to avoid it that freaking mate bond is relentless. It takes absolutely no prisoners. This means I must leave this pack to weaken our mate bond. Kylo was right, I must pray to the Moon Goddess for a second-chance mate because I would never feel or be safe here in my own pack.

With that thought, I say my goodbyes to Zane and his crew and head to my room. The ball was just about over anyway. When I noticed a group of wolves taking the elevator, I decided to take the stairs down on the backside of the house. I just was not in the mood to have to prove that I could kick some of their asses. I will let them keep thinking I am as weak as they like to portray me to be. FINALLY, I make it to the hall that held my room, only to be shocked to see who is leaning on my door obviously pissed.

"What do you think you're doing?" said an angry Meyonna.

"To what do I owe the pleasure, Meyonna?" I say sarcastically.

Before I realized what she was about to do, she violently slapped my cheek. My reflexes took over as I grabbed her by the neck. I could feel my wolf take over.

"KILL THE WHORE, she hurt us, she wants OUR mate!" Amethyst said with so much anger in her voice.

I think my wolf could possibly be batshit crazy behind me and our mate. I am snapped out of my trance by a few pack members who had been trying to pry my hands from around her neck with no luck. When I came back to, I let go as I watched her fall to the floor unable to breathe.

"She attacked me!" she yelled.

Three of them came at me but my wolf was not having it! I felt my eyes shift to those of my wolf.

"If one of you fucking touch me, I will haunt you from the grave and kill your fated mates!" I growled not even recognizing my voice.

It was definitely not me; it was Amethyst! My wolf was badass and I needed her to teach me her ways ASAP! With this, they backed away and I entered my room falling face forward in my pillow. I proceeded to talk to my wolf who is slowly becoming my best friend. I mean, she was me and I was her.

"Why do people treat us this way?" I asked her.

"Babe, because you allow them to. You must begin to defend yourself," she says sternly.

"I'm sorry I lost our mate because of my weak actions," I respond as tears fall from the side of my eye.

"It's not completely your fault, Nova. Our mate is supposed to accept us as we are, protect us, love us, and be there when we need them most," she said sounding more like a mother than my own.

"You're right. His lost," I mumbled.

I stand up, pin my hair up and take a quick shower. I did not want to mess up the curls that Willow worked so hard for, plus I was in love with it. That is when I heard my wolf shout.

"MATE!" Amethyst shouts damn near deafening me.

The knock at the door startled me! That intoxicating scent hit my nose like a train. Before I could stop myself, I was opening the door in nothing but my bath towel. My curls roaming free over my head and a few curls had fallen on my face since I basically ran to the door. I must have subconsciously freed them, weird! His eyes went from those beautiful pools of blue to what looked to be darker gray. I was locked in on his body movements as he slowly made his way in my room. I slowly walked backward until he could shut the door. We studied each other's movements without breaking our intense stare into each other's eyes. I could hear his heart beating as loud as thunder. Mine was no better.

I was infatuated with the licking of his lips as his jaw clenched as if he did not know what to do with me first. He wanted every inch of me. My core was crying a river with the thought of his mouth being everywhere but away from me. I bite my bottom lip as he rests his forehead against mine. He brushed his lips against mine where he stole my very FIRST kiss. It was slow and passionate at first until the kisses became more aggressive and passionate. He grabbed the back of my thighs and lifted me up as my legs found their way around his waist. He laid me back on the bed as I continued to straddle his waist.

His mouth was buried deep within my neck like I was his last meal. My moans were leaving my mouth involuntarily. Kylo drew circles with his tongue around me soon to be where I would proudly wear his mark.

I needed him to match my current state of nakedness, NOW! I tugged at the buttons on his shirt until he helped me finish the deed and he was back at teasing me with his tongue. Pleasuring my bits and every now and then stealing my kisses. He tastes as good as he smells, I thought to myself. I begin to tug at his belt as he cuffed one of my breasts in his hand to begin enjoying it like a baby fresh out of the womb having a taste of its mother's milk/colostrum. Again, he helped me finish removing his pants.

DAMN! Seeing "JR" standing at attention almost made me scurry up near the headboard. He saw my reaction and smirked at me.

"It's all you, babe, there's no need to run from me. I'm going to bury myself in you all night," he said lustfully.

"How bad do you want it?" I ask boldly catching him and myself by surprise.

"You keep talking, that way I'm going to take it," he said confidently.

And there it was, Kylo was devouring my honey pot while he gripped my ass to stop me from sliding from his hold. It was out of this damn world!

"Is this what I've been missing?" I say to myself.

"Yep! Such a shame," he replied.

Apparently, I said that out loud. Can you blame me? I was in an oblivion of lust.

"Oh, baby, please don't stop," I say all but screaming.

When I thought I could not take anymore, he buried his face deeper between my thighs. I could not stop the uncontrollable trembling of my legs.

"Head game on point," I whisper only for him to hear me again.

He was legit killing me softly. Kylo abruptly came up kissing me so passionately allowing me to taste myself and I didn't mind. He grabbed my waist and tossed me on his lap. I was nervous but at the same time, I was willing to let him stick it anywhere if he wanted to. He could have EV-ER-Y hole on my body!

"This was made for you," he said freeing his massive erection.

"I...I... I've never done it before," I say slightly above a whisper.

"Yo...You've never done what, have sex?" he asks surprised.

"No, I'm a virgin," I say blushing and embarrassed.

He flipped me over on my side. Here we go, he is going to leave. To my surprise, he gripped me in a bone-crushing hug saying, "You are too perfect for me."

We ended up talking for hours. We both agreed that my first time should be more than just a fuck one night after alcohol consumption. He held me the hold night whispering sweet nothings to me. It all seemed too perfect. All good things come to an end....

CHAPTER 9: SECRET LOVERS

NOVA's POV

I opened up to Kylo about everything that is happened in his absence. Yeah, Kylo and I do not have the best past, but I am trying hard to forgive him because like it or not, I am fated to be with him by the Moon Goddess. The mate bond is strong and the only way to weaken it is by distancing yourselves for a long period of time and through mutual rejection. I heard it can sometimes take years to weaken that connection. Anyway, Kylo was enraged and even threatened to kill his best friend, my brother, and our future Beta Malik. He is going to END Neko who so happens to be his cousin. I made him swear that he would not end him but punish him. Little does he know is that I want the pleasure of ending that ass clown. It is slowly coming together, sweet revenge! After our discussion, we decided to keep US under wraps until he could weed out those that mean me harm. My true enemies will in time reveal themselves to wolves in sheep's clothing eventually.

Kylo decided that it would be a great idea for me to begin training with the pack again. A Luna's duty to her pack is to be compassionate, levelheaded, and most of all trusted by her pack, basically a Mother Teresa figurehead. He really desires unity among us wolves.

"What happened to you while you were away?" I ask him quizzically.

"What do you mean?" he asked barely opening his eyes.

"You used to be so mean, cold, and standoffish, what changed?" I ask more intrigued than I was before.

I sit up just enough to rest my hands underneath my chin on his bare chest. Oh, shit, he is looking at me like I just asked him to let me put my finger up his butt or something. "Wh... what's wrong, did I say something?" I say nervously.

"No, not at all," he says almost sounding unsure. "I don't want to sound crazy," he says as he stared deeply in my eyes.

KYLO's POV

Why did she have to ask me that? How do I explain to her that SHE happened to me? I used to have both vivid dreams and nightmares all surrounding her. For a long time, I carried the guilt of how I allowed people to treat her. Over the years I have spoken to Malik about the way he used to treat her, and he convinced me that it was water under the bridge, and everything was better now. My intuition told me he was not being truthful. Now that I know I was right; I am not sure if I want him as my Beta if he does not strive toward redemption. My mate was neglected while I was away, and it pains me to think that she feels unsafe in OUR home. She is going to be our Luna and bare my pups, but she is not safe and that infuriates me. I thought it would be better if we kept our bond a secret, at least until the wolves in sheep's clothing exposed themselves.

If I do not banish them, they will be killed on site, PERIOD.

"Nobody will hurt our mate, I will destroy their soul and steal their offspring," Jax interrupts.

Nova has to begin interacting with the pack again, so I thought it would be a great idea that she trained with the rest of us so that they can get to know her, like really know her. As the future Luna, they needed to learn to respect her, know her, and care for her all before the pack knows. This will expose the real and the fake. I am snapped out of my thoughts when I notice a quivering Nova that later beside me. She told me about the nightmares over the years that haunt her daily life, so I tried to wake her. She felt like she had been kissed by the sun her skin was so hot! We were both now laying in a puddle of sweat I presume. Then I heard it, the sound of 206 bones breaking when she let out a loud scream and fell to the floor before I could catch her with my wolf speed. I try to explain to her that she is having her first shift and it always hurts like hell.

NOVA's POV

WHAT IS HAPPENING TO ME? Why am I asking this stupid question when I already know? It was time for my wolf Amethyst to surface. I often wondered what she looked like. Her voice was so angelic yet demonic at times, so could not imagine what her appearance would be like.

"HELP ME, KYLO!" I scream.

I look over at him with his huge smile on his face to hear him say, "You're shifting for the first time, Nova, and it always hurts like hell at first," he says proudly but I can see the instant gratification from his wolf Jax as I transition into Amethyst.

"MATE!" Jax says excitedly.

"WOW, your wolf is beautiful!" Kylo says proudly while looking a little confused.

I look down at what used to be my hands to see midnight black paws. I glance over at the mirror to see my purple glowing eyes and realized that I was huge! My coat is pitch black which is uncommon for any other wolf than an ALPHA. Jax and Amethyst completely put Kylo and me in the background to begin interacting with each other. I telepathically try to reach Kylo and to no avail, that failed. Kylo had not even shifted and his wolf completely devoured his consciousness. I asked Amethyst to let me through to him and she obliged after many attempts.

"Kylo, how do I shift back?" I ask completely clueless.

"Just think about every detail of your human form," he says.

I am stuck and obviously over thinking it. Maybe I am still in shock and infatuated by my beautiful wolf. It was then we heard footsteps moving briskly down the hall and most likely headed to my room because of my loud screams. I must have woken them up.

"SHIFT NOW!" Kylo shouted with much fear in his voice.

Before I knew it, I was lying naked on the floor.

Kylo tossed me my bath towel before shifting in midair out of the window. My father burst into the room to only find me on the floor wrapped inside a towel.

"Nova, are you okay?" he said almost legitimately sounding concerned.

"I am fine," I say nonchalantly raising myself off the floor.

"I heard you scream," he said in almost formed as a question.

Oh, I fell backward in the tub and came out here and lost my balance from the dizziness. I lie and I do not care if he believes me or not as I turned and walked away.

"You didn't shift yet?" he asks surprised.

I stopped in my tracks, did he of all people remember my birthday? No, he could not have possibly remembered.

"Why would I shift tonight, Father?" I asked as if I was dumbfounded.

"Never mind," he says sounding disappointed. "Just get some rest, I heard you'll be training with the pack starting tomorrow," he said as he was closing my door. "By the way, Happy Birthday, Nova," he said making my heart jerk in confusion.

Did he remember, how? And why the hell did Kylo bail on me? Is he embarrassed by me? Is he a coward now? Then it hit me, WE decided to keep US a secret until my enemies are revealed. I better get out of my feelings before I screw this plan up. With that, I went to sleep if that is what you call it because I was woken up by Kylo, which I did not mind. He whispered something l in my ear that I just cannot shake.

KYLO'S POV

I shifted in midair heading out of the window right before Nova's dad burst through the door. I cannot lie, my lust for her only grows as I notice she is quick on her feet and fast in her thinking. She fed her dad a quick lie of the reasons behind her screaming. I am not saying he necessarily bought it, but I could tell she did not care. They cannot know that she is the future Luna of our pack. They would secretly try to destroy her. Yes, her own family. Right as her dad turned to leave, I heard him wish her a happy birthday. I nearly fell from the tree in shock. As I heard the door close, I gave it another 10 minutes before I leaped back through her slightly opened window.

"You cannot show ANYONE that you are a midnight wolf," I whisper to her.

She turned around with a look of disgust, sprinkled with a bit of confusion. I had to explain to her what she already knew. The black wolf symbolizes Alpha blood which is automatically treated as a threat among those with lesser rank and those that hold the highest rank and all in between. I am not sure how it is possible, unless...no, there is no way. I quickly erase the thought of Nova being in relation to me. The Moon Goddess would not mate me with a relative. Something is not quite right here, but I am going to get to the bottom of it.

CHAPTER 10: GET TO KNOW ME

NOVA's POV

After last night's fiasco, I am looking forward to a distraction. My alarm went off at 0430 A.M. It is just enough time for me to throw on a t-shirt and leggings and place my hair in a ponytail with a long braid. I run to the bathroom to wash my face and brush my teeth. I did all this without realizing Kylo had already left my room. As I started to make the bed, I could not help but lavish in the memory we created last night. Even though we did not go all the way, it is the most action I have ever gotten and from my mate to top it off. I can still smell him all over me. I dash my favorite vanilla spray all over my body. Kylo promised things would be different for me from now on. He made it a point that I would not be anyone's slave and I would also pull my weight in training like everyone else. I am willing to try to allow others to get to know me if they tried. Neko was never on my list no matter what he does. He will pay for what he has done to me, that is a promise!

As I exit my room, I am greeted by none other than the pack slut herself, Meyonna. She purposely bumped me calling me a bag lady. It took all the restraint I had in me not to drag her down by her hair and stomping a hole in her face. I looked down at what I was wearing, unfortunately, she was right. I ran back to my room to remove my shirt and through on my favorite red sports bra that once had Nike written in the front. After several years and washes, it read nothing. The material is still great and breathable. I pulled on my grey high-rise legging that cuffed my butt exactly right. I admit that I was super nervous about walking out to training this way. This is how most she-wolves trained. The males were almost always shirtless. It is now or never if I am ever going to reinvent myself and improve my image with the pack. Here goes nothing.

MALIK's POV

I am overly excited that my best friend, our future Alpha has made it home. This means I have to begin my future Beta duties eight away. Good thing my dad has made it a point to have me tag along for all of his meetings and explaining the importance of pack business. It is a lot of work, to say the least, but I am ready for it. My first request to Kylo will be to get rid of Nova. She is the weakest link in the pack. It was not always this way, but after the accident happened with rogue attack, my mom became cold and we blamed Nova. I heard her for it! She was the reason our mother was miserable. When Melody and I treated Nova bad, it caused a shift in my mom's mood for the better. We just continued torturing and dismissing her. It sounds bad, but I would never allow anyone to hurt my mother, physically, or emotionally family or not. Kylo mind linked the whole pack making us aware that EVERY wolf will train from pups on up. The training would be more challenging and demanding. We are ramping up our territory patrols. The rogue attacks have become more prominent on the Northside of our territory since last night. We are not sure why, but it is like they are looking for something or someone. Either way, we must be prepared.

MEYONNA's POV

I cannot believe we are up this early after a night of drinking. My head feels like I have a little live drummer living in it. UGH! I heard that Kylo's leading the drills today. Even if I have to suffer through this, at least I will have a nice piece of ass to look at. I threw on my sexiest crisscross hot pink sports bra with my black biker shorts. I leave my hair free flowing, at least until I have to lay a bitch out. I cannot have her using my hair as an advantage. This is just for show for my man Kylo. He will soon come to his senses and have another taste of my sweet nectar. With that, I am headed out of the door where I bump into Nova. I roll my eyes as I bump pass her in the hallway letting out a small chuckle. The girl really needed a makeover. She is wearing this baggy outdated graphic tee with some hella worn-out leggings. I just look back at her, "Nice outfit, bag lady," I say as I jog to the pack training grounds while letting my honey blonde hair switch back and forth like I was in a shampoo commercial.

I instantly notice Kylo, but my presence has no effect on him. I am low-key pissed! Who is this chick that has his head gone? Is she in the pack? Did he find his mate while he was away? If so, why would he keep her a secret? I will have my way with him rather he likes it or not. That body will be in and up against mine again.

"Hey, Kylo," I say as I bent down pretending to tie my shoe as I gave him a glance at my peach.

As expected, he needed to wipe the drool from his mouth. "Mission accomplished," I say to myself with a smirk.

KYLO's POV

As I prepare the last set of training blocks, I am hit with the most intoxicating scent of none other than my mate. I snapped out of my trance when Meyonna spoke to me. She proceeded to provoke me, but her attempts were ignored when I saw HER! I had to catch the drool from falling from my mouth.

"Hey, you may want to close your mouth before you catch flies," says Malik.

Shit, he caught me. I let out an involuntary growl.

"Dude, she has that effect on us all, we've all had Meyonna," Malik says with his hands up in surrender.

I was relieved because I thought he caught me staring at Nova. She walked onto the pack grounds obviously uncomfortable in what she was wearing yet confident in a sense. How could this young woman not understand how beautiful she is? She is too perfect even in her flaws. I noticed some of the pack members were surprised that Nova was at training, but it seems they quickly brushed it off. I spotted Neko with lust-filled in his eyes toward Nova. I wanted to rip his eyeballs out and shove them down his throat, but I decided against it. Would he act that way if he knew she was my mate? I have to keep my focus.

There is a much bigger threat and we must be prepared for any and all attacks to come. With that, I announced to my fellow wolves of our 5-mile run route and the events that will take place after. We began to run, and I noticed Nova holding back. I drop back as I always do to encourage the weakest link whoever it is for that training session.

"Nova, what are you doing?" I ask.

She looks up at me and shrugs. I explained to her that if she holds back, she will never improve, and they will not respect her. She obviously took what I said to heart and was soon upfront with all of us. I could see the look of disdain in Neko's face when she passed him. No matter what he did, he could not keep up with her.

"That's my girl," I heard Jax say a little above a whisper.

Once we finished our run, I had everyone pair up in preparation for hand-to-hand combat. It is important to train in both human and wolf form. Right now, fighting in human form was by far a weak point for our pack's youth. They were spoiled by their wolf's strength, speed, and instincts. I wanted them to understand that you may not always have time to shift no matter how fast you think you are at it. Once I blew the whistle, each member had one minute to choose their opponent. I watched as Sarah and Nova circled each other. From what I recall Sarah was one of the best she-wolf fighters we had. The girl was lethal! She is about three years older than Nova, but I know she could learn a lot from Sarah. I blow the whistle as an indication for the first round to begin. I am walking around, demonstrating, and sparring when I realize I have not blown the whistle for the end of round 1. I am about seven minutes overtime. I look over and see Sarah slam Nova to the ground. I begin to clench my jaw as I quickly make my way over to their position. I notice there is a slowly growing audience that is watching while blocking my view. I burst through the crowd only to see Nova with Sarah in a chokehold with her legs. She releases Sarah from the chokehold when she spots me and hops up to her feet to bow as a sign of respect since I am to be the new Alpha. Sarah takes this opportunity to take a cheap shot by swooping Nova's legs from under her causing her to lose her balance and fall on her face. With no hesitation, Nova's eyes glow and I quickly shake my head and mouth "Don't." She almost shifted from anger, but instead, she bounced back up in time enough for Sarah to charge at her with her head down in attempts to take her down and Nova met her with this smooth as six-piece combo.

Nova grabbed Sarah by her shoulder blades holding her steady as she kneed her twice in the face. Nova digs down with her elbow right in between Sarah's shoulder blades about four times before did the sexiest shit I have ever seen. Nova took a move straight out of WWE (wrestling) by stepping back while cuffing Sarah's head in a headlock and fell to the ground with her. I thought Nova stood to take her victory lap but instead, she stood there watching her opponent scramble to get up. Sarah is a tough cookie! Yet again, she is back on her feet, barely. Nova is irritated yet admiring of her persistence.

"That's all you got, you weak piece of shot," Sarah said infuriated.

Something clicked in Nova, I felt it! Before we knew it, Nova had toppled Sarah over yet again delivering ridiculously fast and brutal punches to the face. Three werewolves tried to pull her off of Sarah. To my surprise, Nova delivered a kick to the stomach to one of them, struck the other in the chest causing him to lose his breath, and planted a kick to the side of the knee for the other.

"ENOUGH!" I tell using my Alpha tone.

Werewolves of lesser rank cannot refuse this tone. It forcibly makes them submit to my command. Thank you, Moon Goddess, it is only bestowed on those of us that are destined to be Alphas and future Alphas. With that, Nova stops, and they all bow. I decide to dismiss the pack for the rest of the training session. As they all walk toward the packhouse, obviously exhausted, I notice Nova reaching first a crossbow. It was evident that she was not done training. Damnit, Neko and Malik are still here. I order them to take a bloody unconscious Sarah to our pack doctor Olivia. They nod in agreement and leave me to it. I slowly walk toward Nova and asked her was she okay. She looks at me with a huge smile on her face. She is overly excited about how exhilarating it felt to feel included with the pack for the first time in a long time. As she went on and on, I honestly tuned her out because I am so drawn into her beauty. I can tell I have the same effect because I can smell her arousal. I am snapped back to reality when she asked me what I thought about giving her extra training. That is not what I thought she wanted from me. Was this a subliminal message for something else she wanted?

"You're a pervert," I hear my wolf Jax say.

Yep, I am acting like a horny teenager again. I shake it off and agree, but I explained that it would be a great idea if Willow accompanied her for obvious reasons. I do not want anyone in the pack thinking I am showing favoritism or figure out that I am fated to be with her. I feel it with everything in me that something is not right! I had to get to the bottom of it because I am ready for the pack to know that she is MINE!

CHAPTER 11: NOT SO BAD

LEAH's POV

I gaze down at the garden in the courtyard as I do daily. As I admire the newly blossomed rose bushes, something catches my eye that leaves me intrigued. I spot my son Kylo damn near drooling over little Nova. I do not know much about her other than being a nice girl. I suspected something was off with her and her family though. I have directly asked her was everything okay and she usually tried to deflect. I always wondered why she would not look me in my eye. When I enter a room, she nearly runs out of it. It has been this way for years. Judging by the intense look of lust my son is giving her, she just may be the next Luna. I could be wrong, but I have a gut feeling that he is found his mate in her. Just odd, if she is his mate, why hasn't he marked her? Maybe I am overreacting, but I am planning to keep an eye out for it. It is best I do not mention this to his father. He is so distracted with pack business I have not seen much of him lately. I am so excited! If Nova is the pack's future Luna, I better get her up to doors on her duties. She would make an amazing Luna, but something tells me that she does not feel that way. I am going to find out! I am not trying to pry but my son is my business and so will my future daughter-in-law, and my pack.

NOVA's POV

Once Kylo agreed to extra training sessions with the condition of

Willow attending I was ecstatic. Honestly, I have not seen much of her since she found her mate last night. I could only imagine what they were getting into or how he was. There goes my dirty mind again. She only had to the end of the summer to decide if she would depart our pack and join his or vice versa. I really hope she stays now that I know that I will be the next Luna. I called her and right as I was about to hang up an exhausted sounding Willow answers. I explained the dilemma to her, and she was all for it! She along with the other nine she-wolves that found their mates were excluded from training today for obvious reasons. When werewolves find their mates, this is a good thing! It is sacred and appreciated. A bond like that could hardly ever be broken, even though rejection. When werewolves mate and become one, the bond intensifies both the male and female's feeling times ten! Your connection with your mate is like no tiger bond shared in life, even with your pups.

As I am undressing to head to the shower, I pass the mirror to admire my physique. I had to tell my reflection a good job today. I laugh out loud at my goofy actions. I have not heard from my wolf Amethyst today.

"Amethyst, you good?" I ask.

"I'm always with you even if you cannot hear me, you are me and I am you," she says almost poetically.

"Is that your favorite saying now?" I say smiling back at my reflection.

"It wouldn't hurt to let me stretch my legs tonight," she says almost asking.

I agree that it is a fair trade. Plus, I would not mind admiring her beauty again. I am curious about all that she could do to be completely honest.

I head to the shower to wash the crud and blood from under my nails. I release my hair from bondage so I could douse it with shampoo. As I dug my hands in my scalp, I am interrupted by a shadow standing in my door. I could make out his face because the steam in my small bathroom would not allow me too. I immediately grab my razor from the corner of the shower ready to slit the throat of the perpetrator. I look up and the shadowy figure is gone. I have always consistently locked the door as a habit before I take a shower. This means someone either came through my window or picked my lock. Sick bastard! Without any want, the shower door began to slide open. Here I am in all my makes glory with a razor ready to cut someone's throat only to realize it was my Kylo.

As he slid the door closed, I admire his nakedness and again I am astonished by the size of "JR," if you catch my drift. The way the steam made his body glisten had me breathless. There he stood with that sexy ass chiseled body that looks like something straight out of one of those men's magazines with the bodybuilders on the cover.

"Like what you see, baby?" he asks cockily.

I bit my bottom lip in attempts to catch my breath and slow my heartbeat. We locked eyes as he placed his forehead against mine. He slowly teased me with his soft as cotton lips.

"You're going to be my undoing, woman," he says just loud enough for me to hear.

"Why is that?" I ask him.

"You and your damn scent drive me insane, I smell your arousal," he said making my core drip my sweet nectar causing my knees to tremble.

I want him in my temple now and forever.

"I'm not sure how long I can control my wolf from having our way with you," he said sounding as if he was wrestling with what to do.

It was then we locked lips in an aggressive way. He yanks me away and grips my waist spinning me around pinning me against the shower way.

Kylo nibbles on my ear and pulls me to him as I feel his dick hard as steel poking me in the back. I let out an involuntary moan that drove him crazy. He slowly inserted two fingers within my sweet spot causing me to nearly lose my balance. Kylo was killing me softly while stroking every one of my notes with his fingers. He caught me a little off guard when one finger slipped into my butt. It caught me off guard with the pleasurable feeling I received from it. He took his free hand and caressed my left breast so abruptly while burying his head into my neck.

"You think you can handle Daddy, baby?" he asks seductively.

"YES, DADDY, PLEASE, I want it NOW!" I moan. I swear I BEGGED for him to take me right here, right now.

Just when I thought it could not get any better, he looked down at me with lust in his eyes and smiled. Kylo got on his knees, grabbed the back of my legs, and pulled my legs on his shoulders and began to devour every part of me. I shuddered as I had back-to-back orgasms. I had nothing left to give, and there it was again, the most explosive orgasm I could imagine someone could have. He places me down and proceeds to bath me.

"What are you doing?" I ask. "You're just going to get me going not to give me the dick?" I say nearly out of breath.

The way he laughed at me kind of made me laugh at myself. I sounded like a staring child. How could I beg for something I never had? This made me laugh even harder. Once we finished bathing, he carried me out of the shower and lay me on the bed where he proceeded to dry me off and apply my moisturizer.

"You are so beautiful," he says making me blush.

Once we were both dry and ready for bed, he laid next to me holding me tight in his grip.

I could get used to this, minus the no penetration rule. Kylo and I took our wolves out for a long run through the woods near the packhouse. I caught on to the shifting from human to wolf fairly quick. My wolf was badass! She was fast and limber. At some point, I thought Kylo was struggling to stay ahead of us until he pushed his Alpha speed. I do not mind him being more powerful because it gave me this sense of security. When we made it back to the packhouse, we grabbed our clothes we stashed by a tree and through them back on. We climbed back through my window. No lie, this sneaking around is kind of exciting but I know I do not want to do this forever. I do not want our relationship to stay hidden, but I also understood the threat we faced. I will partake in this secret love affair for as long I can endure.

KYLO's POV

I hop out of Nova's bedroom window and sprint across the garden when I spot my mother giving me this almost knowing what I was up to look all over her face. She furrowed her eyebrow at me while crossing her arms with a huge smile on her face. I just tell them good morning to her and keep running. Does she know? Maybe she suspects but does not know. I have to get Nova's scent off me. As much as I cannot wait to bathe in her scent every day, I cannot risk anyone finding out. I rush to my room and hop in the shower once more. Once I am cleaned up, I head downstairs to grab breakfast before handling pack business. I am entrusting Malik to lead training this afternoon. I am let by that delicious scent before I make it downstairs good. To my surprise, I find

Nova chopping it up with a few pack members that wanted it to give her kudos for ripping Sarah a new one. My Nova did not boast or encourage them. She was very reserved and bashful and obviously wanted them to change the subject. Thank you, Moon Goddess, for blessing me with such a perfect mate. I cannot believe I was stupid enough to reject her. It hurt to even think of the fact that she accepted. Yeah, that hurt! That is water under the bridge now because she is MINE and I planned to make everyone know very soon.

CHAPTER 12: AS TIME GOES ON

MELODY's POV

It has been a few months since Kylo returned and he has not shown the slightest bit of interest. Sometimes I feel like there is a spark but when I try to get close to him, he comes up with an excuse as to why he cannot entertain me. The only thing I could think of is that he is super busy preparing to become our next Alpha. I try not to think too much into it because I cherish those moments that I do get with him. I love when we partner up for hand-to-hand combat. I have helped him every time. I could only imagine how monstrously large he is erect. From what I heard, he is a beast with it, and I cannot wait to experience it. I know it is something between us, but I cannot place my finger on it. My plan of bearing his pups before he becomes Alpha has to work. Call it trapping if you want, I call it securing my future as Luna. My mother, brother, and I orchestrated the whole thing. It is slowly coming together. Malik finds every opportunity to slide my name into their conversations. When he reports back, he just says them at Kylo seems distracted and stressed a bit about Alpha business. That is how we know that he has not found his mate yet. This is my only chance!

WILLOW's POV

Over the past few months after meeting my mate, I have been struggling with the idea of leaving my family and best friend Nova. She has been through so much in life and I am afraid me leaving will destroy her. I need her and Kylo to get it together because I am not sure how much more secrecy about their relationship she can bear. I did not agree with their plan in the beginning because I like everybody else, I felt that finding your mate should be celebrated. The more Nova's skills of combat had come to surface, the threats against her were more prominent. At least most of the pack admired her and began to include her, it was her own family that is stirring the pot of hatred for her. When I finally got my father to open up about why he volunteered to train her I was shocked to find the truth. That would explain why her wolf was pitch black, Alpha blood. I feel as if I should tell them both before it is too late! That would not be good for either of them. My father, the Gamma of this pack, whose responsibility is to look out for the Luna, made me aware that I would not utter a word. I am so torn! First things first, I need to let Nova know that I decided to hone the Redstone Pack to be with my mate.

NOVA's POV

It has been months since I have spent training with the pack and Kylo. Neko and Malik have not really laid a finger on me since Kylo threatened the pack members about the punishment for bullying. Either way, I could handle myself in a fight if need be. It is weird because I am starting to think Neko is a thing for me. I always catch him staring at me and I have even heard Kylo growl at him when he catches him. After that, I believe Neko is becoming suspicious after that incident happened, but he cannot confirm it. Kylo and I have to move faster if we want our plan to work. It is. Taking a bit longer than what we both would like. We are both beyond READY to seal the deal. Once werewolves mate you become one. Everyone will immediately know that you have completed the mating ritual based on the Ora you deliver along with the mark you hear us in the open on your neck. I am starting to get a bit discouraged as if it will never happen. In the meantime, Kylo's mom has taken a vested interest in me. My pack members assume I am the personal slave to the Luna, but it is the exact opposite. She has taught me so much about pack business and what her role as Luna requires. I am beginning to feel that is he knows so something, but Kylo swore on his life he has never mentioned it to her. We have to do something quickly because the pack is growing weary of the futures Alpha not finding his Luna.

Everyone knows when an Alpha finds his forever mate better known as his Luna, it provides strength and capability to the pack. As I reported to my everyday duty with the Luna after training and breakfast, today was different. I knocked in preparation to enter. She opened the door with a frantic look on her face while handing me a basket of clothes with specific instructions. She wanted to ensure I separated dark colors away from the light colors while ensuring everything was out of the pockets. Luna quickly shut the door in my face after that. This was odd for me. I have never done her laundry and why was she acting this way? Something was definitely wrong. I held the laundry basket tightly in my hands and headed toward the washers. As I separated two stacks of clothing preparing for the washers, I lifted the last item of the basket a piece of fell from the jeans. It said, *"Read Me in Private."* As applying just the right amount of detergent to each washer, I closed the lids and hurried to my room, locking the door behind me.

I made sure my window was locked as well. I cannot have any naked visitors showing up right now I think to myself causing a smile to cover my face.

"My dear Nova, it has been a pleasure getting to know you over the last few months. I have grown very fond of you so that is why it is hard for me to say this. You should leave this place! I fear that it is not safe for you here based on my newly received intelligence. It is crazy, but I was really hoping that you were my son's mate. That theory left me when I realized that you still did not bear the mark of a mate. I really hope you meet your mate one of these days and he treats you like the queen you are. I am going out of town to visit family in the 'Grey Wolf Pack.' I would love it if you would accompany me two days from now. You are wondering why I did not communicate this with you in person. Well, my spies tell me that we have been having an audience during our daily sessions. I fear that you have many enemies that are close to you. Please consider leaving with me two days from today and plan not to return.

-Love Leah, Your Luna

After reading the Luna's letter I am speechless. I do not know what to do. I fear that we have run out of time. I cannot think about this right now. How was I going to tell Kylo that I must leave for my safety? We tried to keep US being a secret, but it seems it is backfiring. I have decided to leave in two days' time but not permanently. I needed everyone to believe that I would not return. Maybe it is best that Kylo and I cut our losses. I do not want to be his undoing.

I headed out to training as scheduled. It was my turn to be paired with Neko. I had beat all other pack members that I have been paired with. I am now being considered as one of my pack's strongest warriors. I actually believe I made my father proud while my mother, brother, and sister's hatred for me grew by the day. I have paired with Malik a couple of days ago and I swear he intended on killing me. I just barely broke free of his grasp enough to hear the whistle blow. I have not had the opportunity to spar with my hateful sister, but I planned to give her a fat lip. I have studied her technique for months. Her moves became predictable to me. She was an amazing fighter I give her that, but I was better, and I felt it in my bones. These last few weeks she hated me the most! I could only imagine it is because the pack does not hate me as much as they desire them to. The majority actually include me in pack activities.

As I slowly walk over to Neko to get in fighting position, I am disgusted by the way he looks at me. It is like he is dry humping me with his eyes. He hisses at me to hurry up before spits at my feet nearly touching my shoes. Neko is a big guy and he has brute strength. I am obviously not stronger, but I have proven to be faster. Before the whistle blows to start the fight, I see this large fist come against my face, instantly breaking my nose. I start to see black spots. I am immediately knocked down by the harsh kick to the back of moth my knees. I swiftly turn to land a kick to Neko's growing. I take my legs and wrap them around his ankle causing him to lose his balance. I quickly mount him and begin landing blows to his face. I was able to land about four before he knocked me off him like I was nothing. I was getting sloppy. I knew that I should have locked my grip on his torso.

He proceeded to lift me off the ground and repeatedly slammed me until I wrapped my legs around his throat and squeezed for dear life. He began to changed colors trying to fight me off. Neko spotted the audience that began to fork around us. Kylo and Malik were not present for this ordeal form the beginning because they had future Alpha and Beta business to attend to. As Kylo and Malik finished up and headed to the pack training grounds, they noticed the forming crowd yelling, "FINISH HIM!" They were laughing and walking toward the crowd nonchalantly until they heard a growl and my scream to follow. This motherfucker dug his wolf's fangs into my inner thigh and locked in like I was a piece of meat. Amethyst wasted no time on making herself present. Before I knew it, I had shifted midair in my all-back glory and locked on an already shifted wolf Neko's throat. I saw RED.

At the sound of my scream, Kylo shifted midair and made it over to the crowd in record time to see me nearly kill Neko. His wolf Jax pleases with my wolf Amethyst not to kill him. Luna's are looked at to be compassionate and forgiving and not respected for killing a fellow pack member. I surrendered at the sight of him and his pleading with me not to kill Neko. I swiftly turned to make a run into the woods. I was angry because she would not let me have my sweet revenge. I have planned to end his life during our spar for months! But NO, I could not even have that! I'm angry because I'm not safe, I can't mate with Kylo, I'm a secret lover, my family hates me, my best friend is abandoning me, just everything is wrong! the feelings of wanting to cut myself starting to come back.

"They hurt us!" I hear Amethyst say.

She is right! But our mate is not doing anything about it as he promised. I will have my revenge! Neko will die at my hands and my family will wish they were dead when I am done.

CHAPTER 13: LETS DO THIS RIGHT

JOY's POV

Over the years I have not said much to Nova. It is hardly believed that we were once best friends. I kind of always hated that she friended Willow, UGH! That girl never liked me. Anyway, when the incident with the rogues happened it was easier to let Nova be to blame. In all honestly, it was my fault the rogues were there. I informed them of some information about one of their enemies. If this information were exposed to the pack, it would ruin lives. No one in my family knows, but I have congregated with rogues since I was eleven years old and the only person who knew was Nova because she would accompany me. What she did not know was I would meet with them on my own time. A little background, I fell in love with our former pack member Jacob whose family was banished because his father was a known arsonist. His last incident killed a whole family. When my dad decided to banish them, Jacob and I stayed in contact and would meet up and hang out occasionally. This is why the rogues never hurt Nova and me. When I overheard our newly appointed pack's Gamma Emit and my mother, the discussing Nova's family history, I wasted no time informing Jacob who in turn informed other rogues. We set the whole thing up, but it quickly got out of hand. I was supposed to get Nova out into the courtyard to make it easier for the rogues to swipe and go. Things did not go as planned as you already know. You see, I was her best friend, but she was not mine.

I was jealous of Nova's beauty, brains, and physical and emotional strength. Nova was special, but she no idea just how important she would become once she mated. I tried convincing myself that losing her to the rogues was my only option to get rid of her at the time. So, when I woke up surrounded by concerned eyes, it was easier to climb on board to have everyone hate her. That laid the groundwork for no one to ever believe anything that Nova would say. I could not risk exposure! I decided to lay low and stay away from Jacob for a little while. Jacob was unhappy that I ghosted him because he assumed, I was dead. I tried pleading with him, but I have not heard from him since. So now I am the one being ghosted for the last four years. May as well say I have been forgotten.

This made me angrier as the days moved forward. I blamed Nova for causing me to lose the love of my life! So, it was a treat as I watched her spirit to begin dying out over the years. I felt like I had accomplished something, but I fear I was wrong. Judging by her skills she consistently demonstrates during training; I would say it is made her stronger. I thought her broken spirit would delay her receiving her wolf, but I was yet again incorrect in my assumptions. When she shifted into her wolf in midair nearly killing Neko, I was stunned and completely caught off guard! I hate to admit it, but her wolf was gorgeous! It was bigger than most with fur the color of midnight with amethyst-colored eyes. I have never seen anything like it. The whole pack witnessed her transformation and I watched as confusion and curiosity sparked in their faces. Her secret will be revealed to her and everyone else in due time.

I needed a distraction after this freak show. In the meantime, I need to assist my brother in finding a mate! I am trying to lean him toward Melody. We actually became friends shortly after my accident and later bonded over our hatred for Nova. I never disclosed Nova's secret to Melody and Malik. I did not trust that they would not let their mother know that others knew. It is better this way, but I am not so sure if this will last much longer, especially after Malik and I became mates a few months ago. He can sense something is wrong through our mate bond, but I deflect whenever he tries to pry through our mind link. After all, things did not go so well the last time I spilled the beans about this family's darkest regret.

MALIK's POV

What just happened? I cannot even believe what I just witnessed. The Moon Goddess blessed Nova with a black wolf that is nearly as big as our Alpha. I am so confused! We have always been taught that black wolves signify Alpha's blood. It just does not make any sense. Joy, the daughter of the Alpha, my mate, is not even a black wolf. Her wolf is dark brown with amber-colored eyes. I gaze up quickly to see Kylo sprinting after a now angry Nova into the wood line. I would follow but I cannot get my feet to move out of shock. Joy approaches grabbing my chin so that I can look deep into her concerned eyes. She knows something and I can tell she is ready to divulge.

"Joy, what the hell aren't you telling me?" I ask making her flinch and release my chin.

"It's best you ask your mother," she dryly states as she pivots to walk away, clearly annoyed with my reaction.

I wanted to be upset at her, but I just love her too much for it to stick. We could never stay upset at each other, especially now that she wears my mark.

I run as fast as I can in human form to find my mother to disclose everything I had just witnessed. Melody followed suit once she made it to the house sometime after me. I studied my mother's face for some sort of hint or understanding. All she replied was "When was Nova's sixteenth birthday?" she asks clearly unaware. Oddly, none of us realized Nova's birthday had come and gone. Nova did not mention anything either. I guess she figured we would not acknowledge it either way. I would not have minded witnessing her first shift though. Mother do not worry, now that she is of age, she can be sent away to find her mate. I say trying to reassure and calm a now pacing Naomi.

Melody interrupts. "I think she may have found him already, but I think she's he rejected her," she said with a smidge of pity in her voice.

Both I and my mother stopped in our tracks while giving Melody a confused look. My mother urged her to continue. And there it was....

MELODY's POV

I began to explain what I and some other she-wolves witnessed the night of the ball. It all happened so fast and I can remember being embarrassed by her smudged make-up face as she ran pass to obviously

83

fix her make up in the lady's room. To my surprise, a once puffy-eyed Nova was spotted on the dance floor like nothing ever happened. I did not put two and two together at the time. If we can find out the mate that rejected her, we can probably get to bottom of this.

"How would that solve our problem Melody?" she said yelling at me.

Why is she treating it like it is OUR problem? Nova is a black wolf, so what I say loud enough for the two of them to hear.

"MOTHER, what has you so spooked?" I say accusingly.

My mother obviously was not telling us everything and she promised she was not hiding anything. Of course, she fed us with some bullshit story of how the Moon Goddess probably gifted a broken-spirited Nova a black wolf out of pity. We did not buy it! She looked frantic and terrified at this point. Our mother rushed out of the door clutching her purse in the hunt for something or someone. She had some explaining to do and I was not going to stop pushing until she spilled the tea.

KYLO's POV

Wow! Nova was fast in both human and wolf form. It took my Alpha strength to push past her and block her path. Jax and I tried pleading with both wolf and human. She was hurting and I could feel every bit of it. I could only imagine if we had finished the whole mating process that this feeling would multiply! I found myself angry because my mate was hurting.

"Kylo, you're an idiot, he hurt our mate and you're doing nothing about it," Jax interrupts completely throwing me off my objective. "We should END them all," he continued.

I hate that our plan was falling through. Right then, I realized we had been going through this separately. We are better together, and everyone should know it too. I am snapped out of my trance when I realized I am left standing in the tree line by myself. I know where she is headed, and I follow her scent all the way there. It is where she and I usually run our wolves at night. It is mutual territory and there was not usually a threat. Once I find her looking down at the cool spring water I approach and take a seat next to her. We are both still in wolf form. We just sat there for about 45 minutes in silence before we decided to venture back to the packhouse.

Right before exiting the tree line, we grabbed some clothes that we usually keep stashed away in the trees and put them on. When we made inside, we could hear the whispers. At this point, I did not care who watched me follow Nova like a sick puppy. I wanted her and I desired everyone to know that if they have not figured it out already. Nova turned around to face me so abruptly nearly scaring me.

"Why are you following me, Kylo, aren't you worried someone will see?" she hissed at me. "You are not my mate, you REJECTED us, remember?" she yelled as tears fell down her face. "We aren't fit to be your Luna, you remember that?" she continued obviously getting angrier. "You should just leave me alone to find my second-chance mate!" this time crushing my heart into a thousand pieces.

I mean, it physically felt like my heart was falling within the pits of my stomach to be digested. In an attempt to calm the situation and mask my pain, I decided to turn and walk toward the packhouse to get as far away from Nova as I possibly could. I tried convincing myself that she needed time and she would come to her senses. How can I protect her if she acts as if she suddenly cannot stand the sight of me?

When my father and our Beta discovered Nova's huge black wolf, they were on high alert, but because they were out of the country working peace treaties with other packs, I had a couple of days to make a decision to secure Nova's safety. Ultimately, I have to do what is best for Nova, hurt or not she is our mate who we want forever and always.

NOVA's POV

I woke the next morning after my big wolf reveal feeling confused. I think I rejected our mate last night.

"Nova, he was trying to protect us both, cut him some slack because he has been there teaching, protecting, and comforting us through this whole ordeal," Amethyst interrupts.

I know it has not been easy for Kylo to hide this and he honestly has been very patient with me. He is suffering just as much as we were, and I think I may have destroyed his Hope last night. I am so numb right now. I just do not want to talk or see anyone today, so I pull the duvet covers back over my head and drift off into dreamland until I heard a clearly desperate Kylo knocking on my door.

"Are you going to get that?" Amethyst asked agitated.

UGH! I chose to ignore both Amethyst and Kylo. Everyone was getting on my last nerve I swear! Honestly, I just needed time to process all that was transpiring around me. The thought of me not being safe or welcome within my own family and pack had me hitting a downward spiral. I knew I could not stay cooped up in my room forever rolling around at my pity party. I decide to throw on my black sweatpants with a graphic tee crop top. I exit my room to head toward the kitchen to grab a bite to eat. It was weird, but I felt like someone was watching me and not in a romantic way. I stop and scope the hallway behind me and in front, but I could not spot or smell anyone's presence. I just sum it up to my overarching paranoia. When I make it downstairs, I notice a group of pack members huddled up talking about a party they were all planning to attend later in the evening. It looked as if they were drawing straws for who would be the DD (designated driver).

One of the packs she-wolves Sahara was pissed because she drew the shortest straw. "FINE, but I am not the DD next time!" she hissed through her teeth.

I chuckled a bit but did not expect to attract a crowd with my actions. When I noticed that all eyes were on me, I gulped and tried to walk away when I heard Sarah call out to me.

"NOVA! You should join us tonight, when was the last time YOU went to a party?" already knowing the answer to her question.

I had mixed emotions about attending a party with a she-wolf I nearly killed in front of the whole pack. "I may take you up on that offer, Sarah.," I say smiling making my way toward the stairs.

I can hear her sounding excited. This was very odd, and I am not sure if I should trust the invitation. It might be a great idea to get form under the same roof as Kylo for a night. Speak of the devil and he shall appear! Kylo blocked my view as I try to avoid direct eye contact with him. My face was filled with disgust because I felt he was trying to force a conversation on me that I was not ready to have. I could feel Amethyst anger rise from within me.

"You are supposed to be on my side," I tell her.

"I would be on your side if you stopped acting like a moron," she snapped at me.

Miss thang was definitely feeling herself today! I knew she was right, but I did not want to think about that right now.

KYLO's POV

I hop out of bed in a hurry and rush down with messy hair and morning breath in hopes of seeing Nova. Nope, she is not down here. Instead, I spot a few she-wolves desperately trying to present their arousal in my direction. Sorry, sweethearts, but none of you smell as sweet as my perfect mate Nova. It was not until they looked at me with wide eyes and clear embarrassment is when I realized I said that aloud. I take this as my queue to run straight to Nova's room. I knocked and knocked but to no avail, she was not answering. I could hear her wrestling with the covers obviously ignoring me. After twenty minutes of begging and pleading my attempts of entering failed. I was close to just removing the doors from the hinges, but I assumed that would not get her to talk to me. Jax succeeded in reaching her wolf Amethyst. She told him that she has been pleaded with a stubborn Nova since last night. Jax informed me of this so we decided to let her come to us when she was ready, but it had to be within the next day or so before our fathers made it back. Three hours after our failed attempts to get through to Nova, she appeared from downstairs just long enough to grab a beverage and a snack. She was greeted by some pack members that set in the dining area clowning around. I could see in some of the great faces that they were a bit scared and others look of being proud of her.

This made me feel better about the decision of letting everyone know she is my mate very soon if she would agree to it. She notices that I am staring at her and her facial expression quickly shifted to one of disgust. As she waved farewell to her little audience she turned and rolled her eyes at me and walked right past me. No lie, it felt like I was being rejected a third time by Nova. I decided to get some fresh air. I made it out front to our wrap-around porch to take a seat on our porch swings. I fell into deep thought until I was snapped out of it by one of my longtime friends Xander, our future Gamma. He is one of our most fierce warriors other than me of course. He stood at about 6'5" with blonde hair and hazel eyes. This guy was always showing all thirty-two pearly white teeth in his mouth, which drove the females here bonkers. He meant no harm, that is just who he was. I was more than confident that he could help me protect Nova since it was his fated duty. Of all people, I should have confided in him.

In a way, I am making him fail as his duty because I did not tell him that there was a Luna to protect. Everyone assumed I had not found my mate, until now. I should have known better, hell, dude was a freaking bodybuilder in human form and a lethal opponent in wolf form and he was quick. As he set down, I could tell he wanted to get something out.

"Spill it," I say to him.

"So, you mean to tell me that I've unknowingly neglected my duty to protect our newest Luna because you were embarrassed about who the Moon Goddess fated you to be with?" he asks almost accusingly.

I felt Jax rise up in me and I did everything in my power to calm him until I did. Jax still threatened Xander's wolf Zeke against my wishes. I explained the whole ordeal to him and with that, he was left with his mouth wide open. He said he understood and that he would protect her with his life.

"Yo, I heard she rejected your bro," he said with a confused look on his face.

That pain came back tenfold. "Yeah, I think she did, bro," I manage to get out without letting a tear fall.

I ran my plan to get her back with him and made a few modifications with his input. I was confident that it would work, it had to.

"How in the hell did I'll manage to fight the crazy sexual bond that connects mates this long?" he asked almost impressed.

"The hardest thing I've ever done in my life, bro," I say as we busted out laughing.

Apparently, I am now the rejected mate. This quickly traveled to my mother who is not happy with me right now. I will have some explaining to do with her later, but right now I needed to make things right with Nova.

CHAPTER 14: THE FINESSING BEGINS

NOVA's POV

When I walked past Kylo in the common area as I was leaving the kitchen, it was almost empowering yet painful. I thought I was over it but when I saw him, it was like a reminder of all the pain I have experienced. I know all of it was not his fault but a part of me is stuck in the past all of a sudden. I saw the hope that he once had for us making it work to leave his eyes.

"Either you want him, or you don't, Nova," my wolf Amethyst says sounding annoyed.

"Excuse me then!" I say rolling my eyes at her.

Although I am angry at Kylo, I just consider the long-term effects. If I stay here after I rejected him it will pain us both. I must tell him I informed his mother that will leave with her in two days' time in search of my second-chance mate. A second-chance mate is someone the Moon Goddess gifts you with. She mates us to one werewolf in a lifetime, but in some cases, she has been known to bless a few with second-chance mates, such as the mate has died, or they suffered a major heartbreak of rejection. I fall under neither category. I am prepared to spend the rest of my life alone. At least I will not have to experience another heartbreak. I had to muster up the courage to let Kylo know.

"You're making a mistake," Amethyst says closing off the mind link between the two of us. She is not a happy camper right now.

"I'm so sorry, Amethyst," I say falling to the floor sobbing. I am just so confused about life right now. I guess quitting is the easy way out. "Oh, Moon Goddess, please bestow your wisdom down on me so that I know what to do," I plead.

I just lay on the floor until I fall into a surprisingly deep sleep. I awake in the familiar golden field standing face to face once again with the beautiful being staring at me.

"Hello again, Nova," she says making me shiver all over. The power that radiates puts out makes it hard to look in her direction.

"H... Hi," I stutter. "Oh, Moon Goddess, I am confused about everything right now, why am I a black wolf? Am I destined to be an Alpha? Am I cursed? Is Kylo my brother and not mate? Did my mother have an affair? Does my father know?" I ask before she could answer either question.

"Slow down, my child, all answers will be revealed in due time," she says avoiding the answer to any of my questions. "Just know that Kylo is your one true mate and he loves you, but you are making it really hard for him to continue to chase you," she adds.

"I don't know what to do," I say hanging my head to stare at my feet.

"I had a feeling that you do, but you've been hesitant for much too long," she says turning to leave me.

"Wait, please!" I beg.

"Follow your gut, Nova, you've figured it all out, but you don't trust your answers," she said as she sat near the sparkling waterfall. "I gifted you with Amethyst for a reason, she is wise, cunning, and her spirit is strong," she said this time staring directly into my soul. "I know you'll choose correctly, my child, now make it right with both your mate and your wolf," she says as she gives me the warmest hug I have ever felt in my life.

And just like that, I wake up and hop up heading toward my bedroom door to head to Kylo's room to make this right.

I apologize to Amethyst and promised that I would not stop until Kylo and I were happy. It did not take long for her to perk up and cheer me on. As I swung the door open, Kylo's hypnotizing scent slapped me in the face. There he was, staring down at me lustfully communicating with me with his eyes. I stepped out of my door just enough pushing him out into the hallway so that I could move past him. I heard his wolf

Jax growl at me. Amethyst was running laps in my head going crazy trying to figure out what my deal was. Kylo followed me with intense eyes down the hallway. When I reached his room door, I looked back at him to verify if it was okay for me to enter. We decided a long time ago that it would not be wise to have my scent lingering in his room because he frequently had meetings in the sitting area in his room. We always met in my room because I hardly ever had visitors, I heard my wolf purring like a damn cat. Jax must have heard her because Kylo's eyes immediately filled with lust. I see him fighting with his wolf trying to snap himself back out of it. His aroma is heightened as I enter his humble abode. His room is about five of mine.

After all, he is the son of the Alpha and he is the future Alpha. I am tired of playing around and teasing each other. Tonight, was going to change that. I have become so comfortable around this man naked at this point. I was tired of touching what I could of not experience internally. I began to undress to head toward his large bathroom that was drooped in gold from the shower heads to the oversized tub knobs with the accented tile that complimented its beauty. He had one of those removable shower heads that let out the just the right pressure to the body. I did not realize I was staring at it until he nudged me saying, "Should I be jealous?" smirking up at the showerhead.

At this point, I am butt naked standing next to him. I did not realize he matched my nakedness until he walked behind me burying his mouth into my neck and "JR" poked me in the back. No matter what he tried to do to fight back giving me what I wanted, it would not work tonight. Hell, I am at a point that I would take it if I had to. Amethyst let Jax know what our plan was and of course, we had him on our side. With that thought, I smiled sneakily inside.

I turn around and wrapped my arms around his neck, "Let's get cleaned up first."

He squats down and lifts me up and carried me into the shower.

As we teased around lathering each other up it came to an abrupt stop once I locked in on the showerhead. Do not judge me! Before I knew it, Kylo detached it and began to please my sweet spot with it. "How does he know right where to put it?" I can feel that we are quickly becoming one. I begin to release uncontrollable loud moans as I lick my lips in response to this unbelievable pleasure. Kylo sees this as an opportunity to turn the pressure up just enough to make me quiver. He tactfully inserted two fingers within my core as he simultaneously pulled my waist into him. He physically made me feel weak in the knees as he continued to play every string within me. I gasp as he buries his face in my neck devouring my shudders in half mouth. I was not sure how much longer I could stand him not penetrating me something more than his fingers. As he removed his fingers from my sweet spot, I spin around and kissed him with everything in me. I was begging for it and he knew it! Kylo turned off the water and lifted me up bridal style and carried me to the bed. He quickly ran over to the door to make sure he had locked it and the windows. He decided to blast music that only vibes as obvious sex songs as he made his way back over to me. I sat up on my elbows watching him in all his glory run his sexy ass from the door to the window.

"Why did you turn on the music?" I ask.

The look he gave me proved to me that he was on the same of making me cum all night. There will be no stopping tonight. It made my core scream and drip like it was an ocean between my thighs with just the thought. I look down at his dick and I swear he is grown another inch. I am convinced if he puts that inside of me it is going to come out through the other end. I think he can see the concern in my eyes.

"Don't be afraid, we can go as slow as you want," he says reassuring me.

"Do as you please. baby," I respond allowing my body to go limp as he climbed on the top of me.

"Oh, baby. you're trying to kill me with your arousal!" he said so got damn sexy.

This man is MINE and I dare ANYONE to come in between what we have.

KYLO's POV

When Nova came into my room and began undressing, I could not shake my wolf. I did not really want to. Jax let me in on what Nova and her wolf Amethyst planned. They were ready to take US tonight! I am not against it! It was actually my plan to finish the mating ritual and mark her so that the pack knew it was real. She is MINE and I am HERS! After we had our fun in the shower, I made sure to lock every entrance to my room. Shit, she is so damn perfect as she sat relaxed on her elbows ready to take all of me into her temple. I see her eyeing "JR" almost looking a bit scared. I assure her that we can take it slow. I slowly climb on top of her as I felt her relax.

"You sure you're ready, baby?" I ask. "It's going to hurt, but I promise it's the last time I will hurt you," I say to her.

"I know," she responded as she bites her bottom lip prepared to take all of me. She smiled back up at me, giving me the confirmation, I needed.

As I slowly place the tip at her entrance inserting it in and out, I felt her dripping core trying to grab at it. I was driving her mad! When I slid deeper inside her, Nova started to clinch from the pain. I offered to stop but she insisted I kept going. This time my strokes were faster and harder. The way her pussy gripped my dick was inebriating. We moved in sync as Nova begin to guest her hips beneath me as she dug her claws deeply in my skin drawing blood. There was no way she would leave this room not bearing my mark.

NOVA's POV
Kylo tiptoes around my entrance with his fully erect manhood. As he slowly eases his way inside me I clench at the sudden feeling of pain. He looks at me with dread written all over his face.

"Do you want me to stop?" he asked concerned.

"Please don't," I reassure him.

I swear it felt like forever before he could fully fit all of that inside me. I felt pain followed by the most pleasurable feeling I have ever had. As he thrust slowly in and out of my temple I moaned vigorously. I completely understand the reason for the blasted music now. I begin to grind my hips against him as I take all of him within me.

"Wrap those long-ass legs around me, baby," I hear him say in between thrusts.

"YES!" I say in between moans.

I oblige, of course! When I lock my ankles on his back, he grabs my ass in his hands and begins to thrust harder and faster. He is deeper inside me as if this were any more possible. He broke down my walls and left me feeling exhausted and he wasn't even through.

I viciously clawed his back. I could feel the blood seeping from his skin and visibly saw it under my nails. I took every inch of Kylo and it caused a monstrous orgasm to erupt from my core, but he never stopped.

As he brought his face down to play tongue wars with me, I grabbed his neck while simultaneously running my hand through his jet-black curly hair. He smelled so good that I wanted to physically take a bite out of him. I know, weird right.

"Can I mark you?" he asked.

"You can do whatever you want," I say without hesitation.

He ran his tongue around the area just below my neck where he would soon be marked by him. Kylo revealed his fangs and bit down causing me to squeal in satisfaction. Right as he finished, he licked gently wiped the blood away from my new mark. He pulled me in his arms and held me and asked how I felt and if I was tired. I told him I was in awe and no I was not tired. Whatever I said woke up the sleeping beast AGAIN. This is going to be a long night and I ecstatically welcome it!

KYLO's POV

Last night was one of the best moments of my life. Nova handled herself like a pro once she was comfortable with my size. I wake up to my beautiful Nova still sleep from having an exhausting number of orgasms. I decide against waking her. I do not care if my room smells like her and she smells like me. She's MINE and it is time everybody knew that. I jump in the shower and throw on my Nike gray sweatpants and a Nike white tee, with that matching kicks and ready myself to head out of the door. I left a note for Nova letting her know I was going to handle pack business, AKA let my mother know. She wakes up as I turned the know reading my note. Nova stops me in my tracks by saying, "I think we should do this together," with a smile.

I run over and kiss her on the forehead which then turned into me trying to catch her lips. She shies away complaining about her morning breath. When she notices I do not care she kissed me back more passionately than last night. Here we go again, I cannot hide my obvious arousal when I am hit with the scent of hers. She pulls me down to her and mount me. Mind you, she is not wearing underwear. I gave her one of my black T-shirts to sleep in last night after our shower.

Nova's arousal has the front of my gray sweatpants drenched. She sees this and is a little embarrassed, but I am turned on even more.

Nova assists me removing my shirt as I stand to remove my pants and boxer briefs. Before I could get out of my pants good, she has knocked me over on my back. I watch as she exhales as she sits on top of me taking in every inch of me inside her. I feel her temple walls grip around my dick, and this only causes Jr to grow within her. She moaned loudly as she begins grinding back and forth as I grip her waste directing her movements. I thrust my hips ups so that she could devour all of me inside her. I cannot lie, she is surprising me with her riding skills. She leans down to plant a passionate kiss on my lips as she rocks the lower half of her body in an up and down motion. I swear this girly has no spine.

"Baby, you feel so damn good," she pants in between moans.

This woman drives me crazy. I am not sure how I would live with myself if something happened to her. I am brought back to reality as Nova slides into an orgasm. I lift her up by her waist allowing her to lay on her chest. I then climbed on top of her as I admired her caramel skin that looked as if it had been kissed by the sun.

I insert myself in her and lean down telling her to lift up. She seemed a little confused.

"Lift your ass up for me, babe," I say and like a good girl, she arched her back allowing me to go all in. As I spread her cheeks to go deeper, I felt her quivering on the verge of another orgasm, "Hold on, baby, not yet," I tell her. I grab stroke harder and faster leaving down locking my hands in her gorgeous locks. "Now," I whisper.

We both release at the same time. If we keep going like this, we will never leave this room. I swear we are going to fuck her into an oblivion. We both decided it would be a good idea to shower and grab a bite to eat and replenish everything we lost during our sex-capades. I throw on another set of gray joggers, and the same white tee and kicks. I give Nova a pair of my camouflage joggers and a black t-shirt with a camouflage Nike check on the front with my Nike slide on slippers. She decided to let those long back curly locks glow free. How does she look flawless in men's clothes, my clothes? She looks better in them than I do. Nova heard my thought, damnit I forgot to block the mate link. Now that we started the mating process, we intertwined for life. Her thoughts are mine and her are mine. If you do not block that person out everything is transparent between you two. She just looks up with a smile as she blushed. She nudges me lovingly. Once she was done moisturizing her face and finger combing through her hair we were out of the door.

CHAPTER 15: FACING THE LUNA

NOVA's POV

Before heading out, Kylo mind linked his mother informing her that he was on his way and he was not alone. He did not give her too much information over their exchange. We headed in the direction of the Luna's quarters. Kylo and I looked at each other before entering. He gave me a reassuring nudge as he announced himself as he opened the door. As he entered, I insisted on following directly behind him. To my surprise, there our Gamma stood there with a look of concern. Oh, no, what if he does not approve? The Gamma has been a father figure to me these last four years. I think he sensed my reservation, so he softened his facial expression and embraced me in a hug. I always found comfort in him and his family. They were always so generous to me. He pulled me away and just looked at me with such pride.

We were interrupted by Kylo's possessive growl. Seriously, Kylo, I think to myself as I playfully punch him in the arm.

"Well, congratulations, you two, I can tell you have begun the mating process ," Luna interrupts.

I must have been the color of a tomato if it was humanly possible for my caramel complexion to turn that color.

"As happy as I am to watch this display of pure love, we have some serious business to discuss," she says with seriousness.

"Yes, Luna," I respond bowing my head with respect.

She proceeded to explain to Kylo how it would be best that I depart with her a day from now to stay with one of her relatives until the threat against me die down. He was not happy about this revelation, but he also agreed that it would be best. They were going to move fast, and I could not be here for whatever they were planning.

"I want to help, after all, it is a threat against me," I say sternly.

Kylo pleaded for me to listen until I withdrew my attempts to help.

LEAH's POV (PACK's LUNA)

"Kylo, Nova honey, please do not take these threats lightly. You have enemies that want you out of the picture so they can not only mate with my son but bare his pups. I have informed KYLO's father of our concerns and pressed the importance of not disclosing this to our Beta, your father. He is meeting to discuss one last treaty agreement in the morning, and he will be on the first flight home. But Nova, you must leave with me in a days' time. I am not risking the future if this pack because of someone else secrets and neglect. Tell me you both understand," I ask the both of them.

They nod their head in agreement. "Well, it is settled! We leave tomorrow night."

EMIT's POV (PACK's GAMMA)

I am over the moon when I find out the Luna's and I revelation rang true. Nova and Kylo are fated to be together for the end of time. Naomi is punishing her daughter for something she did to that child. Instead of making it right, she decided to treat our dear Nova like trash when she deserved so much better than that. Our Beta was no better because he condoned it by not intervening. He was hypnotized by Naomi's beauty and cunning attitude. When were young Naomi had all of our attention, including other werewolves that came for visits? She was out-of-this-world beautiful! She would remind you of Stacey Dash with a sprinkle on Angelina Jolie. Not only did she carry herself as a warrior, but she could also back it up too. I would have never thought in a million years that she would turn into this cold-hearted being that she had become. Enough of that, let us get down to business.

"My spies confirmed what I suspected for weeks now," I say catching their attention. "Your mother has dabbled in witchcraft in order to destroy the bond between you and Kylo, leaving him open to falsely mate your sister Melody," I say disgusted.

"Kylo could never fall for that, my scent would be overpowering that he would not be able to deny it," Nova said blushing.

"Nova is right, I could never resist her," Kylo interrupted.

I went on to explain the effects of witchcraft and how powerful it can be, especially if she found a powerful enough to break a mate bond or at least mask it. "Nova, they are going to get rid of you someway somehow," I say with seriousness in my voice. "STAY READY!"

KYLO POV

"Why do I smell your arousal after the news we received?" I ask Nova.

"It's something about a forbidden love that turns me on, but I do understand that I'm in real danger Kylo," she reassures me. "Seems to me that I'm not the only one," as she looks down spotting the bulge in my pants.

I cannot believe we are standing in my mother's office thinking about fucking each other after processing such terrible news of Nova's family suspected betrayal.

"We have to get you to safety, babe," I say.

"I'll do whatever I need to do in order to survive and live out my days with you forever and always," she says making my heart skip a beat.

Nova leans on my chest and I wrap my arm around her with sadness written all over our face.

Before we make it out of the Luna's office good, Nova is dragging me in the nearest laundry closet in the hallway just feet away from the pack's common area. She tips toes in order to plant a passionate kiss on my lips as I wrap her tightly in my arms. Nova found her way to the inside of my joggers grabbing my manhood in the cuffs of her palms and fingertips. As the stroke intensifies, she goes down on her knees and takes me in her mouth. Both her boldness and forcefulness caught me off guard, but I was not complaining. I guided her head and forth as she fondled my jewels and captured ALL of me in her mouth. I could tell that she relaxed her throat to accommodate my inches. Just when I thought I was about painting the inside of her mouth she pulls it out just enough to tease the head of my pen is with her tongue.

She moved down to my testicles and took them in her mouth sensually moving them around with her warm tongue. I wanted to be inside her in more than one way. As she rises from the floor wiping her mouth, I spun her around a pull-down her joggers to expose her naked ass. I insert me in her and dared her to scream. As I rammed over and over inside her, she whimpered with pleasure. She placed her hand over her mouth as I pressed deeper and deeper inside her smacking her on the ass. We heard someone coming but she would not let me stop and I did not want to! I spread her cheeks just enough to penetrate deeper inside her with every stroke. Nova was on edge and it just made my wolf kiss his mind. I had the most intense explosion inside her as I still stroked in and out. I just could not get enough of this delicious specimen. She is trying to kill me, and I will cooperate!

CHAPTER 16: UNWIND A BIT

NOVA's POV

After Kylo's buddies begged him to hit up the party Sarah and some of her friends were discussing, he decided it may be nice to unwind. It was being held by a neighboring pack and our two packs often partied together. I ask Kylo not to mention us being mates to anyone just for tonight, especially going into unknown territory. He agreed because he wanted the announcement to be in front of the pack. We decided to keep them guessing. Willow was all for it!

"Nova, oh, my Moon Goddess, what are we going to wear?" she says jumping up and down with excitement.

"Girl, it is just weird that Sarah invited me to this party," I say but in the form of a question.

"Yeah, it is, but we will watch her like a hawk and end her if need be," Willow says to me as I am knowing she is not joking.

We scrounge around Willow's closet to find the perfect outfits for tonight. I am actually excited to get dolled up again. I decided on a sexy RED form-fitting dress that stops right above the knees. This dress was simple but perfect for the occasion.

It ties around the neck allowing all of my shoulders to be visible, just enough to carry my mark. It revealed my obliques and most of my back. I decided to complement it with some gold open toe two-inch heels, golden accessories, black blazer, and a majority black clutch with gold accents. I am not trying to be too far from the ground tonight. I am not that comfortable in heels. Me and Mr. Floor and Mr. Ground would be awfully familiar with each other tonight if I decided to more than two inches from off of it. My hair was bone straight, thanks to Willow. She has a gift and she know it. Willow hopped back and forth from my makeup to her own. Just a little gold eye shadow, mascara, and lip gloss for me. We were ready to leave once Willow threw on the royal blue dress that fit her slender figure with her open-toe black heels and her all-black clutch. She decided to wear loose curls in her shoulder-length hair. She was remarkable! As we headed out of the door, I decided to carry my blazer in hand ready to party. We had Emit's car tonight. He knew we were responsible. I doused myself in my favorite vanilla scent, trying to mask Kylo's scent. NO one knew we were mates except for the obvious people that were close to us.

Once Willow and I made it down the stairs, we were greeted by Zion and a lot of eyes glued on us by some we knew and others we did not. I immediately noticed Kylo licking his lips from across the room. I am immediately aroused at the sight of his appearance. He had his same messy curls, white t-shirt, dark blue jeans, with a navy-blue blazer, and the Jordan sneakers to match. He was on a phone call that I clearly distracted him from, although it seemed serious. Once Kylo realized he was staring at me along with all the others, he departs the room to continue with his phone call. How does this man have this effect on me? Geesh! As always, I could feel the hate radiating off of Joy, Meyonna, and Melody. The crazy part is, Meyonna and Melody both want the same thing and that thing was MY mate! I cannot wait for the big reveal, I had to laugh at that myself.

I head towards the door to leave when I was stopped on my tracks by Sarah. She grabs my hand and escorts me to the kitchen. The look she had in her eye was of pure concern.

"Nova, I do not want you to feel uncomfortable by me, we fought, you won, and that is what it is," she says sounding genuine. "I want to apologize if I ever made you feel uncomfortable or made you feel like I was angry with you," she finishes.

Sarah went not to explain how that fight gave her a different perspective of me. She gained a greater level of respect for me and always knew I was a fighter. Her last statement had me in shambles,

"Nova, please be careful and watch your back with those three out there, they mean you no good," she said pulling me close.

"Why would you think that, Sarah?" I ask acting completely oblivious to the fact.

"They want what is fated to you and only you," she whispers.

"Okay, cut the shit, Sarah, and stop talking in riddles, what's going on?" I say annoyed but low enough for only her to hear.

"They want YOUR mate, Kylo!" she says boldly. "I will NOT allow anyone to hurt our future Luna!" Sarah adds with seriousness in her voice.

"How do you know that?" I ask curiously.

"Nova, it may not be clear to most, but a blind man can tell that Kylo cares deeply for you. He was about to snap my neck the day I slammed you to the ground, I saw it in his eyes that he wanted me dead," she said sounding frightened.

I pulled her into a tight hug expecting her to push me away, but she did the opposite and held me tighter.

"Now let us unwind a bit," Sarah said as she wrapped her arm around my neck.

We drive up to this huge fenced-off mansion. It is almost enchanting. We see someone vomiting on the front lawn and others holding a beer bottle in their hand relishing in each other's company. I see Kylo, Malik, and Reggie get out of the car in front of us. Kylo did not deal with Neko after what happened and for other reasons he could not discuss yet, but mostly because of what he did to me. Malik is on his hit list next, but he has to be strategic about his next move. Kylo is secretly finding replacements for Malik as the Beta. He has some prospects. They enter the mansion and are recognized by some old friends. They immediately pulled them in handing them a drink. Willow and Sarah exit the car first and I am wrestling with my clutch that ripped a small hole in my dress. Once I withdraw from the car, we head inside. Willow of course abandons us for her mate Zion who is standing to wait with a drink. Sarah spots her mate Reggie and nudges me to talk to Kylo. I decide against it. For the first 40 minutes of the party, I'm approached by our pack members and others and partake in small conversations. I kept filling like I was being watched.

NOVA's POV

"Kylo, I feel like I am being watched by someone other than by you," I say through our mate link.

"Who says I am watching you?" he sheepishly asked.

"I am not crazy, Kylo, I know you are watching me, and you have not stopped since I entered this house," I snickered.

"How do you know I am watching you if you are not watching me?" he asked smirking.

"Man, I am going to withhold myself from you if you keep talking to me like that," I said laughing.

"Why do you want to punish me, queen?" he jokingly asked.

"Because I know you cannot resist me," I teased.

"So, if you know that why are you trying to punish me? You are MINE," he finished.

"Am I?" I jokingly asked.

"I can smell your arousal, Nova," he said hinting at something other than a conversation.

"You only think you smell my arousal, Kylo," I giggled.

I suddenly felt chills on my skin and a slight gust of wind in the back of my dress. He had his hand under my dress in one swift movement.

"Kylo, what the hell?" I said slapping his chest.

"Scared?" he teased.

"Are you trying to expose us?" I asked looking around trying to ensure no one saw him.

"No, baby, you just look immaculate in your attire tonight," he whispered in my ear.

"I am going to walk away now. Besides, I need to use the ladies' room," I replied walking away.

XANDER's POV (FUTURE GAMMA)

Nova heads to find the ladies' room and I notice Kylo inconspicuously follow behind her from a distance. He wants to ensure her safety, even if he has to follow from a distance. As Nova enters the restroom, she turns to shut the door when Kylo places his hand on it and walks in. Kylo waves back at me to make sure no one enters or comes near the door. I did not care because my boy was finally being a mate to HIS mate. I was later joined by who I wanted to be my mate, Julissa. They have been in there a while and I am growing impatient, but I know I cannot rush the process. My duty is to protect our future Luna at all costs. I am willing to lay my life on the line for her and I barely know her. It is odd before Kylo told me about Nova and him being fated mates, I already felt drawn to her the night of the ball. I cannot explain it, but I wanted to protect her. I NEEDED to protect her.

NOVA's POV

I head for the ladies' room to catch a break from the unknown eyes of the crowd. I met some pretty cool wolves here tonight. It has been exhausting doing this alone and not alongside my mate and he is within arm's reach. As I arrive at the ladies' room, I feel Kylo's body heat, and his scent wraps around me. Is he seriously following me to the bathroom? What is he thinking about his sloppy actions? I enter the restroom and turn back to close and lock the door, Kylo stops it with his hands and quickly enters and locks the door behind him. There are no words exchanged before he has my back against the wall simultaneously lifting my dress up to my stomach and pulling my black lace to the side preparing to enter me. I straddle him and hold on for dear life as he quickly undoes his belt. He slides in me with no hesitation as he plants passionate kisses from my lips to my neck, and down to my breast that is now cuffed in his hands as he rams me against the bathroom wall. My moans are getting louder. Kylo cuffs his hands on my mouth as he jives his hips in a circular motion as he thrusts deeper inside me.

He forces my ankles to unlock from behind him and lifts my legs to his shoulders and his rams deeper into my soul. I am slowly losing control and I cannot control my loud moans through his cuffed hands over my mouth.

"Scream for Daddy, I want you to cum all over this dick when I tell you to, okay, baby?" he said more like an order.

"Yes, Daddy.," I weakly respond.

He gyrates his hips in a motion as if he is doing mountain climbers, making me lose my mind until I hear "Now." I let go of everything I had in me releasing my monstrous orgasm. Kylo releases my legs that have gone limp from my power loss. He holds himself up against the wall and me as I listened to his racing heartbeat and loud breathing.

"I do not deserve you, my queen," he says nearly out of breath.

I look in his face to see a single tear fall from his eye. I grab his chin to kiss away the lone tear. "What is wrong, K?" I ask a bit worried.

He steps back and we begin to fix ourselves and wipe away the signs of sex. "I should not have let them treat you so bad when we are growing up and I should not have pretended you did not exist," he said. "You were my world even back then, but I refuse to allow myself to feel anything for you, especially after you slapped me when I tried to kiss you, I felt rejected even before we were fated by the Moon Goddess," he finished. "That is one reason I rushed to reject you when I found out, I was afraid you were going to reject me first. When you accepted without even a fight, I felt my heartbreak, physically!" he added.

I spent the next twenty minutes reassuring him that I have forgiven him, and I did not blame him for all of it. Once we were done exchanging pleasantries, we exited the bathroom strategically one by one. I doused myself in my portable vanilla spray and decided to enjoy my time with the rest of my newfound crew, which so happens to be Kylo's circle. I was happy, I mean really happy!

CHAPTER 17: WHEN IT HITS THE FAN

Today was like any other day except the fact that I cannot shake the conversation I had with Kylo, his mother, and our Gamma yesterday. When I woke up, I decided to continue on with my morning routine seven-mile run, pull-ups, ab and bag routine, and hand-to-hand combat.

"There you go, you're getting stronger, No-No," said our Gamma.

So yeah, I forgot to mention Willow's dad still gives me private lessons before the pack wakes. I could hear my name and the disgust behind it.

"Nova, you WHORE!" said my mother.

"Mom, what's wrong?" I say terrified.

"Are you trying to FUCK your Gamma now?" she yells loud enough for him to hear.

Here we go, is all I could think. "Why do you hate me so much, Mother?" I ask in search of reasoning in her eyes. "Just because you're a whore, does that make me one too?" I spit back at her.

"C-c-come again, Nova," she stutters.

"You heard what I said, it seems like I'm not the one that has some explaining to do," I yell loud enough for most of the pack to hear.

The Gamma grabs my arm and gives me a look that would have killed me if it could have.

All I heard was "RUN!" his inner wolf Malcolm says to me. As I run into the tree line with tears streaming down my face, I mind link

Kylo to let him know what happened. I could hear the Gamma try to calm my mother from coming after me. Whatever he said, it stopped her dead in her tracks. She would not have been able to catch me because I had already tied my clothes to my ankles and shifted at this point. I must have zoned out because I ran nearly to our border where I met the most beautiful scene I have ever seen! It was a river flowing so peacefully while accompanied by a waterfall. The water was so clear that I could see the fish that swam in it. I sat next to the water until I was tempted to jump in, but I decided against it. Kylo knew where to meet me because we had come here quite a few times before. I shifted back to my human form and threw my clothes back on. Unbeknownst to me, I was followed.

"What are you doing here, STUPID?" yells my brother Malik and his friends Neko and Sloan in unison.

Right as I began to shift, I was being held under the water fighting for my life, hitting my head on a huge rock. All I could hear my brother say is "It's better if you died that day, don't you ever speak to my mother that way, why can't you just disappear for good?" This HURT!

You know when they say your life flashes before your eyes, let me tell you, all I could focus on was fighting until flashes came flooding at me like it was a dream. My limbs felt like 100-pound sandbags and I could no longer fight it as a succumbed to blackness. This must have had my brother and his friends scared shitless that they believed had killed me, but honestly, they probably couldn't be prouder that they killed the pack slave, weakling, whore, moron, and any other ungodly insult they'd like to throw at me. This was the day I was broken mentally and emotionally. When they released me, my body was drug out of the water is all I could imagine as my chest was being pumped until it was in excruciating pain. I began to regurgitate water from my diaphragm.

Next thing I know. I am surrounded by about seven wolves I did not recognize. They did not smell rogue, though. I blacked out again from the trauma.

"Am I dead?" I ask as I enter the golden field as I face the most beautiful being, I have ever seen or imagined.

"Do you know who I am, my child?" asks the beautiful woman.

"No, ma'am, I do not," I say. "For a second, I was going to say Moon Goddess but that would be silly!" I chuckle.

"Why would that be so outrageous, my child?" she asks as a quizzical expression rest on her face.

"Because a person like me would NEVER be so lucky to have the Moon Goddess appear to me, I am nothing," I say sadly. I am not sure what happened under that water, but it is just too difficult to want to continue living.

"NOVA!" she yells completely snapping me out of my thoughts. "You are a special young lady that was created from both lust and love!" she states lovingly. "You just need to be strong and your wolf will guide you when the time is right, hold on just a little longer and the truth shall be revealed," she states confidently.

With that, I feel like I am on fire as my body screams from what feels like every bone in my body has been broken. Yeah, I am being a little dramatic, but hell, I am tired!

I woke up in a room that I did not recognize as I listened to yelling outside my door by two males who obviously held status here. Who are they, I wondered to myself?

"Hi, sweetie, you're awake," states a small woman with light brown hair, green eyes, and black glasses.

"Where am?" I ask. I had so many questions that I could not get them all out. I was weakened from my near-death experience.

"You're in the Gray Wolf Pack's hospital," she says grabbing my chart.

She asked for my name and could not for the life of me, I did not know it. I started balling uncontrollably. I know I was running from something, but I could not for the life of me remember a thing.

"It's okay, love, I'm sure you're important to someone and they will come scouting for you," she says attempting to calm me down.

I could not help but have this feeling as if I were running from something. "Please do not put out the word that you have found me to neighboring packs," I plead with her.

She noticed that I had been marked. "Young lady, are you possibly running from your mate?"

That woke up something in me, but I was unsure if it were a good feeling or a bad one. "MAYBE!" I yell.

I made her promise to not announce my arrival to anyone else. I told her that once I was feeling up, I would leave. She begged me to stay and meet their Alpha Azrael.

After eight days in the pack hospital and a little rehab therapy, I was ready to meet their pack Alpha in hopes that he would let me stay. Here goes nothing...

CHAPTER 18: MEETING ALPHA AZRAEL

AZRAEL's POV

I was informed about a young female being fished out of the lake and brought to our pack hospital. I have been told that she is awake now but cannot remember a thing. This immediately sparks my interest and makes me feel this young wolf is untrustworthy. I have been so caught off in pack business that I have not had much time to give that situation much attention. Jacob, one of my pack members along with two of his comrades have been keeping an eye on who enters and exits her room. She could be a spy from a neighboring pack, and I am not taking that chance. I will personally rip her to shreds if I find out she has been lying to us all. A little over a week has gone by since our pack doctor Victoria has attempted to nurse her back to health. It is clear that she has grown fond of her.

My son Xavier made a visit to her a couple of days ago and came back saying that something feels off about her. This sent me into high alert because Xavier is usually right when it comes to reading people. Guess he inherited it from me. Victoria informed me that this young female was well enough to entertain an audience with me if I was open to it. She left me saying that she believes it is way overdue that I have met her. Why would it be overdue for me to meet nobody, a stranger? I shook it off and cleared my schedule to listen to this newcomer plead her case on why I should trust her enough to allow her to run with my pack.

"Keep an open mind, please, she just may surprise you," Victoria said as she walked away.

I wrestled with her words for a good fifteen minutes before I was graced with my pregnant mate Hannah's presence. She could see the uneasiness in my body language.

"What's got you all riled up this early in the day, babe?" she asks furrowing one eyebrow as she sat on my lap.

She is aware of our visitor and I explain that I will be meeting with her today.

"I'll come with!" she says excitedly.

I have done my best to keep her out of that strangers' quarters. She is carrying my pup and I cannot risk the chance that I am being targeted, therefore so is my family.

"That's won't be necessary, sweet pea, I got it covered," I say trying to reassure her, but she was not lacking down.

"I do not think so, I was fated to walk by your side and that's exactly where I'll be when you speak to the young wolf," she says putting her hands on her hip giving me no hint that she was willing to back down.

If I have not learned anything over the years, I learned not to challenge a pregnant she-wolf. "FINE," I say not really agreeing with my outburst.

NOVA's POV

The day came for me to meet the pack's Alpha Azrael. I could not imagine what he must have thought of me, weak, runaway, spy, liar, and the Moon Goddess only know what he assuming about me. Hell, I did not even know me. I mean, how does someone forget their own name. I have not heard from my wolf and maybe it is because I do not know how to call on her. I hate that I even remember my wolf's name to call on her. I have made many attempts and to no avail, nothing. I am snapped out of my thoughts by their pack doctor Victoria. She has really looked out for me during the short period of time I have been here. She even gave me a name, Star. I know, sounds like she is naming a puppy, but she thought it would be a good idea to greet the Alpha with a name.

"Why Star?" I ask her.

"Because I would always catch you staring into the night through that window every night and I have followed your gaze a many of times and you seem to lock in on this one particular star, hence the name.," she chuckles while tossing me a loose-fitting white t-shirt shirt and some black leggings.

I was nervous because I do not know if danger is following me and I have led it here or if I was kicked out of my pack and classified as a rogue. I was driving myself stir crazy with all the unanswered questions I had. It has been very frustrating, to say the least. I have prayed to the Moon Goddess for answers and I consistently receive, you are exactly where you are supposed to be at this very moment. She would not give any hints of my name, where I am from, my wolf's name, I mean nothing! Why am I supposed to be here I wonder? Guess I will find out in due time.

It has not been all bad. I met a fellow wolf named Xavier. He was breathtakingly stunning for a male wolf. He towered over home standing at about 6'5", caramel skin, muscular build, a mixture of hazel and green eyes, with just one dimple on the left cheek. He has not mentioned it, but I am certain he is the son of the Alpha. From the look on his face when first laying eyes on me, made my skin tingle a bit from his overpowering Ora. It was like I was familiar to him as he was to me. We sit and give each other curious looks, not the kind of attraction but more so "Do I know you?" type of stares.

"Oh, Moon Goddess, please do not let this be the mate that I may be running from.," I said out loud.

He laughed so hard that tears were falling from his eyes. "Trust and believe that I am not your mate and you are definitely not running from me, I do not know you.," he said in between laughs.

It was weird because we had a strange pull between us. He felt it too, but he never uttered a word of it. Xavier was intrigued to find out, so he popped in every day for the next few days to follow. We would have simple conversations and quite a bit of laughs. I found out he found his mate; her name is Chloe and she hates some girl named Amber. We laughed at how I could remember everyone else name but my own. Xavier has been great, to say the least, but I still can tell he is a little uneasy about divulging too much information to me and that was smart of him. He even helped me through my rehab when Victoria was not around. It was nice to be around wolves that seem to care so much about me that did not know me. I guess they are getting to know me as I am myself.

XAVIER's POV

I have visited this she-wolf our pack doctor is now calling Star a couple of times the past few days. It is some sort of connection between us and I am unsure of what this means. It is not like a mate pull, but more of a... honestly, I am not so sure. She expressed her concern about addressing our Alpha, my father. Yeah, I never disclosed that I am Alpha Azrael's son, the future Alpha of this pack. I did not want her to assume that she was in good for me that she would be a shoo-in. I trailed carefully because I am not big on allowing my feelings to determine the outcomes of my decisions. I decided to skip a day of visiting because I could feel our bond forming. It had me restless at night just wrecking my brain of who sent her here and why is she here right before I take my oath to assume the role of Alpha upon completion of my two-year training and leave for training. My ceremony will occur on the night of the full moon three weeks from now. My wolf O'Rian has been losing his mind since she has been here. He keeps saying, "We will find out soon enough," but that is not enough for me. To say that we are part of each other, O'Rian is really good at keeping secrets from me, it drives me mad! I thought it would be best that I informed my father of this. As I watched his look on his face go from interested to concerned. He knew I had a gift for reading people. I tried to calm him and let him know that it was not so much of a bad feeling, more like she is supposed to be here. Listening to me say this calmed him a bit, but my father had always been paranoid and on high alert for any threat. He had his reasons.

STAR's (NOVA) POV

I jumped in the shower, brushed my teeth, moisturized, and brushed my now matted hair up into a bun. That is failed as all my hair ties popped from the thickness of my hair. I decided to let it flow free and slid on the red Chuck Taylor's Victoria had latex out for me. She could tell I was nervous and offered some advice.

"Be completely honest with the Alpha, he can sense when someone is lying to him fairly well," she says with all seriousness in her voice.

I have no intention of lying to him, but I nodded in appreciation and walked by her side as she escorted me across the pack grounds in the direction of his office I assumed. It was absolutely gorgeous here with the surrounding gardens and the breathtaking waterfall just near the tree line. The thought of seeing the extravagant view made my head hurt. It was like someone was trying to get through or a memory that I had intentionally locked away nearly broke a barrier in my brain. I stopped and let out an involuntary squeal from the pain as I held my head in both my hands until it subsided. I explained to Victoria what I felt, and she thought I was correct in my assumptions.

We kept walking one cent finished explaining and I continued to take in the view. As we walked past the courtyards, I saw warriors training, some swimming, barbecuing, climbing, cleaning, etc. I could stay here forever if the Alpha allows me to that is. I just hope this meeting goes well and I can begin to live my life again, whatever that looks like. As we approached the oversized brick mansion, I was in awe as the huge steel doors parted. The interior was absolutely breathtaking! There were wrap around stairs that greeted you with the foyer with fancy steel designs etched in its black foundation. Once I picked my jaw up off the ground from admiring the so incredibly detailed cream, soft orange, and golden fixtures and furniture, we headed down a wide-open hallway. It was like every room had its own theme and scent.

Once we came to a halt at an extravagant cherry wood color door, that clearly weighed more than I did, we stopped. Victoria knocked until she heard "ENTER." Once we step foot in the Alpha's office, he locked in on me and my eyes were drug from the floor to his. It was that same familiar look Xavier gave me every time he would see me. I am starting to wonder if they may know who my family is and how I could make it back to them. But what if I was running for my family and reached out to them and they are planning to ship me back to whatever I was running from? I gulped at the thought of this. Alpha Azrael stare became uncomfortable. He could sense this too it too but he did not let up until this beautiful sun-kissed diva around my height with what looked to be auburn-colored hair, with a long black sundress on and sandals struts in the room holding what looked to be a fresh cup of lemonade she was bringing to Azrael. When she turns and realizes I am standing there all we heard was a glass shatter that had fallen from her hands.

"I should leave.," I say making my way to the door.

"Victoria, leave us.," I hear her say. "Who are you, child?" she asks quizzically.

"I... I am not 100 percent sure of how to answer that question.," I say barely above a whisper.

They went in to ask me what the last thing I remember was.

"I remember running until I couldn't breathe, it is like I was trying to get away from something or someone.," I answer honestly.

I explain about the flashes I have been getting the last few days but each one has given me a monstrous headache.

"Why are you two looking at me that way?" I asked stepping back nearly falling backward.

"Sorry, love, you just look like someone we used to know, that's all," the lady whose name I still do not know. She must have read my expression before introducing herself as Hannah, Luna of the pack I am trying to become a part of. I had my guards up for sure but them stepping back a bit eased my tension.

There is something I know they are not saying, and this is me more intrigued more than anything. When it felt like the air was being sucked out of the room, Xavier walks through the door.

"Hey, Star, how are you feeling today?" he asks obviously in a good mood.

Alpha Azrael has not said a word to me since I walked in, he just stared, awkwardly.

"Dad, can we discuss the arrival of the neighboring packs for my ceremony around noon?" Xavier says confirming that he is the Alpha's son.

I did not look surprised and he caught that.

"You knew?" he asked.

"I assumed but I did not find it relevant to discuss it, Xavier.," I say shrugging my shoulders and looking out the window.

Alpha Azrael left the room so abruptly rubbing his head in frustration that it made us all flinch.

"I think I may have offended him somehow, I should really leave," I say frantically trying to gather my shaken composure.

Hannah asked Xavier to escort me to the dining hall. He obliged and we were on our way. I kept looking over my shoulder waiting to be mailed over by an angry Alpha.

"What are you doing?" Xavier asked laughing.

"I do not think your dad likes me very much, I believe I remind him of an enemy he once knew and that is not good.," I say almost yelling at him. I had to be talking at a million miles per minute. If I run, I look guilty, but if I stay, I may not wake up tomorrow. I need to get past the patrols, but how?

CHAPTER 19: AWKWARD EXCHANGE

STAR's (NOVA) POV

We made it to the dining hall, and it was immaculate like everything else on the premises. Even with all the amazing things surrounding me, I still felt uneasy, yet comfortable. Oxymoron, I know! I cannot shake this feeling, but I will not allow me to let this delicious food go to waste. Besides, I need my strength if I am going to formulate a plan to make it past the border patrols. I begin stacking my plate with different kinds of pasta, salads, and bread rolls. Did I mention it is Italian night at the dining hall tonight? Everything looked so scrumptious! I made it the dessert area and grabbed a huge slice of peach cobbler. The kitchen staff prepared it as if it was an apple pie. Either way, it was about to get in my belly! I sit down and forget it is like the world is watching as I am doing my happy dance, I mean, rubbing my hands and staring at the food and all.

"Eh-hm, are you really going to eat all that?" Xavier asks drawing my focus from my plate.

"Now why do you have to spoil my mood, young man?" I say playfully pouting and folding my arms like a child.

That did not last long because I was burying myself in my decadently stacked food tray. I could feel eyes burning a hole through my head before I looked up and saw an intense Alpha whispering something to the pack's doctor Victoria through the window. Whatever he tasked her with had her in a frantic state. I watched as she walked away, well ran away I should say. I look away from the window suddenly losing my appetite when I am greeted by who I am guessing Chloe, Xavier's mate.

"You must be Star?" she says while reaching her hand out to greet me. "Babe, why didn't you tell me that she is fucking flawless?" she says nudging Xavier.

"Yeah, because that would have gone well for me," he said shrugging his shoulders.

She rolled her eyes at him and turned her attention to me. This girl could talk, but she was super sweet, and it was easily understood that she was a force to be reckoned with. Chloe was stunning to say the least. She was beautifully tanned with long curls that complemented the shape of her face with pure blur eyes and pouty lips. I could see why Xavier gushed about her every time he would speak about her in her absence. Her personality further made her a unicorn, pretty, intelligent, and neither arrogant nor vain.

Chloe dropped her hand on the table grabbing Xavier's attention from his tray. "If your little want to be girlfriend bumps me in the hall again, I am going to have to relinquish the future Luna title because I will have kick her ass.," she said with all seriousness.

I am sitting there silent the whole time listening to her talk. I only responded when a question was directed at me. Xavier turned in his seat and looked her dead in her eyes, I could tell they were mind linking each other. Whatever he said to her made her turn beet red before she got up and stormed out.

"Oh, my goodness, Xavier, what the hell did you say to her?" I ask really wanting to know.

"I explained to her how important a Luna's actions are before and after she assumes the role. If she continues to entertain drama from the she-wolves that desire me, she will eventually lose both her Luna title and me.," he said coldly and went back to eating.

I reached across the table and smacked him on his arm.

"What was that for?" he starts laughing.

"Xavier, that is not cool, do you know how much you mean to her, how you probably just crushed her soul?" I said not battling an eyelash.

"It is not cool to play with your mate's emotions or have her thinking you are one foot in and one foot out," I add.

I went on to explain how it was unfair of him to hang those things that she cared deeply for over her head. I could only imagine that it would feel like shit to always feel that there is a lingering ultimatum for you to have what you desire. Who would want that?

By the time I was done lecturing him he shook his head in agreement.

"I bet you are really special to someone and I honestly hope you two are reunited," Xavier said as he exited the table leaving me there in my thoughts.

I decided to follow suit and dump my tray and head back to the pack's hospital. After all, this was not my home and I could not even effectively navigate the grounds. I decided to follow the smell of fresh linen in the wind which led me to a fellow she-wolf hanging freshly washed sheets over a laundry line.

"You guys do not have dryers that plug into the wall?" I asked seriously curious without trying to sound judgy.

"Oh, my, you know nothing, princess, this is the freshest way to dry your sheets. Some say it helps you sleep better at night and prevents nightmares.," she says with a smile.

"Sorry for my outburst, my name is Star," I say a little embarrassed.

"It is nice to meet you, my name is Italia.," she said with a smile and continued hanging her sheets. "You are not from around, here are you?" she asks clearly picking up on my nervousness.

As I began to walk away, I hear her yell my name.

"Would you like to join me for a walk through the gardens, I could show you around if you like?" she asks.

I quickly accept her invitation because I feel so alone now that Xavier is not around.

We walked for nearly an hour until we came eye to eye with the pack hospital. She told me how she was rejected by her mate but later received a second-chance mate. Italia was still broken and trying to heal from the trauma of her past heartbreak. Funny thing is, he rejected her for the same Amber that Chloe despises. Apparently, that is her thing, sleep with other she-wolves' mates. Evidently, she has been trying to sleep with Xavier again. They had a one-night stand before Xavier recently found his mate Chloe. Amber was a persistent little unmated jezebel. We were stopped in our tracks by a tall dark and handsome

121

young man. He reached down and lifted Italia up and swung her around. It was like a scene right out of a movie.

"Put me down, you are being rude!" Italia said playfully slapping him in the chest.

"Babe, this is Star, Star, this is my mate, Jacob.," she said gushing.

"You look so familiar.," he said sounding like everybody else.

"Yeah, I have been getting that a lot.," I said reaching out to shake his hand. "Ow!" I groaned.

"Star, are you okay?" Italia asked with worry in her voice.

I grabbed at my head, which felt as if it was going to explode. All I remember is the darkness that took me over.

JACOB's POV

I cannot shake the feeling of not remembering where I have met Star before. It is right in the back of my mind and I cannot for the life of me put it together. As I lay back in the bed cradling Italia, she senses my restless body.

"Jacob, what is going on? You have been acting really weird since I introduced you to HER.," she said with emphasis looking me dead in my face accusingly.

"Babe, I assure you; you are the only she-wolf for me. It is nothing like that.," I say while grabbing her chin to plant a sweet passionate kiss on her lips.

We drift off a bit when I am woken up by a memory. "NOVA!" I say jumping from the bed heading straight for the Alpha's office.

I was stopped in my tracks by the pack's Beta Wyatt. I explained to him how urgent it was and what it was in regard to. He knew something, I could tell. I did not give him full details because I did not want him to relay the message in his own way. Wyatt agreed that it should come from me. As I entered the Alpha's office, I immediately bow my head as a sign of respect. I spill my guts to him of all that transpired all those years ago with Joy and the orchestrated rogue attack to have Nova taken to get back at him. Joy never explained why Nova was important to Azrael and his wife, but she assured the rogues that he would care. We had our assumptions, but most were made rogues by Alpha Azrael after a few pack members planned an assassination attempt on him and his son Xavier. I ended up a rogue from the Shadow Moon because of my treacherous father being a known arsonist.

They did not band my mother nor me, but my father left us no option but to become rogue just as he would. Being a rogue is worse than death if you ask me. I hated him for that every day. I watched him murder my mother in cold blood because she was barren, and he wanted more pups to build a mini-Army. That man is sick! I had no escape from him until I concocted the perfect plan. I conspired with Alpha Azrael's border patrol warriors to bring them the entire rogue Army to their door. I divulged attack strategies and plans of infiltration all in exchange to be a part of a pack. I was just a pup at the time and posed no real threat at the time. In the end, my pops escaped but all others were destroyed in the attack. I was taken in by the Alpha himself. Xavier and I consider each other as brothers, and I are the next Beta. I will serve faithfully at his side until my dying day, "On My Honor."

ALPHA AZRAEL's POV

I instructed Jacob not to disclose this information with anyone else. It is evident that Star does not remember a thing. He may have just confirmed my suspicion, but how could it be? If I am not crazy, I know her and her family. But why was she running and what was she so afraid of that made her do it? I wondered. Good thing I asked our pack's doctor Victoria to look into something for me to confirm what I fear is true. As my Beta Wyatt poured us both a drink, we watched as Jacob exited, clearly shaken up by his revelation.

"Wyatt, this would be crazy if it is true?" I asked.

"Yeah, man, I told you she was a witch.," Wyatt said with disgust in his voice. He never cared for Naomi because of her conniving ways as he calls them.

Sadly, I do not have much time to consider the possibilities. We will have wolves from all walks of life in my territory a few weeks from now for peace treaty discussions, Xavier's ceremony, and to strategize around a common rogue enemy, none other than Jacob's father. This crazy mother fucker has formed himself a rogue Army twice the size of a regular pack. Our spies have told each of us that a war is brewing, but we have not been able to penetrate their camp out. They have been very smart about their tactics, which has us all on edge. The timing of everything is just odd, unexpected, and coincidental.

To top it all off, I have been trying to calm an anxious Hannah. A little background, Naomi and Hannah used to be best friends. Once Hannah turned sixteen, we found out we were mates and she would be the future Luna. Naomi was furious when she found out. She started running with the witches and dabbling in black magic. One of her good friends Shasta was a witch and cast a spell on Hannah to be barren. But catch this, the only way Hannah would be able to carry a child would only be allowed if the witch that cast the spell died. Hannah announced her pregnancy to me a few days ago on Xavier's sixteenth birthday so it is my assumption that the witch is no more. DING DONG THE WITCH IS DEAD! I am elated that I am having another child and with Hannah this time Xavier is my son my blood, but he is not Hannah's, but she is the only mother he has ever known. She raised him from a brand-new pup fresh pup out of the womb and has not looked back since. We orchestrated it so that it would look as if Hannah had given birth in the countryside when the whole time she was caring for young Xavier. Once she returned holding baby Xavier, no one gave it a second thought. They were simply happy to have an air to the Alpha throne. Enough of that, we have to get ready for our guests. Naomi usually does not attend these events all out of avoidance of myself and Hannah. I am honestly afraid of what Hannah would do to her if she ever saw her again. Naomi is good at hiding the truth from people. I rather she stays away versus partaking in an awkward exchange of pleasantries.

CHAPTER 20: I CANNOT FEEL ANYTHING

KYLO's POV

It has been a rough here lately. It felt as if I had not seen Nova in forever. My heart feels like it has been placed on pause. The day she vanished into the tree line no one has seen her since. I can sense that something is definitely wrong, but I do not feel our mate bond anymore. The last thing I remembered was falling from the feeling of being suffocated the day she disappeared. I remember her calling out to me through our mate link. When I woke in the pack hospital a few days later, I was told that we had possibly lost a pack member. Only a few knew that Nova and I were fated mates. Why did I not feel torn up about it? I felt absolutely no emotions about it. My Gamma Xander said he felt the same. His need to protect her was no longer burning within him. We knew this was not normal and we planned to get to the bottom of it. Our number-one suspect was Naomi, Nova's mother. I was beginning to hate me soon to be mother-in-law even more than I had before. Before I could get out of the bed, my mother and Gamma Emit entered my room asking me to sit. The feeling of urgency filled my body like an IV. There was no time, I needed to make sure my mate was okay. I head for the shower before being stopped in my footsteps by my mother.

Emit and my mother began to hash their plan in hopes to catch Naomi red-handed. It is hard to banish a high-ranking pack member without solid evidence no matter how bad we wanted her gone. My father and his Beta were in on our plan as well. Beta Malachi was fed up with Naomi and her antics. He said he has been trying to get something on her for years after he witnessed the way she treated Nova. He knew we could not kick her out without proof. He never saw her lay a hand on Nova but had other suspicions of her behind the scenes actions. When he found out what his son and daughter had been up to in order to appease their mother it infuriated him. I swear I believe he was going to kill them. Beta Malachi looked me dead in my eye and asked me to reconsider my selection for Beta versus choosing his own son Malik. I know it was not easy for him to reach this decision, but it was a necessary one. We were going to take them all down, even if it were only by title. He did not wish to hurt either of them, but rather shame them in the end.

Gamma Emit interrupted to deliver the worst news I have ever heard in my life. He was told that Nova had been drowned and her body dragged off by what looked to be rogues as if they were vultures. And yet, I could not feel anything for her, although I knew I hated the sound of this.

"There's more," he interrupted again. "We speculate that Naomi had black magic at her disposal and her accomplice was just found dead in the wood line obviously dying from a werewolf attack. The marks around her jugular indicates that the wolf that killed her may have been desperate. Naomi broke the mate bond between the two of you. We are unsure of how to break the spell. We have searched for Nova's remains and to no avail, there wasn't a single shred of her left," he said sounding angrier this time.

No matter what we did now, it would never bring Nova back. She is so much good in her. Nova had become to finally come out of her shell and something like this happened. Gamma Emit wanted Naomi to suffer and we all agreed. We had to move fast and most importantly smart.

ALPHA KADE, LUNA LEAH, AND GAMMA EMIT's POV
"Do we know why Nova ran in the first place?" Alpha Kade asks.

"It is fine, Emit, just tell him."

"I told her to run and now she is dead because of me," Emit said as tears formed in his eyes.

"Tell him why you told her to run. It was for good reason," Luna Leah stared.

"Her and Naomi got into a yelling match on the field and I saw Naomi's eyes glow as if she was going to attack Nova," Emit frantically out of his mouth. He further explained how it was not a normal glow at all. "I was afraid for her at that moment but prepared to kill Naomi or give my life if I had to. I made a vow after witnessing how she came into this world and what happened to her freshly delivered from her mother's womb that I would look after young Nova. That was the day I realized my hate and frustration for Naomi. Malachi deserved so much better than her and I pray to the Moon Goddess that he is gifted with a she-wolf that is worthy of him."

"Was Nova aware of her conception?" Alpha Kade asked.

"No, but I think she was beginning to put everything together, which had Naomi scared shitless.," Emit said ending the conversation.

BETA MALACHI'S POV

I failed Nova; I failed my baby girl. I cannot hold back the tears that I have held on to all these years. I was WEAK! I should have confronted my suspicions. And my own children, how could they turn out to be just like their mother? Now my baby girl is DEAD, and we cannot even find a trace of her remains. She did not deserve this, not at all. I would do anything to give her a second chance on this earth. After about three weeks of Nova's disappearance, we decided to organize a memorial service in her honor. We at least owed her that much. We informed her best friend Willow of what happened, and she was in the first thing smoking headed back to the Shadow Moon Pack with her mate in tow. She was shattered, but still did the honor of ensuring we had everything perfect for Nova's memorial. The moment she came bursting through the pack mansion doors she attacked Malik with all of her might. When she was pulled from him, she went after Melody, shouting...

"It's all your fault! You are the reason she is dead! She did nothing but love you and treated her like shit! You know what I think, you are the shit, the nastiest scum on earth. You did not deserve her. Why couldn't it be you two son of a bitches who died? I hate you both! I swear on my life I will be the one to end you!"

Both Malik and Melody shuffles out of the room like they were hiding something. We watched as they crossed the open field yelling in anger at each other. Even with our heightened werewolf hearing, we could not quite figure out what it was about. Either way, Melody had fallen to her knees and left hysterically crying in the open field. If we were going to get to the bottom of this, Melody was going to be the weak link we needed.

After witnessing the brief controversy between siblings, we informed Willow of our plan and it took her no time to volunteer her services. She decided to stick around a little longer to ensure everything goes according to plan. Naomi was no longer me fated mate and I prayed to the Moon Goddess to heal me from my soon to be broken heart. What if I met my true mate and could not even acknowledge her because of Naomi's trickery? The only reason I have not ended her is for the sake of our children, but that bitch is dead to me in this life.

WILLOW's POV
When I arrived at Shadow Moon, the feeling of dread came over me. The realization of my best friend no longer being here with us shook me. I could not stop the tears from falling from my eyes. My mate Zion held me the entire car ride. I was trying to hold it together and be strong like Nova would want me to be. It was one of the hardest things I ever had to do. I just could not shake the need to fall apart. I looked up and realized we had approached the oversized doors of the Shadow Moon Pack Mansion.

My sorrow quickly turned to rage as I entered the room and spotted Malik and Melody. I could break their fucking faces. Before I realized or understood what happened I let out a ferocious growl catching the attention of all that were in the walkway. I launched at Malik first before being prayed away from him, before I found myself slicing the chest of Melody with my now extended wolf claws. I wanted to pry her heart from her chest and make her watch as I crushed it at the bottom of my feet.

After they scurried away from the mansion, I noticed everyone ran to watch what was transpiring between the two of them. Apparently, they were arguing about only the Moon Goddess knows. I did not give a shit what it was about, I wanted them both dead. When they were a good distance away, the others made their way to my direction, my mother Elena included. They began to inform me of their plan to bring Naomi and her pawns to justice. It did not take me a hard second to hop on board, but for now we had a memorial to plan.

Memorial Ceremony

The ceremony was absolutely gorgeous. It attracted all who had come to care for her, all the way from the pack members, kitchen staff whom she spent a lot of time with thanks to her mother, to the gardeners, and groundskeepers. I cannot believe I am back here, and it is for this reason. I will not attempt to fight back the tears. This is tragic. This is wrong. This cannot be life. I break down and was caught by my mate before my bottom touches the surface.

"She deserved to live, got damnit!" I yell in between my out-of-control cries.

My mate stood there as I beat on his chest while trying to gain my composure.

He has been so great through all of this. I thank the Moon Goddess for blessing me with my rock. It just really sucks that Nova never had the opportunity to experience real-life with Kylo. At first, I thought it was terrible that Naomi broke their bond, but now I think it is more of a blessing at this moment because he would not survive the pain of losing a mate, especially one who died.

I watched his emotionally confused face nearly the entire ceremony. He was barely breathing, and I think we all noticed the tiny rises and falls of his chest. He was now pale with messy hair and huge bags under his eyes from lack of sleep. It seems to be the new him. What had Naomi done to him? The fact that we could not prove she was behind this was infuriating. I will not give up until she is brought to justice. The moment she entered the ceremony alongside her minions, Melody and Malik, you would almost believe she gave a damn about Nova. We could all see through her hysterically fake cries. When it came time for the reception part of the going home celebration, I am more than certain my eyes burned a hole within her.

"Don't look a time like that!" Naomi shouted.

"Excuse me?" I asked.

"You heard what I said! I know what you're thinking and you're wrong," Naomi stayed coldly.

"The guilty will speak, and I will he waiting to listen," I said rolling my eyes turning away from her.

"If you were such a good friend you would have gotten her help when she was harming herself or when she is being abused if you were her true friend," she said accusingly.

"Are you fucking serious right now? Did I give birth to Nova? Let me check, nope, hole still intact. You are her mother, you should have cared enough not to inflict pain on her, but you did not. Because your offenses were about to be exposed, you decided to get rid of the one person who figured it out," I hissed.

"You got me there, but offenses? Not sure what you are referring to," she responded sounding as if she were mocking me.

"She was my best friend and I did what I thought was right for her. That is more than what you have ever done for her. You were okay for her taking the blame for something she didn't even cause," I said shaking my head in disappointment.

"Willow, you know nothing to me and my daughter's relationship. She was a habitual liar, but I'm sure she would never lie to you," Naomi responds sarcastically.

"Fuck you!" I said storming away.

This will not end until Naomi is exposed, DEAD, or both!

CHAPTER 21: ON MY HONOR

STAR's (POV)
I have been with the Opal Moon Pack for a few weeks now and I have already learned to love them. I spend most of my time with Chloe and Italia. We all have a common enemy in Amber. How on earth did I get roped into their drama?

*FLASHBACK TO A COUPLE DAYS AGO
Here I am minding my own business when Amber aggressively bumped into me knocking me into the table while I am talking to Xavier. She yells at me telling me to "WATCH IT!" and "YOU BETTER BE CAREFUL, NEW GIRL!"

Mind you, I do not know this she-wolf. Naturally, my reflexes took over me when I realized I had a hand full of hair followed by a head attached to it in my grips laying punch after punch to her face. This devil tried to shift on me, and I grabbed her by her throat and put her to sleep. As I drop her limp body to the ground, I notice there were a creepy number of eyes on me and I felt a blow to the back of my head. I turned around to tackle the culprit landing right on top of the second she-devil Jennifer and started mauling her body blow after blow. No lie, she was strong as shit. Jennifer caught my arm in mid-swing and tried to gain the upper hand. I noticed she was attempting to flip me over, so I locked my thighs down and intertwined my legs with hers. It was useless of her to try to get out of it as I flashed out and begin to bang her head senselessly against the pavement over and over. Next thing I know, she locked her canines into my arm. She reached behind my neck and brought my head down and start delivering blows. I found myself becoming livid and I started to claw the skin from her face in attempts to get to her eyes causing her to stretch out in pain. I heard Amber coming, but Italia intercepted with a heavy blow to Amber's stomach with one of those street fighters' kicks. Italia has been waiting on that for a minute. As chaotic as it was, I saw Chloe fighting for dear life for Xavier to release her from his grasp. She was angry that she could not get to me once she saw about five or six other, she-wolves crowd me and Italia. Xavier saw this and before he lost his mind, we locked eyes causing them to glow. We simultaneously shifted into our huge black wolves, except he was slightly bigger with red eyes and mine were obviously purple. This made the crowd bow and back away, including Chloe and Italia. I look down and spot my huge black paws and just thought to myself, I shifted, and I have not even spoken to my wolf in weeks. And there it was, "Hello, doll," my wolf said sounding ashamed.

Before I could ask her where she has been, Alpha Azrael entered the dining hall using his Alpha tone causing us all to bow in submission. He pointed in the direction of the door. Once we made it to the corridor, we heard a loud and thunderous "SHIFT, NOW!" Alpha Azrael ordered.

We bowed and obeyed. As we stood there being handed our asses, I zoned out because what just happened was too overwhelming to say the least. I shifted for the first time in weeks of being here and I do not even remember allowing it to happen. I tried reaching my wolf, but she was silent once more until she said, "The time is upon us and all will be revealed tonight."

What is crazier is Xavier and I shifted at the same time. I could feel the stares burning holes in me once everyone saw my midnight black wolf. Everyone stepped back with a gasp as if I was an abomination. I am unsure if they were impressed or afraid. Instead of running away, I felt I needed answers and I needed them now. I think his wolf was able to reach mine and he used his Alpha authority to make her arise from the surface. That is the only answer I could come up with after what just happened. If he could do that this whole time of knowing me, why didn't he help me out before? I feel myself getting angry! It must have been visible judging by the red glow in Alpha AZRAEL's eyes. My wolf yet again was made to submit. I did not realize that my eyes were glowing. Instead of Azrael snapping my neck, he just gave me a stare and began to chuckle. He mumbled something under his breath, but I heard him, "You two are one of the same." If I did not know any better, I would assume that Alpha Azrael was becoming fond of me. I mind-linked Xavier and had a whole conversation before we realized what we had just done.

"What the hell was going on here?" I ask Xavier over mind-link.

If you are not officially a part of the pack then you are unable to reach anyone in it through mind-link. I have not taken the Opal Moon Pack's oath because they are unsure if I am trustworthy yet and after today, I am not so sure if I am either. First things first, I need to have an overdue conversation with my wolf. She had some explaining to do.

"Yeah, that was some freaky shit, Star. Maybe the fact that we have grown closer over the weeks. I am not sure what's going on," Xavier said sounding confused through our mind link.

"I'm going to figure it out," I said cutting off our mind link.

STAR's POV - PRESENT DAY
We must have made hanging out in front of the pack's mansion in the center of the gardens a part of our daily ritual. We would play silly games and rag on each other as if it never got old. Jacob decided to play "Never Have I Ever." I stopped him at the thought.

"Now how in the hell am I supposed to know what I have never done when I can barely remember a thing from my past?" I asked.

Everybody was crying tears from laughter at my comment. I could not help but laugh at myself. I mean, it was true! We decide to all go our separate ways to give Xavier some time to prepare himself for tonight. I dart in the direction of the Pack's Hospital to see if Victoria needed any help. As I enter through the double doors, I was greeted by the secretary, Sharon. She pointed me in the direction of where she last saw Victoria. The door was a bit cracked and I heard her on the phone with someone whispering, "We cannot wait much longer, Star deserves to know the truth." I wanted to stay and listen outside of the door, but I was interrupted by Italia with a huge smile on her face.

"Hey, Italia, what are you doing here?" I ask a little irritated she interrupted me. I give her a soft smile so she could continue to explain why she is here.

"Jacob asked me to marry him!" she said excitedly.

"Oh, my Moon Goddess! Congratulations!" I say as I picked her up and swung her around. "When? Where? How? Can I see the ring?" I ask back-to-back not allowing her to get a word out.

"Hold on, honey, I am still processing it myself," she said sounding a bit unsure.

"Woman, are you not happy?" I ask looking dead into her eyes.

"I am, just nervous that he will get bored with me," Italia says shrugging her shoulders looking away.

I turn her back toward me and grab her shoulders and say, "YOU ARE ENOUGH!"

"You're the absolute best, Star, and I mean it!" she says pulling in me into a bone-crushing hug.

I am, huh, I thought to myself bringing a smile to my face.

That news nearly distracted me from my mission. What was Victoria not telling me? I am tired of being left in the dark. I am already on extra kitchen duty for getting into a fight I did not start. Or maybe I did, I do not know, whatever! I decided I am just going to be direct and ask Victoria what she knows about my past. Over the last few weeks, I have had glimpses of what I escaped, and I am okay with never going back. The thought of asking my scarce wolf for questions left me because yet again, it was radio silence. Where the hell is she?

XAVIER's POV

I am blown away at the fact that Star was able to reach me through mind-link. How is that even possible? She is not officially a part of our pack. I will save that for another time, tonight is my ceremony in preparation to ship me off to begin my official Alpha training. Chloe is not happy but understands the importance of the role I am assuming. I am sure she will visit while I am away, but under no circumstances could I return once I depart for the next two years. I am excited, but I know I will miss the pack. There will be at least five packs here tonight discussing peace treaties, business, and uniting within the packs. Hard to believe that it will be me calling the shots for the largest pack on this continent. I am more than ready "On My Honor."

ALPHA AZRAEL's POV
Everything is in order for the incoming packs to arrive. Shadow Moon Pack has always been a close ally of this pack. They are the second to largest pack on the continent. Their Alpha is fearless and fair. I fear that Naomi may make an appearance tonight. I cannot risk her running into Star, I mean Nova even if she is her mother. She will pay for her crimes once I validate my already suspicions about Nova. I pick up the phone to dial Alpha Kade to verify his attendance at tonight's ceremony.

"Hey, Alpha Azrael! What is going on brother?" he said loudly into the phone.

We went on exchanging pleasantries and catching up like old times. When I found a way to mention Naomi, Kade went mute on the other end.

"Kade, man, are you still there?" I asked thinking the phone went out.

"Yeah, man, I am here, you just caught me off guard inquiring about Naomi.," he said sounding disturbed.

I ensured him I was not asking about her for any other reason than to keep her away from my premises. He sighed in relief on his end which made us both break out into laughter. He knows Naomi and my history of hating each other. That woman is the devil and I will never forget all of the pain she caused to me and my mate. We could never prove it; therefore, we could not prosecute her without looking like revenge seekers to our newly inherited pack. She still carried a part of me with her and for that, I am grateful and angry all at the same time. After I hang up the phone with Alpha Kade, I hear a knock at the door. I could sense that it was our pack doctor out of breath behind my closed door.

"VICTORIA, enter!" I yell.

She runs in frantically trying to catch her breath as I stare at her.

"Please, sit.," I say staring down at the chair facing my desk.

She sat down and proceeded to hit me with some much-expected news.

VICTORIA POV
"Alpha, I think everyone was surprised at the sight of them. I am still

not certain of what happened, and I could tell they did not either. I say still trying to catch my breath. Those two have bonded and they deserve to know the truth before it is too late and after tonight, I am sure it will come out one way or another. What are you planning to do, Alpha?" I ask.

If we do not quickly move this just may backfire on us. Star overheard me on the phone with Gamma Emit. She did not hear much because she was interrupted by an excited Italia. Star does not know I heard her. I cannot and do not want to continue to lie to her anymore.

"Victoria, I plan to address her before the ceremony.," Alpha Azrael says certain of this.

"Thank you, Alpha!" I say excitedly, but mostly relieved.

BACK AT SHADOW MOON PACK

Alpha Kade, Luna Leah, Kylo, Beta Malachi, Malik, Xander, and Gamma Emit were all ready to head to Opal Moon Pack stomping grounds for their future Alpha ceremony. After Nova's memorial, Kylo has not really spoken a word to anyone. They could barely get him to eat. He still was not ready to declare her as dead. He felt guilty that he did not feel anything, thanks to Naomi. He felt as if he betrayed Nova somehow. Kylo kept repeating how he was her mate and he did not protect her. Although he was not in good shape, they could not risk leaving him behind. Kylo has actively tried to kill Naomi and each time his father intervened. Willow and Elena agreed to stay behind to keep an eye on Naomi and Melody. If she were to witness anything suspicious, she was to report to us immediately. There is much to discuss in regard to business and territory for each of the pack, so they had to keep focus. After about a three-hour drive, they arrive at a secluded mansion with steel doors blocking their entrance. Once they are buzzed in, they enter the premises and are escorted by one of the gate guards. They are brought to one of the guest houses and begin to download their luggage.

ALPHA KADE's POV

I rung Alpha Azrael to let him know that we made it and we were in guest house number four per his instruction. Before I could hang up, Azrael was leaning in the doorway. We embraced each other and exchanged pleasantries and joked with each other about each of us getting old.

"Kade, I really need to talk to you before I unbury some skeletons," Azrael says sternly.

I grab my coat and proceed to follow him to what I am guessing to his office. "I'll be back before the ceremony.," I say waving at Leah.

Once we made it to Azrael's office, he seems a bit paranoid.

"Azrael, what is going on, brother?" I ask concerned.

He opened the door and looked around before he shut it and locked the door. This had me on high alert and my wolf let out a discerning growl. He stood across the desk from me and stared me in my eyes.

"What I am about to tell you cannot leave this room.," he said as if it were life and death. "On Your Honor?" he asked.

"On My Honor.," I reply.

I shook my head in agreement as he laid everything out to me. It was then I understood why this had to be revealed immediately. Our lives will never be the same, especially Kylo's and Xavier's. I had to warn them all and I had to do it now minus the details per my promise to Alpha Azrael. It is not my secret to bare or divulge to anyone other than the audience it is intended for. May the Moon Goddess carry him through this time of need.

CHAPTER 22: ASHES OF THE PAST

STAR's POV

After helping Victoria out at the pack's hospital, I decided to go for a stroll through the garden. I ended up running into a nervous Xavier.

"Hey, Xavier! I thought you were resting?" I asked.

"I was trying to, but I am a little nervous about tonight.," he replied.

"Oddly, so am I!" I exclaimed.

"Really, why?" he asked.

"I am not really sure. It could be that one of my closest friends is assuming a huge role and then he is leaving me for the next two years to fend for myself," I respond nudging his shoulder.

"Aw, Star, that means a lot, it really does. You will not be left alone. You will have both Italia and Chloe that as you can tell will not allow anyone to hurt you," Xavier says as he wraps his arms around my neck as we continue to walk.

"You make a good point, young Alpha!" I say jokingly.

"Hey, let's do something, call it a rite of passage,," Xavier says with a huge grin.

I somehow understood where he is going with this. "Well, what did you have in mind?" I asked.

"Let's GET TATTOOS!" he says while dragging me to the vehicle parking lot.

"Xavier, are you serious?" I asked.

"YEP!" he exclaimed.

As we hopped in his all-black Camaro, I admired the red seats with the matching threading made within the black steering wheel and dashboard. The floor mats were black with the word "CAMARO" etched in red. His headrest had just one "X" engraved in them. I was feeling its fly, but I was not going to let Xavier know that. His ego was already big enough, yet he was one of the humblest people I think I have ever met.

"Conceited much?" I ask with a smirk while sliding in on the passenger side.

"You know I am dope, Star, stop pretending not to notice," Xavier said barely keeping a straight face.

We both laughed uncontrollably at his corny remark. Although we have known each other for a short period of time, I feel that we have this undeniable connection. It is seriously freaky! On our short twenty-five-minute drive, we talked about the tattoos that we chose and why. I decided on a burning phoenix to cover this hideous scar on my shoulder near my neck and Xavier decided on a badass tribal tattoo shoulder and arm sleeve, how cliché? We are going to be late to your ceremony doing this!

"Star, out of all the tattoos you could choose, why a burning phoenix?" Xavier asked genuinely interested in my reasoning.

"Because phoenixes represent renewal, rebirth, the beginning of new life, ashes of the past, and celebrating a victory of life over death. Is that not currently my life? I will not be defined by my past and like a phoenix, I will rise from it," I respond confidently.

"You aren't upset that you cannot remember your past? Or the fact that you have been placed in this situation?" Xavier asked.

"Everything happens for a reason and in order for a phoenix to rise, it must burn. Besides, I would not have met either of you if I were not disposed of by the Moon Goddess only knows," I say shrugging my shoulders.

"Wow, you really thought this through in a short period of time," he says clearly impressed.

"Why choose something as cliché as a tribal tattoo? Just about everyone in the pack has one?" I ask hoping he changes his mind.

"See, everyone has their own meaning as to why they elect to permanently stamp their bodies with a tribal marking, and mine is my own," he says deflecting from the question.

"Stop talking in riddles, man, and answer my questions," I yell while slapping his arm.

"Okay, okay!" he says placing his defenses up. "My tribal tattoo will be accompanied by an anchor at its center. Its meaning comes together as a representation of the courage and strength I want to possess as an Alpha; the loyalty I expect from all pack members; the success at the hunting of our enemies; the hope and salvation I will pray to the Moon Goddess for; and the wisdom to keep my composure, calm, and steadfastness," he says with so much passion in his voice.

"That shit was deep! As if you could not get any more perfect, Xavier.," I say smiling at him.

Paxton is a well-known tattoo artist among the pack. He works in one of the local tattoo parlors. This is the only way two sixteen-year-olds could get tatted up. Paxton was able to have us in and out after five hours. The time and attention to detail he placed on each of our tattoos was phenomenal. Werewolves have incredibly high pain tolerances and stamina, so he barely took a break in between tattoos. Yes, we are part human, but we are forever tied to our wolves and they shoulder most of our pain to allow our human side to survive large amounts of pain.

XAVIER's POV

Star was a bit worried about Chloe feeling some way about us running off to get tattoos together, but I placed her mind at ease when I let her know I cleared it with her beforehand. I understood where she was coming from. Chloe was not the jealous type of girl, but she was very possessive around those she did not trust. She learned to trust Star very quickly. Star must have texted her the whole way. This made me feel even more trusting of her because it was evident that she was not that chick! Any who, before heading back to the pack premises, we grabbed food to eat since we missed dinner. My dad was ringing my phone off the hook and mind-linking me. I shut it off because I was already nervously lost in my feelings. He was anxiously ready for me to meet the neighboring pack's Alphas.

"Dad, I am fine and on my way home with Star," I tell him reassuringly.

"Why are you with Star?" he asked completely ignoring my well-being.

"Really, Dad?" I question him. "It is not like that, I assure you."

The link goes quiet for about five seconds before he cleared his throat and said, "Son, there is something that I must discuss with you and Star both."

Out of the corner of my eye, I see Star straighten up in her seat before saying, "Your father wants to speak to us." I did not realize I was giving her an inquisitive stare before she finished saying, "He mind-linked me, what the hell?"

Does this mean he is allowing her to join our pack? Chloe will be so excited! I am excited my mate will have someone to help her through the next two years in my absence. Where will she stay?

I am interrupted with all my thoughts by a touch to my shoulder by Star saying, "Slow down, Xavier, I hope this means I can stay. I am hoping Chloe will be excited if this is true. Of course, I will help her not miss you as much the next two years, and I am perfectly fine staying with Victoria."

What just happened?

"How did you hear my thoughts?"

Star shrugs her shoulders and a look of confusion flashes her face accompanied by a smile. It was then Star screamed out in pain cradling her head in between her hands.

STAR's POV

After an awkward moment of listening to a goofy Xavier's thoughts, my head hurt as if someone began cuffing my brain in the palm of their hand and crushing it. My flashes have been becoming a lot clearer, but I did not tell anyone. I did not want to risk the chance of being wrong about what could have happened to me and later have to rescind one version of the story making me lose credibility. Victoria thought it would be a good idea if I kept a journal so I could start putting the pieces together. They all knew I had flashes, but I never fully disclose what I see during them. I was embarrassed about the abuse I saw myself taking. From the flashes, I could not have been older than ten to fourteen maybe, that part was still unclear. I realized that I know Jacob, although it still is not clear. I remember meeting him some time ago. I was with this other she-wolf and it looked like they were in love. I cannot recall her name, but I know my real name is Nova, but for now I am comfortable with Star. It would be easier if I could reach my wolf. I have asked Xavier's wolf, O'Rian to reach out to my wolf, but he says that it seems that she is an abyss. Black magic was definitely at play. He was not sure how he had reached her before, but it felt as if he was not being entirely truthful. I know when the time is right, I would require his help, so I did not push the issue.

ALPHA AZRAEL'S POV

Xavier and Star should be here any minute I say to Alpha Kade and his Beta Malachi. We thought it was only right that he knew the truth as well. He was over the moon to discover that Nova-Star was still alive, but unhappy of how it canes to be. We were not ready to let Kylo know. This news was going to shift his whole existence and is not in the right headspace. After several hours of trying to reach Xavier through mind-link, text, and phone calls I could not reach him. I would have been worried if Chloe would not have told me that he decided to go for a drive to clear his mind for the ceremony tonight. I understood until Xavier linked me letting me know that both him and Star were heading back from town. Those two have rightfully so grown awfully close. It is inevitable and I hate that it was brought to our attention this way. The two of them were headed home after grabbing something to eat. I instructed both of them through the link to come directly to my office without detouring. When I mind-linked Star, I could hear the shock in the way she stuttered to respond. It has been hard not linking her before this time, but I had to be certain that I was correct. I am more than certain that she is suspicious more than ever. She is a very curious little wolf. I look down and realize the time quickly approaching ten o'clock. The ceremony begins at eleven o'clock, so it looks like the big reveal has to wait until the conclusion of the ceremony. We have to keep Star and Kylo away from each other until we can figure out how to break the news to Xavier and Star. I am not so sure of which name to call her now. This is a lot to take in.

MALACHI's POV

Being told that your pup is alive should feel enlivened and do not get me wrong I was. I am just very confused as to why she was unable to remember anything. Alpha Azrael filled me in on how savagely beaten she looked and how his pack fished her out of the river. This was earth shattering to hear. I could not help but wonder what had her so spooked. We have to find a way to pull her memories to the forefront. I am snapped out of my thoughts by Alpha Kade, my best friend.

"Are you sure you are ready for this, Mal?" he asked noticing my uneasy body language.

I am not sure if the part of not remembering bothered me or the fact that my suspicions are confirmed that I am not her father. When Naomi gave birth, I was out patrolling with Kade when we encountered a rogue attack. It was almost calculated it seemed. We always knew something was seriously wrong with the timing and the look in the rogue's eyes that attacked us. Present-day and the ashes of the past are coming back to haunt us all.

CHAPTER 23: WHAT ARE YOU DOING HERE?

XAVIER's POV

My father advised me to prepare for tonight's ceremony after practically rushing us to see him in his office. I hurry and jump out of the car banging my head up against the outside of my door. I hear Star yell out in pain. I am assuming she did the same thing. I cannot control my laughter at this point.

"It is not funny, you and this stupid tiny car," Star yelled rubbing the top of her head.

"The car is stupid, yet you ran into it while it was sitting stationary," I said shrugging my shoulders.

I had to duck after she tossed her shoe at me. We laughed and waved goodbye as we parted ways in opposite directions. My arm was still a little tender from my tattoo. I hope it does not affect my shift tonight.

"Be cool, man, let me take full control, I got you," my wolf O'Rian interrupts.

"I know you got me, and I got you," I respond while heading for the shower careful not to get my new tattoo wet.

"Tonight, is a special night for you, Xavier, the Moon Goddess has deemed it so," O'Rian says speaking in riddles.

"What are you going on about? You have been anxious all day," I say to him as he growled in laughter while cutting our link off and completely ignoring me.

I mind-link Chloe to let her know that I made it back in one piece. I listen to her go on and on about Amber and Jennifer and their drama. I could listen to my sweet mate talk forever, but I had to cut her off so I could finish getting ready. I throw on my black slacks, crisp black button-down shirt, a jet-black blazer, and a blood-red handkerchief in my pocket. I decided against a tie and left my top two buttons unbuttoned. I gently slick my messy curls so that they complement the fresh line up I got yesterday. I douse myself in a little Giorgio Armani Code and headed out the door. I was more prepared now than I ever have been, but not ready to leave my mate, Chloe.

STAR's POV

I am low-key excited and nervous for Xavier. I can already tell he is going to be a phenomenal Alpha when the time comes. Italia, Chloe, and I went to the mall about a week ago to find the perfect outfits for the occasion. We used Jacob as our personal chauffeur. It is exceedingly rare you see Italia without him. He really does adore her. My wolf has been shuffling around in my head all day. She has been giving me the silent treatment, but I am starting to wonder if it was voluntary or has, she been forced into an abyss as O'Rian mentioned. I have to help her in any way I can. After tonight, I need to hit the pack's library harder than I already have been. If my wolf is in trouble, I would feel awful that I failed to assist her in a time of need. I am her and she is me. This whole time I have been angry at her, but never considering the fact that she may be in trouble. I have been selfish and thoughtless, but that is about to change. I throw on my signature color, black! I elected to purchase a two-piece set I saw on a mannequin in store. It cuffs around one side of my neck, exposing the entire right side of both my neck, perfectly advertising my new phoenix tattoo. The halter extends to sit right above my top two abs and the high-waisted form-fitting skirt rested right above my knees. I decided to throw on some pointy-toe all-black Christian Louboutin red bottoms Chloe let me borrow. I decided to throw my hair into a high bun with some simple accessories to accompany my outfit. Italia hooked up our smokey eye make-up. Chloe decided to do a natural beat and I so did I. Italia decided on a long linen royal blue form-fitting romper, while Chloe elected for a blood-red spaghetti strap dress the crisscrossed in the back to compliment Xavier's attire. We looked like we walked straight out of a Charlie's Angels movie.

MELODY's POV (BACK AT SHADOW MOON)

I was furious that my father did not consider allowing me to accompany him to Opal Moon, especially since Kylo was going. It is only right that I am by his side. After all, I am destined to be the future Luna of this pack. I am certain the Moon Goddess will bless our union. It was odd that Malik was told that he would not be attending such a prestigious event. My father has been acting suspiciously distant for some time now. Malik agrees that our father has been very dismissive of us both. He is grieving over Nova, but I would suspect that he would be over it by now. UGH! Not only has my father been a bit peculiar, but my mother and Malik as well. He made up an excuse saying that Malik needed to stay back and look after the pack in their absence in case rogues decided to attack us in the absence of its leaders. I caught my mother coming from the wood line at about three A.M. dirty and fidgety a few weeks ago. When she saw me, all she could say is "I was here all night, you understand?" she said a little above a whisper.

My father was out with Alpha Kade per usual. The next morning as we headed down for breakfast, I asked her what last night was all about. She told me that she needed to clear her head because everything was becoming all too much. I could tell that she was anxious just by listening to her breathing and noticing her mannerisms shift over time. I have never seen my mother cry, scared, or anxious about much in our lifetime. She is by far one of the most fearless and combative she-wolves I have ever met. I strive daily to try to be at least a quarter of what she is today. Malik, on the other hand, has been acting uncomfortably guilty about something. He keeps saying, "Maybe we should not have treated Nova the way we did when she was alive." My all-time favorite, "How were we unaware that Kylo was her mate, that is my best friend and I did not know?" Today I had just about enough. I was pissed because my mate is visiting another territory, Dad is acting weird as fuck, and my mother is probably a got damn serial killer as far as I know. Somebody better start giving me some answers!

MALIK's POV

"What does it matter either way?" I hear Melody snap at me.

I begin to rub my hands over my head and sliding them down past my face.

"We killed her, Mel.," I said not believing what I just said aloud.

"Malik, what the fuck are you talking about, guy?" she said pushing me in the chest. "SPILL, NOW!" Melody yelled.

"It was right after she embarrassed Neko on the training grounds. I was upset but I was enraged when I witness her pretty much call mother a whore. It was Neko's idea," I continue to explain barely stopping to catch my breath because Melody hit me right in the jugular.

She lunged at me, but I already had her up in the air by her throat with her feet off the ground. "Mel, I love you, but you put your hands on me again, you will face the same fate as Nova, you understand?" I throw her to the ground and hover over her as she tries to catch her breath.

"I wanted her gone but I did not need her dead, Mom and I were taking care of that and you two idiots ruined everything," Melody shouted.

"Okay, now what the hell are you talking about? Mother knows exactly what we did," I said purposely bursting her bubble.

I could see the evident shock on her face.

"You all froze me out?" she hissed at me.

"I would not call it 'freezing you out,' consider it a favor. We needed you to pimp yourself out to Kylo and bear his pups and you have not been able to even get that right. Why on earth would we let you in on something as big as this?"

"You two are disgusting!" she yelled damn near knocking me out with a fire poker.

I mushed her head backward so hard I nearly knocked her out with the impact of the fireplace made with her head.

I needed her quiet so I could focus. Honestly, I did not intend to kill Nova. We just wanted to remind her of her place. It has been weighing heavily on me knowing that I killed my childhood best friend's fated mate, my sister. I did not need Melody to remind me of what I had done. When Mother told me, she buried their mate bond and Kylo would feel numb to her pain and would not be able to grieve for her because their connection would feel as if it was severed. Now that at

Nova is dead, Kylo may be gifted with a second-chance mate. We instructed Melody to have sex with Kylo enough times to become pregnant. She tried on countless occasions, but Kylo has not been the same since Nova's death. Although he cannot feel a thing for her, he is holding guilt knowing that he should. He has not said much to me of Neko who happens to be his favorite cousin. I have never seen him in a state such as this, and we are to blame for it. In some way, I feel if I can find him another mate it may heal his heart. That is where I and my mother seriously began forcing Melody on him. She is obsessed with him, so it was easy to have her tag along with the plan. Upon Kylo's return, the plan is to have Melody drug him with a sleeping pill doused in crushed Sildenafil, AKA Viagra, and have her way. She is judging me for accidentally killing our sister, but she is planning to rape my best friend and conspiring to do this for however long it takes for him to impregnate her and appoint her as Luna. I think we are both equally responsible for what happens next.

NAOMI's POV

My wolf Annabelle is stirring in my head. She is hell-bent on heading to Opal Moon Pack's future Alpha ceremony. It took about thirty seconds to convince Melody and Malik of my plan to attend the ceremony. It has been several years since I have step foot on my old stomping grounds. My ex-best friend Hannah would not be thrilled to see me, but the bitch should be grateful that I gave her a gift, two if you count what was supposed to be MINE! I especially wait to see the looks on Azrael's face when he sees me. I am sure he will regret his decision all those years ago when he sees my ageless beauty still intact. I have grown to love Malachi with everything in me, but he could not handle that ruthless part of me the way Azrael could. Malachi is one of the most caring yet fiercest warriors I have ever seen go to war. He could be coldblooded when he needed to be. This is the reason I targeted him to become my mate. He was not my chosen mate by the Moon Goddess. Did not see that coming, huh? No one knows this but my acquaintance Kaza, whom of which I nearly got caught slaughtering the other night by Melody. I had to end her life because Alpha Kade and Luna Leah were becoming suspicious. Kaza had it coming, but I needed her to carry out my plan. I was happy to end her life because miss thang was getting beside herself. She threatened to expose me if I did not allow her night with my husband the night he returned from his latest mission. Before I knew it, I was cradling her throat between my fangs as I tore her apart limb from limb. My wolf Annabelle did it before I could have a say in the matter. She knew I would have done the same. If I were in my human form at the time, I would have slit her throat just enough for her to slowly bleed out and tied her limbs to two horses and made them ride off in a separate direction as they ripped her limb from limb. Slicing her throat would have been me doing her a favor. Over the years she has hinted at desiring Malachi. This made my blood boil, but I tolerated it so I could maintain my beauty, plans, and any other matter I required. I needed to keep her around to ensure this all remained untouched. I snapped back to reality as I packed for a two-day trip. I had the perfect all-black cat suit that hugged every curve I owned with some black thigh-high three-inch boots I just purchased from DSW. It is only right that I rock my Ruby Red lipstick and throw in my makeup pallet for the smokey eye look to make my hazel eyes POP. I am probably going to pull my jet-black curls back into a long French braid. I am ready to steal souls tonight. I instruct Melody and Malik to meet me in my red Bugatti Veyron. They did not question it, because they know and understand their mother does not come to play, EVER. As they approach, I notice a third.

"Neko, what the hell are you going?" I ask him clearly against the idea of him tagging along.

He gave some weak-ass excuse about being concerned about Kylo and he wanted to make sure he was okay. It is apparent that this fool has no clue that I know what they did to my baby girl or my problem you could call her. Took me a few days to process what these two had done. Yeah, she was a constant reminder of my infidelity, but I did not want her dead. I hated that she was so much like me, but weak! I could not stand it and could not chance her exposing what I had done all those years ago. The day she practically calls me a whore, I was enraged that she had suspicions.

I felt my wolf rise up, but she stopped me by saying, "We will not hurt our pup, she is a part of us."

My wolf was never on board with how I treated Nova. It confused her. One time she said to me, "Instead of getting upset, why not make a sex God sandwich with both Malachi and Azrael?" I cannot lie, it was a thought! It should be illegal for how deliciously sexy both of them are. I always felt Malachi should have been an Alpha instead of a number two. It has crossed my mind to take Kade and Leah out several times. To be honest, it is not a forgotten thought either. When we near the premises I mind link Malachi making him aware of our arrival.

Instead of this joker being excited that we made it safely, he responds with "What are you doing here? You should not be here!"

"Well, tough shit, we are here."

"Who is we?" Malachi asks.

"The entire family, babe, surprise!" I sarcastically state before cutting our mind link.

CHAPTER 24: HOW IS THIS POSSIBLE?

ALPHA AZRAEL's POV

Watching my son prepare to take his oath to finish Alpha training and stand ready to take my responsibilities makes me proud. We have over twenty-five hundred wolves in attendance to witness my son shift and him taking the oath of a future Alpha. This is a big deal among packs, and it is an honor to be in attendance. This night will determine if the Moon Goddess will bless his reign or condemn him to rule over a pack that will not pledge their loyalty and will experience hardships throughout his reign and until his death. Xavier must possess a pure heart and I am certain that he will have no issues with this once the Moon Goddess looks upon his him. I am more concerned about Kylo running into Star prematurely. I am in high alert when I see Alpha Kade, Beta Malachi, and Gamma Emit briskly walking in my direction with purpose written all over their faces.

"Alpha Azrael, Naomi is here!" Malachi says pissed beyond calming him down.

"We knew something was off when Leah and Willow called to inform us that they followed Naomi and the others to the border and saw that she blew some sort of a purple powder in the warrior's face that were patrolling the pack's territory. We suspected that they were headed this way, but we could not be certain," Kade finished.

"That bitch is crazy!" I hear Kylo say walking up to us.

"She just cannot let lying dogs lie, can she? This is on you too, Alpha!" Malachi shouts at me naturally causing my wolf to surface.

"Stay in your place, Beta! I don't need you to remind me how I fucked up.," I said trying to calm myself.

"If you two wouldn't have been sneaking around like two fucking high school kids none of this would have ever happened!" Malachi yelled getting upset himself.

"And neither Star nor Xavier would have been here. I'm not saying it wasn't wrong, but I wouldn't change shit I did," I yelled back causing the attention of the crowd to be on me.

"That's enough! Both of you! You are acting like two messy-ass females fighting over a male that is not theirs. Now cut it out! We have a common enemy. If we spent more time focusing on bringing that demon down," Luna Hannah said storming off toward the stage in hopes to redirect the crowd's attention.

We shifted our anger toward each other to hatred for Naomi. I had more important things to think about that we are currently happening. This thing with Naomi has come back to haunt me. I need to focus on my son, Xavier.

"Alpha, Naomi will be dealt with. She's smart, but even the wicked fall short," Kylo said walking on side of me.

"I hope you are right. She is a cunning one and if she does not want to be caught, she will not be. If it did not go against the counsel's wishes, I would kill her in sight for all I know she has done and for the things I assume she did," I responded causing us both to laugh.

Kylo really is a sharp young man and I can see why Star was paired with him as a mate. I have known Kylo since he was a pup. Always brave, cunning, and quick on his feet and mind. He reminds me a lot of Xavier just a little older. The Alpha Academy raved about his level of combat fighting skills and professionalism with his dealings with other packs. I hate that he is not in a good head space after what he suspects as a loss of a mate. I am hoping revealing the truth does not do more harm than good. To be honest, I do not foresee how this will play out. I shoot Hannah a quick mind-link with the update. I could hear the frustration in her voice when she says, "Are you fucking kidding me?"

I quickly reminded her that she is carrying our pup and it would be wise not to engage Naomi once she has spotted her in the crowd. I assure her that I plan to take care of her for good.

HANNAH's POV

When Azrael linked me to let me know that Naomi decided to show up to OUR son's ceremony unannounced and uninvited, it sent me into overdrive. As I felt my wolf Cristal rise up, Xavier came up from behind me unaware of what was about to go down. Thank the Moon Goddess for his touch. It quickly reminded me of why we are here, and I did not want to ruin this for Xavier. I swung around and offered Xavier a huge smile indicating how proud of him I am.

"Xavier, are you ready, my baby?" I ask sensing his nervousness.

"Mom, I am almost man, I have not been a baby since I have found my mate if you know what I mean," he says furrowing both of his eyebrows up and down at me.

"UGH, too much information!" I say swatting him with my handkerchief that would soon be filled with tears of joy. "Where is Chloe? I am surprised she is not standing alongside you," I asked.

I know he could sometimes he could be hard on her, but I love how they level each other out. After heading to the stage, I take my place by my yummy dessert of an Alpha husband. I stare at him in awe as he exchanges pleasantries with the crowd. He feels my intense stare and turns in my direction and licks his lips and winks his eye.

"Alright now, you keep eye-fucking me I am going to put a second pup in your already occupied womb," he states through our mind link.

"You promise?" I asked lustfully.

"You know I have no problem punishing you, my little submissive," he says clenching his jaw.

I look down to see his belt holding on for dear life trying to keep his animal contained. "Yes, my sexy DOMINANT, I will be ready for my punishment later," I say closing the link between us because it is evident that he has lost his focus when he cleared his throat and attempt to inconspicuously cover his bulge with his speaker notes.

I blushed long enough to blink because it was quickly wiped away when I saw HER in the front row. Azrael turns back and continues addressing the crowd not realizing she had approached the stage from a pool of faces. It did not take long for his face to be drawn to her with his face displaying pure hatred. I will never forget all she has done to us. Naomi and I were thick as thieves back then. Naomi was about fifteen months older than I was. When she turned sixteen, she still had not found her mate, at least that is what she told us. She was sneaking around with my future mate Azrael at the time. As her best friend at the time, I advised her that they were both unmated wolves and should not be messing around out of the fear of them falling hard for each other and they end up finding their fated mates. Naomi swears it was just something to do, that he was just filling a temporary void. Naomi would not listen to me, so I spoke to Azrael and tried to reason with him once he realized that Naomi was in deep. He informed me that he had broken it off with Naomi months ago. I realized that she had been lying to me for months and I was her best friend. Azrael expressed how possessive she had become over him. His mom intervened and forbid them from continuing to mess around. The woman that acted as Azrael's mother was a firm believer that you should reserve your temple for your fated mate or be cursed by the Moon Goddess. Naomi did not care.

When I turned sixteen, Azrael and I discovered we were mates almost immediately. I almost rejected him because of Naomi. I knew she loved him, but I always loved Azrael and Naomi would always make fun of me for my fascination with him. Naomi betrayed me and slept with him after a drunk night at a party and continued to after that. I still feel stupid for remaining her friend after her betrayal. I stayed true to our friendship to the very end of it. She stalked Azrael for a long time until she found her fated mate as Malachi. She met him when Opal Moon came to town for a ceremony just as this one, except it was for Azrael.

I hate everything about that bitch, but I am also grateful for her. She gave me my exceptional son, Xavier. Even though she cursed me to be barren, I was still gifted with such an immaculate son to be the air of the Opal Moon Pack. She tried to destroy us and ended up making our bond stronger. I searched high and low for proof of what she had done and every time I would come back with nothing. There were rumors of me being paranoid and I was possibly making excuses for why I could not provide their Alpha with an heir. I was in a very dark place until we got the call of Naomi being pregnant and it was believed that it was for Azrael. We had not spoken to Naomi or laid eyes on her for years after she departed with her mate. I could not wrap my mind around it until Azrael looked me in my eyes and told me the reason for my physical burn and excruciating body aches a night long ago. Basically, it was because he had a moment of weakness and fucked Naomi. He claims he barely remembered doing it, which sparked suspicion in my mind. My heart was shattered into a million pieces and I found myself not able to breathe. I should have known already, but I was in denial.

When a fated mate engages in any sort of intercourse or affection with another, it physically hurts their mate. When I was in the darkest place of my life, my mate was basking in the juices of another woman. In this case, it was my ex-best friend. She was not going to stop until she took everything from me because of her own reasoning's. I could not bear children and she took the ability of me being my mate's first sexual adventure. She ruined everything! What the she-devil meant for bad, the Moon Goddess meant it for good.

I was uncertain back then as to why I hopped in Azrael's truck with him the night Naomi gave birth. When we burst in the small cabin together, that bitch could have jumped out of her skin. If looks could kill, we all died in that cabin that night.

First off, why are they not in the pack's hospital? I guess she could not explain that you were birthing another wolf's child, an Alpha at that. Gamma Nathan from the Opal Moon Pack was there to deliver the baby. I could sense that it was involuntary. He did not want to be responsible for holding such a secret, but Azrael begged him to and he nodded and obliged. The secret died when Gamma Nathan's untimely death came years ago. When Xavier was born and he came out crying, I instantly felt an overwhelming connection to him. It was my idea to take him off to the countryside until enough time passed so I could return home, and no one would really question if Xavier were mine. He was and still is MINE. Azrael says he fell in love with me all over again that night and he vowed to make it right and treat me as his queen through both the good and bad times. I was over listening to the bullshit, but I stuck it out, partly because of the hold baby Xavier had on me and the mate bond was just too strong to fight. I cannot help but think that it was supposed to happen this way. Now to find out there are two...how is this possible? I was there that night, but thinking back, we left so quickly. The best excuse I assumed Naomi would have given Malachi is that the pups died, but because there were two, she passed Star off as his. Sick motherfucker!

CHAPTER 25: OH, YOU DIDN'T KNOW?

KYLO's POV

When I walked over to where Alpha Azrael, my father, and Gamma Emit stood having a heated conversation, I thought I would add my two cents. I could sense the hesitation to tell anything in their faces. Luna Hannah must have linked him because he looked in her direction and gave her a smile and excused himself and pivoted to the stage. That was a change since Hannah had just handed them their asses a second ago. I told Alpha Azrael what I thought just as he left. That left the three of them standing their staring at me and later redirecting their attention toward Naomi. I meant what I said. That bitch is off her rocker. Beautiful woman with a despicable existence. She may have wounded my bond with Nova, but she definitely heightened my senses of wanting to end her life. According to the elders, wolf law does not allow us to banish a pack member without undeniable and solid proof. She is smooth with her exploits, but I plan to end that. I will have revenge for Nova. It hurts to even think of her these days, but I cannot help but to feel guilty. I should have been strong enough to get to her.

"Kylo, I need to speak with you. It is an urgent matter," Gamma Emit says with seriousness.

I could not make out what he is saying after the sweetest smell of vanilla and freshly baked cinnamon buns infected my nose. It is a familiar smell, but it is not possible that anyone else could affect my nose the way she did. Emit realizes I am in a trance and now on a hunt.

"Kylo, please, you have to listen to me," he said pleading.

I shake my head at the thought of my mate still living and breathing. I started to feel the familiar feeling of heartbreak. "Yes, Gamma Emit, what is it?" I say with a slight bit annoyance.

"It is about Nova," he says catching my full attention. "She is—"

Before he could finish his statement, I lay eyes on the most astonishing she-wolf I thought I would never see again.

"MINE!" Jax growls.

It all came back to me and I felt my soul trying to leave my body from all the pain my body and mind had been compartmentalizing. I rush over to her causing her to immediately be on guard. Why is she acting as if she does not know me? I reached for her hand and she stepped away from me with wide eyes indicating that I was making her uncomfortable. She takes her fellow she-wolf that she was had her arms interlocked with and turned and walked away from me. I wanted to fall to the floor and pick my heart up, but instead, I stood there looking stupid and in a state of shock.

Then my dad, Malachi, and Emit walked within my view. My dad placed his hand on my shoulder and said, "Son, she does not remember us, she does not remember that you are her mate." They went on to explain everything to me.

I felt like my world have just been shaken up. "This cannot be life."

They pulled me deep into the crowd in hopes they could calm me down after they instructed me to be patient. The fact that they knew she lived pissed me off, but I was too fractured after what had just happened. How can I sense her now, but her not me? Jax cannot sense her wolf either.

"You all want me to be patient after finding out that my soul mate is still very much alive, but she doesn't know shit of my existence?" I yell at them.

Right then and there I saw the glow of two very agitated Alpha's eyes glow red. "You WILL not fuck this up, Kylo," they say calmly in unison.

"All will be exposed to them all tonight, just hear us out," Emit interrupted in hopes to break the tension.

I wanted to snap at him too, but I know Emit is a force to be reckoned with and I did not want to cause a scene. I respected him and so I decided to listen to all that was kept from me. I am boiling hot right now because this is the very information that could have placed me in a better headspace. Azrael headed back to the stage once the time came for the ending ritual of the ceremony was upon us. I am beyond livid, anxious, and ready to end Nova's entire family except Beta Malachi; however, we cannot prove that either of them had anything to do with Nova's disappearance. We know they all did, though. They will pay in blood. It took every fiber of my being to continue with this night pretending like I was unbothered by everything that transpired tonight. I ran into a nervous Xavier and decided to give him some words of encouragement, not to mention finishing out that he is Nova's brother. What in the actual fuck? He was shaken up because he went out on a whim and got a tattoo. Go figure that he and Nova or Star I should say, decided to experience a tattoo in basically the same area of the body on the same day at the same time. He was concerned that his throbbing arm would affect his shift tonight. I assured him that with our healing abilities and extremely fast healing times us werewolves possess; it would be no issues. We hugged it out and said a few outlandish things, laughed, and parted ways. I have known Xavier since he was a pup. He would always call me and ask advice on different things over the years while I was away at Alpha training. I am unsure of how I never put two and two together. I stop myself at that thought, there is no possible way I would have known.

STAR's POV

"Girl, who was Mr. Hot Buns over there trying to grab on you?" Italia asks making Jacob raise an eyebrow.

She placed her hand on his chest. "You are the only wolf for me, Jacob McIntyre."

He was like putty in her hands after that. Jacob knew Kylo from his time spent in Shadow Moon before his father's banishment, but he did not know our connection. Hell, neither did I.

Sadly, I could not even answer Italia's question. It was like he was familiar to me, but I could not quite place him. Maybe instead of running away, I should try to get some answers. As I head toward the young man that tried to grab my hand earlier, I realize that he and Xavier must be friends because they were in the middle of bear hug. You know, that hug-like "Man, it has been a long time" type. When the two-second embrace ended, they were smiling and joking about something then quickly parted ways so Xavier could take his place next to his father.

Chloe followed behind in tow because she is fated to be the future Luna of Opal Moon. They are perfect for the Alpha and Luna roles. Once Xavier faced his father and raised his right-hand vowing to always be strong, loyal, and steadfast as a future Alpha. Luna Hannah sliced a small section of Alpha Azrael's palm as well as Xavier. The two of them locked hands while interlocking their arms. You could see the blood draining from their palms down their arms within their blazer tops. The elders begin chanting the same incantation in unison. This caused us all that were not Alphas to bow our heads in submission. It was absolutely breathtaking to see the passion in each Azrael's and Xavier's eyes. There is no doubt that Xavier's heart has been found true among the Moon Goddess. Once the full moon is at its highest peak, Xavier has to shift, and this would seal the ceremony. I am so proud of him! Forever shall he reign. I am knocked out of my awe moment when my wolf kept insisting that I join hands with Xavier on the stage. When he motioned me to the stage, I found myself already making my way in his direction. Chloe was confused by my actions, but whatever Xavier linked her set her right back in her place where she stood.

"Hello, sweetheart, how are you holding up?" she asked knowing I am stressed out about life.

Although I have a million questions, instead I ask, "What is your name?"

She chuckles and begins to speak in riddles. "All will be revealed at the moon's highest peak and you, my dear, will be made anew."

I was so agitated and of course, she could sense it.

"I hate that it must be this way. I am not particularly fond of being held captive in our own mind," she says with a whimper.

Once I made it to the stage and conjoined hands with Xavier, I felt the tingly burning sensation all over my body and the familiar sound of cracking bones. Xavier and my eyes burned bright orange as we looked deep into each other's soul and proceeded to shift.

MELODY's POV

Malik, Neko, and me missed the entire ceremony because these two are complete idiots. I was instructed by mother that I could not depart without either of them in tow. I ended up falling asleep a little longer than I planned. I set the alarm, but my phone died. I woke up startled with the thought of the possibility of me oversleeping. I woke Malik and Neko up, plugged my phone up for a charge, and began to get dressed. Once we arrived at the reception portion of the ceremony, I try to slip out of Malik and Neko's view. I did not see our mother anywhere and she was not responding in our link or text messages. My search for her did not last long because I needed to find Kylo, my future mate. Tonight, is better than any other night to consummate our bond. I got distracted by a text from Meyonna. I roll my eyes at the thought of her fucking Kylo before I had a chance to make him mine. I look down at the text to see that it reads,

"You whore! It is not fair that you get to have my sexy man meat, he was mine first!"

This she-wolf has some serious issues. I do not even know how she knew that we were here. Meyonna has been running around like an unmated dog in heat! I will be glad when she finds her second-chance mate so she can shut the fuck up before I end her ratchet ass. The fact that she rejected her mate the night of the ball for a wolf that is not fated to be hers only proved that she was dumb as hell. Let me get back to finding my man. I could never forget his scent. It is not as intoxicating for a she-wolf that is not his mate, but it is delicious enough to want to devour every inch of him. That is exactly what I plan to do tonight. I plan to deep throat every inch of him until he shoots his warm juices within me as I vigorously massage his balls. I am immediately aroused by the thought of this. Why does this man have to be so got damn delectable and not MINE? UGH!

NAOMI's POV
"Hello, Luna Hannah, Alpha Azrael," I say addressing them both. I know both of them noticed me in the crowd earlier.

Neither of them returned my greeting. We were then accompanied by Alpha Kade, Gamma Emit, and my dear husband Malachi who I have not seen since I arrived. Before I knew it, I was surrounded by them all and their stares. It was as if they were waiting for me to speak.

"Why are you all staring at me?" I ask trying to sound innocent.

"Naomi, I think it is best that we speak in private," I hear Malachi say while pulling my arm.

"Babe, did something happen, are you okay?" I ask while checking his body for puncture wounds.

Say what you want, I am still madly in love with this man. If I would have known what would have transpired next, my performance would have been a bit different. I notice the time was approaching when the moon burned its brightest in the night. We all turned our attention to the center of the stage. I could have jumped out of my body and when the walking dead appeared in my view when Xavier called her to the stage. I hear Hannah in my ear, "Oh, you didn't know?" I could hear her sarcasm and I wanted to snatch a hole in her ass, but I was in such a state of shock I could not move or utter the words of disgust.

XAVIER's POV

As my instincts arose from the moon's queue for me to shift, I felt the need to invite Star up to join me. This was not planned, but my wolf O'Rian was going crazy insisting that he is guiding me on what should have been made right years ago. I did not understand what he meant at the time, but I trust him, after all, we are each other. Before I had the opportunity to call her, Star was already making her way to the stage.

I saw Chloe stand to her feet before I linked her. "It is okay, babe, my wolf is adamant about wanting her here and I fear that I cannot complete the ritual without her on my side, please sit."

What the hell is going on right now? We did not utter a word to each other, but we knew we should join hands. This was followed by us locking eyes long enough to revel in the bright orange coloring of our eyes. We never released the intense gaze we gave one another. Just like that, we shifted into two of the most beautiful big black wolves with blazing orange eyes right before the eyes of the crowd. We knew we both possessed black wolves that are bigger than most, but it seemed we were slightly larger and more muscular. I towered over Star's a bit, but she was bigger than any other she-wolf I had seen including a Luna.

I heard one of the elders gasp and whisper, "It cannot be, I cannot believe I am witnessing the transformation of the Gemini Twins."

CHAPTER 26: DIDN'T SEE THAT COMING

STAR's POV

As Xavier and I sit there being admired by the thousands in the crowd, I am even more confused than I ever have been before. Xavier mind-linked me to see if I was okay and if I heard what the elders whispered.

"Gemini Twins?" I ask him curiously.

"Yeah, but I didn't see that coming, I mean, how is that even possible?" Xavier asks sounding more like a statement.

"I do not know, but something about what we did seems right, but I have at least a thousand questions," I say as we howled up at the moon.

It was a sign of respect and a way of us thanking the Moon Goddess for the gifts she has blessed and reveled to us. It was time for the pack run and I was more than happy to not be sitting on the stage. This was halted when Alpha Azrael joined us on stage to have a closer look at both of us as he shifted into his enormous black wolf with bright yellow eyes.

"My children are reunited" is all he whispered just between the three of us.

As I am about to ask my first of a thousand questions all we hear is "ROGUES!"

ALPHA AZRAEL's POV

As I enter the stage where my not one, but two children sat in all their mid-night black glory, my mind begins racing almost as much as my heart did. I saw Hannah frozen in her thoughts until she links me.

"There were two of them, but h... how, we were there!" she says as tears form in her eyes.

I informed Hannah of my suspicions of Star being Naomi's daughter, but I did not know how to tell her that Naomi and I shared a daughter even if it was one time around. I had already hurt her so much in the past with this Naomi mess and I could not stand to make her relive that pain again. Hannah was in a state of depression when she was unable to bear my heir for the pack. She became unaffectionate, distant, and careless of her appearance. Hannah couldn't have cared less about whether I would come or go. She allowed the pack's rumors to devour her very existence. No matter what I did to pull her out of the oblivion she was falling into, and to no avail, would always make things worse. Alpha Kade called me about a business opportunity that could possibly extend our business into Asia. Once I arrived at the Shadow Moon Pack's territory I ran into Naomi after one of our evening meetings. The more I think about it, I am sure it was not by chance. I found myself involuntarily breaking down bit by bit in a tucked away cabin while she fed me drinks. I would not have ever thought this would have led to a night of pure passion. I could not stop myself; she was giving me everything I had been missing with Hannah. There were times I became lucid realizing what I was partaking in, but I could not fight my temptation any longer. Yes, Naomi was gorgeous, but I felt no attraction to her once I mated Hannah. During our sex rendezvous, I heard Naomi say, "You will forever be linked to me," as I shot my future Alpha into her womb. It all became a blur after that. I woke up in my bedroom every single time. This continued to happen for all five days I was in Shadow Moon's Pack territory and each time, I woke up alone in my bed. A part of me thought I was losing my mind and maybe my dreams were becoming so much more vivid until they felt real. When I received a call that Naomi was in labor with MY child, I could not deny it. The timing was right on the queue from the last time we saw each other. I did not share what I felt was a dream with Hannah because I thought it would hurt her. While I was away, my mother called me to let me know Hannah had fallen sick, but it was nothing to rush home for. Hannah was not very responsive to me while I was away on any of my other business trips. As I stare at my pups, I am proud, and all those feelings of regret no longer exist.

Right as we are ready to take part in a pack run, I hear my Gamma Wyatt yell, "ROGUES!"

MALACHI and NAOMI's POV

"Do you want to explain to me how my daughter is a twin with another wolf's pup?"

"You do not have the right to ask me that?" Naomi hissed to me.

"If you do not tell me the truth, there are other ways of making you talk," I say hinting at torturing her.

"I really do not feel this is an appropriate time to discuss such matters. I just found out my baby girl lives," she says with tears falling from her eyes.

I did not care how she felt at this moment. "Cut the shit, Naomi! No one is buying your little act. You hated that child and always have because of what you did!" I yell at her yanking her small frame toward my chest so that she was looking me dead in the eye.

"Mal, how could you say those words to me? I loved my child! I would never hurt her!" she said as she starts bawling her eyes out.

I felt nothing but anger, and the more she cried I felt the need to snap her in half. "We are done here, I am embarrassed to call you, my mate!" I say walking away because we have attracted quite the audience.

I am stopped in my tracks when I hear Wyatt yell, "ROGUES!"

I shift in midair and head in the direction of the threat. I needed this outlet more than anything right now. Sinking my teeth in the throat of a dirty nasty rogue would have to suffice. I look over to see a now shifted Naomi head towards the threat. We were met with at three hundred and fifty rogues coming from every corner. This was a well-trained army of wolves. Someone has been planning this. Why attack now? What did they want? I was fighting off three rogues when a fourth and fifth charged right at me knocking me over. I see an angry Naomi dive and take out two of them as I proceeded to sink my claws in the side of one and rip the hind leg and head of the other two. Instead of gratitude, all I could think was, well at least she is worth more than sex and scandals. She paid me absolutely no mind and proceeded to claw away at the rogues. As I look around to aid anywhere needed, I spot Nova taking on at least six wolves, and might I say, her fighting skills were impeccable! It was not even a challenge for her. She was accompanied by Xavier. It was like they sensed each other's struggle and fed off of it. It was almost like they channeled each other energy. It was amazing to witness this.

XAVIER's POV

"ROGUES!" It is all I heard before Star and I ran toward the wood-line in search of the threat. I could sense her anxiousness and her anger as we moved deeper and deeper onto the battlefield. We took every rogue out in our sight. We moved in unison and anticipated each other's moves. We had no time to focus on the fact that we were twin or how it all came about. I spot Chloe ripping the jugular from one of the rogues while hovering over it when she was attacked by another one from behind. By the time I moved toward her she had already ended its life one blow to his ribcage, digging at its heart.

"I LOVE YOU," I said through mind-link.

"I KNOW YOU DO!" she said as we ran further into the woods in search of clues as to where the rogues were pouring from.

Once I spotted a black wolf a little bigger than star having her back, I knew it was Kylo protecting his mate, my sister. Once all the rogue's bodies were spread across the fields, we all headed back toward the pack's mansion in search of some clothes before there were thousands of naked bodies walking through the fields. That would be bad business for all involved. Werewolves are already very sexual beings, and this would be the honey pot for those mated and unmated. More wolves would die tonight if this happened. We usually keep clothing stashed in trees right before you exit the tree line. I know we did not have enough because I saw naked bodies running to cars and guest houses.

"It is like an involuntary streaking party," I hear Star saying coming up behind me in a long t-shirt that had to be at least a size 5X.

Shortly after, a lovesick Kylo approaches with nothing on but some blue basketball shorts. I saw lust immediately fill Star's eyes. She may not remember or feel their mate bond any longer, but her wolf definitely knew what it wanted or needed rather. I can tell that her wolf Amethyst had a lot to talk about. My wolf O'Rian filled me in on all the details. We were interrupted when my father summoned us to the pack's bottom floor to have a discussion with the elders. We only meet down there when something must be kept under wraps. There were very few who know of its existence and its whereabouts. Before we could head in his direction, we heard a frantic Italia running in all her glory toward our direction before falling headfirst. Star and Chloe shift in midair to check on their friend. Kylo and I followed closely behind still in our human form. Kylo quickly snatches a tablecloth from one of the decorative tables on our way.

"JACOB, JACOB, they took him!" she says screaming out in pain. "They are hurting him!" she moans in between screams.

"It has to be his father behind this! He is the king of those disgusting rouges!" Italia says before her skin begins to burn beet red under her ribcage.

You could smell the stench of her flesh burning. Star grabs the tablecloth from Kylo and her and Chloe begin to wrap her to make it easier to carry her to the pack's hospital.

"Why would his father want to hurt him?" I ask.

"Because he betrayed him to become a part of this pack. His father would never forgive him for that. Before you ask, Jacob witnessed his father murder his mother in cold blood," Italia says before passing out.

"We have to get him back, guys. We need to inform my father."

"OUR father," Star interjects.

I give her a nod and we head to the bottom floor of the mansion.

CHAPTER 27: MINE!

STAR's POV

As we head toward the bottom floor, it felt like forever because I had a million things running through my mind. This stranger I could tell I had an inevitable attraction to never left my side since the battlefield. Instead of me making attempts to kill him for stalking me I decided to figure out what connection I shared with him and his wolf. I desperately called out to my wolf whose name came to me during our shift.

"Amethyst, please tell me everything in a nutshell. It is the least you can do since I have been left in the dark all this time," I say trying to expedite the process.

"Well, someone placed a curse on us. I could not reach you no matter how hard I tried. Whatever happened to us before we were found is still a mystery to me. When I woke in your conscience, it was like I was in an abyss. It was not until Xavier's wolf began trying to reach me. He could not fully understand what I was trying to relay to him, but he never gave up trying. Every time Xavier visited you in the hospital, his wolf tried to get through to me. I could sense his frustration. It was something that kept our persistence to reach each other through our link. It was not until the Moon Goddess revealed to us that we were siblings, Twins, that it finally made sense to us both. I could not tell you what was going on even if I tried. Hell, I am still processing this as well," Amethyst pauses long enough to catch her breath.

"How did I shift when I was in a fight earlier this week and my eyes were my beautiful purple, but now they burn fire orange?" I ask her to hope she could fill in the blanks.

"Because, love, the full moon was close upon us and O'Rian sensed our stress. It made him want to kill at least a dozen she-wolves and he would have if Alpha Azrael would not have appeared and forced us all into submission. That was the longest contact through the link we had. Xavier's powers were strong enough to snatch us clear of the fog. The Moon Goddess appeared to both O'Rian and I letting us know that all would be revealed to you the night of the full moon when it is at its brightest peak. She instructed us that you two must shift together to be blessed with the gifts of the Gemini Twins that came before you," she said finishing.

I could easily hear how excited Amethyst was to share this with me after all this time. I just really wish this explanation had come sooner.

"Why does everybody keep calling us Gemini Twins?" I say right before the two heavy Mahogany doors swung open in front of us.

The elders were ushering us in as if it was a matter of life and death. When we entered into the room, I noticed this beautiful older woman with a freshly dyed full head of bouncy curls just freed from a bun that fell a little past her shoulders, caramel skin, and hazel eyes staring at me as if she had just seen a ghost. She was gorgeous, but her demeanor screams criminal, I thought to myself.

"Yeah, she really is, she looks like anyone to you?" Xavier asked turning me toward the mirror.

"Um, how would I know?" I asked in frustration before it hit me.

"This woman cannot be my mother," I accidentally say aloud. My awkward outburst was overshadowed by one of the elders.

"You kids sure you were not followed, right?" Elder John asked needing to be reassured.

We all nod our heads in unison.

Elder Christopher interrupted, "Let's get down to business, there is much to discuss."

"What are the Gemini Twins and why does everyone continue referring them to Star and I?" Xavier asked reading my mind.

Elder John began speaking, "Gemini Twins was once thought of as a myth until the first set appeared almost over 100 years ago. The

172

legend says that the twins could only be born to an Alpha that is true of heart and by a dominant female she-wolf that deceives him into conceiving. This is accomplished between the months of September and October, under a full moon and the twins must also be born during a Lunar Eclipse. Greek Mythology speaks about Pollux, the son of Zeus, seducing Leda, the wife of Castor. Honestly, all the required factors seemed impossible, but what we witnessed tonight proves we were wrong all these years," Elder John finished with a long pause.

"Why were our eyes glowing blood orange instead of our usual purple and red?" I asked more curious than ever now.

"Because, my dear, it is said that your bond is strengthened when you are together. You sensed Xavier's obvious nervousness so you let him borrow your strength so you could calm him in his time of need. Call it an example of a shared power. You can also tap into Xavier's power of discernment as he can tap into your power of healing. Some Gemini Twins bonds have been to become closer than mates," Elder Christopher says with an unbelievable huge grin on his face.

"Your eyes will return to their usual color when you are not in need of each other's care," Elder Simone says turning toward the beautiful lady with the now grimace on her face.

"Looks like you have some explaining to do Naomi," Simone says to her with a "Do not play with me because I am not here for it" voice.

We all turn toward Naomi awaiting her reasoning for how everything went down. I for one cannot wait to hear what her excuses are. I do not remember much about her, but I have a feeling that she is part of the reason I was on the run and ended up in the river. I could see Kylo's eyes fog over as he was in a mind linking with multiple wolves. Once his eyes cleared, he informed us that he sent Melody, Malik, and Neko back to the guest house Togo get their things to head back to Shadow Moon without Naomi.

"They were trying to beat down my mind link walls ever since they realized I was alive. I never responded to them, because as far as I am concerned, I am still dead to them," I said to the crowd hearing a few gasps by my outburst.

Kylo was the first to speak and agree with me. Who was this freaking sex GOD? I am starting to pray to the Moon Goddess that he is mine. If that were true, I should have known tight away. The way Xavier and

Chloe explained the mate bond it is almost unbearable to be away from them or deny them without excruciating pain to follow. Somebody was about to start delivering truths or it was going to be hell to pay.

"Don't look at me like that. I just have a nagging feeling to not trust their sneaky asses," I say to everyone in the room.

"You are right to trust your instincts. I just hope when the time comes you will trust them with me as well," the sexy-ass stalker said to me.

I am ready to trust my libido right now if I could have one piece of that I thought to myself. I had to keep my focus. I felt my mind slowly clearing the more I spent time standing next to him staring in his eyes. His mans was Kylo and that much is true. I watched as he begins to listen as he filled me in on their treatment of me and how they have reason to believe that they are partially responsible. He never mentioned this woman that calls herself my mother. I think he wants me to save her for him to take care of judging by his looks of rage toward her. I pushed that thought out of my head as I prepare to take in Naomi's excuses, with my arms folded directly in front of her.

MALIK AND NEKO's POV

"Bro, what if she remembers what we did to her and she exposes us to the pack, Kylo in particular?" Neko said pacing back and forth.

We have made many attempts to reach her through mind-link, but her wolf is not allowing us past her barrier, but I know she senses us trying to get through to her. I feel myself freaking out because I know a Kylo is the last one you want to be indebted to or hurt someone he cares about. We are fucking DEAD already!

"Calm down, man, we cannot begin to act suspicious and losing control Neko," Malik says catching NeKo's attention.

He listens and begins to throw his things in his overnight bag. Kylo instructed us to head back to our territory without Naomi. I am certain that he does not know about what we did to Nova because he was extremely calm when delivering the message.

"It was almost like he was himself again," I say aloud to a now relaxed Neko.

We both agreed it would be best to leave while we had the chance and hope and pray Nova did not remember.

Melody has been blocking me from mind-linking her. I attempt to call her cellphone and she does not answer. I am getting a sense that something is not right and her sudden disappearance. I inform Kylo and he promised once he was done handling business, he was going to come as soon as possible to locate his pack member. I could sense that he was in no rush. Maybe she was with him doing the Moon Goddess only knows and now he feels guilty learning that his mate lives.

"First off, any business you have going on, I should have been included. Why are you shutting me, your future Beta, out?" I yell angrily through our mind-link to Kylo.

It was met with silence until he growled through our link, "SHALL I REMIND YOU OF YOUR FUCKING PLACE, MALIK?" Kylo says using his Alpha tone to force me into submission.

"No need," I respond.

"Good! Now stop being a pussy and find your sister so the both of you can as far away from me as possible," Kylo said with disgust.

"Say no more," I replied before listening to him shut off our link.

KYLO's POV

After hearing the theory about the Gemini Twins being sometimes closer than mates, it made me worry a bit. I wanted to be the only one who penetrated the walls of Nova's heart in such a way she could never deny me. Would she not want to leave this place now and take her rightful place as my Luna? I mean, she just found out that she has a twin brother, for Moon Goddess' sake! You can feel their bond like an aura that reaches far beyond this room. How could I even fix my mouth to ask her to leave not only her twin, but her father as well? I can see both of them wanting to kill me, but I am not afraid, she is MINE!

"Jax, buddy, what are we going to do if she does not want to leave her family?" I plead with him in my mind.

"Kylo, we will put a pup in her and she will come back with us," Jax says laughing.

"I am being serious, you dick!" I yell at him in all seriousness.

"Exactly my point, give her just that and she will be ours forever!" he says visually turning his back on me.

Before I can utter a word Jax interrupts like his normal rude self, "Look, if you would have just handled your business with her a long time ago versus waiting months to seal the deal, she would probably remember us by now. Maybe you should allow me to take the lead the next time you decide put your banana in her smoothie," he says mischievously.

"More like a cucumber, but whatever," I snap back at him cutting the link between us.

Nova catches me staring at her in mid-conversation making me blush a little. It was like no one else existed in that room, but her and I. Although we hear the Elders and Alphas going at it with more questions than answers in the background, we are locked in on each other. I hear her breathing increase as her eyes fill with lust. Her wolf was fighting to come to the surface and of course, Jax does whatever the hell he wants so he is all for it. I feel the bulge in my pants, and I notice she has already drawn her attention to it. Her pouty lips separate in anticipation to take me in her mouth. Everyone drew their attention to us at the sound of "MATE!" our wolves said in unison. Right as I cuffed her lower back snatching her body to mine and prepared to plunge my tongue down her throat, her eyes turned back into their naturally stunning light green and hazel eyes when the she devils herself began to speak.

"Are we going to talk about this or what?" Naomi asked interrupting our moment.

She pulled away from me as if I were a stranger all over again. Nova quickly redirected her attention to a now annoyed Naomi. If I did not already hate her, this would be the moment I smashed her head up against the concrete wall.

"Cock blocker!" I heard Jax mumble.

"I second that, brother!" I say out loud not caring who heard me.

"Yet again, Naomi, you are the center of attention, just the way you like it," I hear my father Kade say.

"Very funny, Alpha Kade, but I am certain Luna Leah would like to hear just how much you like giving me attention," Naomi hissed catching everyone in the room's attentiveness.

He is obviously tired of her antics, along with the rest of us. Can we just kill her already? There are enough witnesses here to cover it up and make it seem like an accident, I thought to myself.

"Can we get this over with so I can get to know my mate?" I say looking over to find a blushing Nova looking at me licking her lips in agreement.

"I'm so sorry I didn't remember before," she said through our mate link.

"It's okay. It will never be your fault that I did not do my due diligence to protect you," I respond pulling her into my embrace.

"I'm guessing you could not have known it would become this bad. I just wish I remembered what the hell happened," she said laying her head up against my chest.

"We will figure it out, TOGETHER," I respond before cutting our link to listen at this devil spawn's lies and excuses that stood before us.

CHAPTER 28: CUT THE SHIT!

NAOMI's POV

Alpha Kade's remark rung true, but I did not like the way he said it, but the expression he had on his face after I spilled the beans about our past nearly ripped his soul from his very existence. I rolled my eyes at him without him noticing. I am not trying to get his wolf Maxwell twisted and ready to kill me on sight as I know he wanted to and would give the opportunity. I have witnessed what he does to those he feels are traitors. If he were a good boy, I could have my way with him again too. Luna Leah was always attached to his hip these days, but I always find a way. I cannot believe I am honestly thinking about seducing my Alpha right as everyone is this room wants to kill me. I snapped out of my haze when I hear Kylo's growl toward me. Clearly, he was growing impatient. The whole room could see his excitement for his mate, for Moon Goddess sakes! Hell, I am excited for Nova to get it too. I am impressed with VERY noticeable excitement in his pants, I might add. Guess I should not be surprised, like father like son. Naomi, pull it together because now is not the time I thought to myself. Any who, where do I start?

"How about you start with your reasoning as to why you thought splitting the twins up was a good idea? Or how you managed to seduce my father? Or why you felt it was best not to disclose this to me that I also had a daughter? What about how you got away with it? Who helped you? Who else knew of this damaging secret? Did you think Alpha Azrael would leave his wife? Were you planning to black male him with it? What did you know about the Gemini Twins myth?"

I listen to all these questions formed as one as each of them shouted one at me.

"STOP, I will tell you everything, let me get it out!" I yell to hopefully silence the room.

I turn and address them all from a new vantage point. I had to be on guard in case I was attacked by someone who did not like my answers.

"Are you all ready to listen or are you all going to continue to throw eye daggers in my direction?" I asked not receiving a response.

"It was not my idea to split the twins. By the time I realized I was about to push out another baby, you and Hannah had already ghosted," I said pointing at Azrael.

"What was I supposed to do at that point? Malachi knew I was pregnant, so it was easy passing her off as hers versus faking a miscarriage or stillbirth," I said hoping to get a reply, but nothing came out any of their mouths.

"I did not seduce your father, Xavier; we were both pretty hammered and took advantage of each other! By day three it was basically voluntary. I didn't drag him to that cabin in the woods," I said to my estranged son who looked nearly identical to his father Azrael.

"Azrael, I did not disclose to you that you had a daughter because I could not stand you taking something else from me like you did over the years. You were supposed to be MINE, but you chose the lesser," I say hinting at my ex-he's friend Hannah causing her to stir in her seat and let out a growl.

"What did I take from you exactly other than your virginity and now I am not so sure that I took that?" Azrael responded. "I love my mate and would have been choosing the lesser if it were you. If the Moon Goddess wanted us to be, she would have made it so," Azrael said with so much passion never unlocking eyes with his mate Hannah.

I was immediately turned on by this and I did not try to hide my arousal.

"Really, Naomi, while I am standing here?" Malachi interrupts.

"How do you know my sudden arousal isn't because I'm staring at you, my love? You're still sexy as shit in my book.," I said sending him a wink.

180

When Malachi growled at me is disapproval, it made me soak a bit back in the chair. I saw that fire he had for me that use to burn in his eyes go out. I could hear Hannah growl trying so hard to calm her wolf, Cristal. I turn way from Malachi's intense grimace to lock in on the crowd. He was suddenly making me nervous. His anger streak is what initially drew me to him other than his obvious God-like features.

I continued to explain the partial truth, but I did not feel I was getting away with anything.

"My heart hurt knowing that there was another part of me that I could not ever see because I was banned from returning home by you two!" I say pointing at Hannah and Azrael. "Gamma Nathan, Moon Goddess rest his soul, he delivered both babies. If I recall correctly, Alpha Azrael pleaded with Nathan not to tell a soul and he did as he was told being the loyal warrior he was. I knew nothing of the Gemini Twins myth," I explained before being rudely interrupted by Gamma Emit.

"CUT THE SHIT!" I hear Gamma Emit yell.

I knew he was close to exploding after realizing his brother was complicit in the whole thing. It was only a matter of time that the truth was going to be revealed. Why not let it be now I recite to myself?

"Why did you place a curse on us, Naomi?" Hannah asked while fighting back tears of pure rage.

"I did no such thing. You would like to blame that on me, but that is on you and your broke-down womb," I said staring her dead in the eye.

"At least my womb is intact! More than I could say about your trashy pussy!" Luna Hannah yelled trying to get free of Alpha Azrael's hold to make her way to me.

"You knew I loved him Hannah, regardless of the Moon Goddess' pick for me. It broke my heart how you quickly dismissed my feelings for him without so much of a warning. Eventually I would have gotten over it, but you did not even allow me the opportunity to discuss matters of the heart with you. You were my best friend and your excuses me the moment you found out he was your mate. I never even uttered the words you told me right before your sixteenth birthday. You loved Daniel, not Azrael!" I shout actually sounding sentimental.

"That is not true, Naomi! Sure, I loved Daniel, but it is nothing compared to my feelings for Azrael," Hannah responded.

"Are you trying to convince us or yourself?" I asked furrowing an eyebrow as she fell silent.

"That's enough with your unburying the skeletons trick. Stop deflecting! What is your angle for trying to bury Nova and my mate bond, she is your daughter, for goddess' sake?" Kylo asks getting angrier.

"Did you have anything to do with my disappearance?" I hear a voice in the back of the crowd directly toward me.

It was like looking in a mirror when she approached me.

"Hannah, Nova, and Kylo, I am not a witch and I would have absolutely zero reasons to place a curse on either of you. Hannah, you blame me for you not being able to carry a child, but I gave you one of mine. Word around the pack, you are no longer barren anyway. If I cursed you to be barren, how are you carrying Azrael's seed now? Or is it Daniel's?" I respond before changing my train of thought.

"Kylo, you are my son-in-law and the future Alpha of our pack and Nova is my youngest daughter. I have everything to gain. Why would I sabotage that? I was barely surviving when no one could locate you. When they pronounced you deceased, I was a nervous wreck and Malachi could attest to that," I say looking at Malachi for validation, but he turned away.

I got upset because that is all I needed for the others to believe me. This man has been married to me for nearly twenty years and could not come to my aid the one time I really needed him to. Guess I need to do this one on my own.

"I would never hurt anyone if they were not a treacherous rogue. Here I am, mated to the second in charge and being treated as if I am a filthy rogue, how dare you!" I yell because of their audacity to treat me this way.

"You would make this all about you," I hear Hannah mumble under breath.

"Excuse me, say that again," as I inch toward her direction.

"I said, yes, the fuck you would, you stupid bitch. You would destroy all that stand in your way of getting exactly what you want!" Hannah yells as she shifts in mid-air into her wolf Cristal lunging to attack me who of course shifted incredibly fast into my wolf Annabelle.

I was not worried about Hannah now her wolf because I am already knowing my wolf like myself takes prisoners and everyone knows that Luna or NOT!

NOVA-STAR's POV

I stood in shock watching these two warrior she-wolves nearly kill each other. Luna Hannah in her wolf clawed at Naomi's face as Naomi's wolf went for her jugular. It was evident these two loved each other at one point and now they wanted to see each other dead like yesterday.

No one even flinched to stop it either. There were a few times I assumed someone would give the bloody mess the two of them were, not nope everyone stood frozen in the moment. I think everyone forgot for a second that Hannah was pregnant including my father Azrael. I am sure Naomi couldn't care less; she did not discriminate. Naomi would her men, women, and children if she felt it would gain her some sort of advantage.

I was seriously surprised as the way even the elders were so reserved about it. I felt this fire rising up within me. Before I knew it, I had shaken the room when I yelled, "STOP!" I failed to realize that it physically sent shock waves throughout the pack grounds. We heard some of the pack members outside through the barely visible windows scream in shock. They thought it was a mini earthquake. The two of them shifted

"Would you look here; seems we have a second elemental wolf in the family?" I hear Alpha Azrael say.

"A what wolf?" Nova asked him.

"Every century, the Moon Goddess blesses a wolf with a gift to control the elements, such as earth, wind, fire, and water. They call them the chosen wolf or wolves in this case, but it is usually developed by one wolf and handed down if the Moon Goddess deems it so," Azrael responded before being interrupted by Elder Marion, his sister.

"Azrael is the chosen wolf," Marion said.

"So basically, my so-called mother knew this from the time we were children until now. She kept that part a secret too, I see. At least we know that I have been gifted with the power to heal and control the earth beneath me. Xavier has the gift of discernment and the ability to control smaller bodies of water. We were not blessed enough to be able to control all others like our father that we know of. Do I have it right?" I asked.

"That sounds accurate," Elder Marion responded.

Malachi steps forward after our revelation and landed a hard question on Naomi that had everyone's attention. Not even Naomi could swivel herself out of this or so I thought.

"When you were allowing yourself to be fucked into an oblivion by Alpha Azrael, why was I not in pain?" Malachi asked her without breaking eye contact.

"Oh, shit!" I hear Chloe says unexpectedly.

"Seriously, when a mate shares affection with another, it usually brings about a heart-aching pain followed by rivers of torment in nearly every part of the body," Malachi finished awaiting an answer from his mate and wife Naomi.

NAOMI's POV

When Malachi asked me about my time with Azrael and why he was not in excruciating pain, I could have died on the spot. I was tempted to sprint for the door, but after my scuffle with the bitch Hannah, I injured my calf because I held her in a death grip, and she tore away at my hind leg. I thought of the first thing that came to mind.

I am tough as nails when it comes to spinning the truth, but tonight had me in overdrive. Yes, it is true, when a mate partakes in sexual activities with another that is not their mate, it nearly kills their fated mate if they have been blessed enough to find one another. Call it a cheating radar or painful alarm. I was not ready to reveal my entire life as a lie. I just could not do it. I did the only thing I could think of and faked a panic attack. They all just stood there staring at me until I took drastic measures and stopped my heart allowing myself to blackout. I woke up in what I figured out to be the Opal Moon Pack's Hospital with an IV attached to my arm along with a few other cables. My vision is blurred at first, but I was able to recognize a familiar face.

"Victoria," I say barely getting her entire name out before she stopped me.

"Hello, big sis, it has been a long time since we have seen each other. How are you feeling?" she says with a smile.

"I am feeling better now that I have seen your pretty face.," I say hoping I could get her to go along with my plan.

I need Malachi to believe I am pregnant. Desperate times call for desperate measures. I did not want my husband, my mate to leave me. He may hang in there just long enough for me to have him plant his seed within me. He is one step from being a nympho so it will not be hard to seduce him.

"Baby sis, I may be pregnant," I say winking my eye at her.

"Naomi, you are still up to your old tricks, I see?" she says with a sarcastic attitude.

"I do not understand what you mean?" I say innocently.

"Okay, if you say so," Victoria says dryly.

"Can you help your big sis out this one last time?" I say pouting like a child.

Victoria looks to have transformed into something out of the exorcist. She was staring at me like I had two heads. I could tell that I hit a nerve, but I needed help shit.

VICTORIA's POV

"HELP YOU, I should end you!" I find myself shouting while in Naomi's hospital room.

The audacity of this fool to ask her fool someone I care DEEPLY about. Her and my mother ruined my life with their selfish decisions. Not once did they think of my feelings in all their planning and how it would affect me.

"You ruined my fucking life! You ignored me growing up until you needed something. I have always been a silly little pawn to you. Naomi, you selfish cunt! I gave you EV-ER-Y-THING I had including my future does not like I had much of a choice in the matter! You promised me that I would have a second-chance mate because I still had time, but you LIED! It was no different than anything else that came out of your filthy good-for-nothing mouth. You are not shit, Naomi, and you are never going to be shit, but a lying sleazy whore that gets off on other people's misery and their MATE!"

I could not stop the words or the tears flowing from my eyes. I felt the rage in me multiply at every word that came flying from my mouth.

"YOU stole everything from me and out of everything you took from me, you elected to steal MY MATE, MALACHI! He was rightfully MINE!" I say falling to the floor.

I could not continue to give her the satisfaction of seeing my upset and crying. Her face and demeanor screamed, "I do not care!"

"You are still weak, Victoria. Both you and Malachi were easy targets. That mother you wanted to please so bad was the same one that orchestrated the entire thing. When she found out me fated mate was a human, she was ashamed. When I told her that you found out that Beta born Malachi was your fated mate, she insisted I send you on that wild goose chase to go check up on Uncle Ron up at Cannon Woods Pack. She knew I had the witch Kaza at my disposal. She always hated you in school, so it did not take much convincing to have her whip up something to sever your mate bond. She created a fake one for Malachi and me. He still has no clue that you are his mate and you will not have the opportunity to tell him. It was not perfect, but it was enough having him believe that I was his fated mate. Kaza despised me after getting kicked out of her coven for dipping into werewolves' business. She stayed on the run until her untimely death brought on by herself and her selfish desires. She was hidden in plain sight the whole time too. Did you know she only helped me all those years so she could fuck Malachi? Yeah, I made sure that never happened," Naomi said rubbing it in.

I pulled a scalpel from my lab jacket and begin slicing away at her most prized possession, her face. Because werewolves heal about ten times faster than humans I moved quickly because I wanted her to bleed out beyond repair. I watched as she tried to fight and become disconnected from the IV and other tubes. She began to convulse and roll out of the bed from the wolfsbane I plunged into her system through one of the tubes that she could not identify. I hated her with everything in me and I wanted her to die a slow painful death.

It was not until Malachi burst into the room along with Alpha Azrael stopping me from killing her. Luna Hannah leaned in the door with a look on her face that seemed a little upset that she did not think of killing her this way first. I prayed to the Moon Goddess that I had done just enough to kill her. She lay there unresponsive and I showed no remorse. I was taken to the cells to be punished for my crimes. This bitch can steal mates, use her kids as pawns, dabble in black magic, hide witches among her pack, drug, and rape people, and nearly kill her child and nothing happens. I try to kill the evil spawn for her sins and transgressions, and I get pack jail time. Something is seriously wrong with our justice system.

CHAPTER 29: THAT DIDN'T GO AS PLANNED

MELODY's POV

After witnessing my supposedly dead sister shift right before my eyes had me in a state of shock. Finding out that she is a twin has my mind racing a million miles per hour because that means I have had a brother out there in the world I knew nothing about. I search high and low to reach my mother with no luck because she had some explaining to do.

It is like she disappeared in the crowd before I spotted her having what looked like a heated conversation with the two Alphas and Kylo. Now would not be the best time to intervene, especially if I wanted Kylo on my side for what I had planned. This day has been so crazy! I needed to get away from this Gemini Twin and adulteress freak show. I decided to take my mother's Bugatti to a nearby small town. I found a quaint little coffee shop and decided to enter it to collect my thoughts. Before I could sit down good , my wolf Isabelle started losing her mind, "MATE!" I hear her say.

My eyes were then drawn to the most scrumptious mocha-skinned, 6'1", grey eyes, muscular back, and a six-pack you can see through his tight white t-shirt, straight grown MAN. He could not have been more than 23 years old. He was carrying what looked like two lattes in his hand. The names on the cups were Kaleb and Julia.

"KALEB," I say a little above a whisper.

When he sat down with a blonde-haired bimbo, I let out a growl scaring the waitress who was now standing to my left.

"Sorry, terrible acid reflux," I lie to her.

Never judge a book by its cover but come on! The chick was wearing a sweater buttoned to her throat with buttons hanging on to dear life trying not to pop from her oversized protruding breast that were obviously FAKE. She had a bad dye job, way too much make up on and she could barely pronounce the simplest words. Yeah, I was eavesdropping! How could he want a girl so simple and unable to properly articulate herself in public or private? I am both annoyed and disappointed at my mate at that thought alone. I snap back when I noticed he was leaving for the restroom. It looks like he is trying to fish something out of his eye. He is about to learn in more ways than one what a real woman can deliver, better yet, what she is supposed to look like.

"Oh, baby, I'll help you with that stubborn lash," my wolf Isabelle growls inward at me.

Before the barista could make it back, I would be gone already. I follow behind him like a true stalker as he entered the bathroom. I needed a fix and I wanted him to desire me now and forever, even if I had no intention of making him my mate. My mother would die, rise from the dead, and die again if she found out my mate was a simple human. Yeah, I had butterflies and all that jazz, but my overwhelming need to hump him all night was overpowering any damn butterflies I thought I felt. I have had a boyfriend before and we messed around quite a bit, so this is not my first rodeo. My first actually introduced me to dominatrix, and I ended up making him my submissive. I have no issues with taking charge and KA-LEB was about to find out firsthand.

"I can help you with that," I say standing in the door.

"Can you? Wait, what are you doing in here?"

"Does it matter?" I express seductively.

"Umm, no, I guess not.," he says turning away from the mirror.

"Would you like my help or not?" I asked staring into his pools of gray.

"Do you think you could get it out? Got damn eyelash giving me hell.," he says sounding little kid. It was kind of cute.

"Why are you really in here... Mel," I say finishing his statement.

The sound of his voice makes me clinch in my jeans. He has no clue how I am about to turn him out. I slowly blow on his eye successfully fishing the eyelash from the brim of his eye. Oh, he feels the undeniable chemistry too. He is neither an Alpha nor a Beta. He is not good enough to carry my shopping bags, but it will not stop me from enjoying his flesh.

"Is that better for you...Kaleb," he finishes my statement.

Yeah, how does it feel, KA-LEB? I inch closer to him so he could feel my rapid breathing.

"It is a lot better now. Thank you.," Kaleb says flashing a smile at me.

"No problem, handsome," locking my lips and lowering my eyes to take in his entire physique up close.

I bit down on my bottom lip and pouted trying to make him feel bad. Then some dude walks in the bathroom and proceeds to the urinals. He just eyes me as he passes me.

"Um, ma'am, this restroom is for males only," the strangers say.

"I am aware, but I am trying to get Kaleb here to taste me," I say using my sexy voice.

"Ahhh, I zipped my fucking dick in my pants," again the stranger interrupts.

I roll my eyes at him. Right then, I see Kaleb's manhood jerk in his jeans and the button holding on for dear life!

"My, my, my, you want to keep all that to yourself. There is no need to be stingy, mister," I said moving closer to him.

"Man, if you don't bend her over, I will," AGAIN, the stranger interrupts.

By this time, I am close enough cuffing part of his manhood in my ENTIRE hand. This man was blessed, and I could not wait to wrap my legs around his waist and take every inch of him deep inside me.

"I should really be getting back, I do not want Julia thinking I ran away," he says rubbing his head clearly wanting me to object.

I slowly step outside to let him believe he was leaving out of the door. And to my surprise...

"You were really going to let me leave," he said placing his forehead up against mine simultaneously locking the door behind him.

All I could hear is his ferocious heartbeat and heavy breathing.

"Julia is going to have your head, mister," I say searching his eyes for a reaction.

"Fuck Julia," he says as he plunges me into a stall burying his tongue down my throat.

He tastes like fresh French toast on a Sunday morning, LAWD!

"Hold on, baby, because Daddy about to make you beg me to stop eating your pussy," he said ripping my yellow lace thong off damn near throwing me through the door.

"Slow down, Daddy, I am not running," I say hoping to get him riled up.

He spun me around pressing his hard body against mine. "I will let you know when you can speak to me like a good girl," he said nibbling at my ear.

Oh, shit! This man is dominant! "Yes, Daddy," I say like a good little submissive I pretend to be.

Kaleb wasted no time grabbing behind my thighs and lifting me on his shoulders as he buried his head into my sweet flower.

"Oh, baby girl, we may have hit the jackpot with this one," I hear Isabelle say sounding as if she wanted a turn with him.

"He is mine, love, even if it is just for one night," I tell her hinting at my plan to reject him.

She did not object because she would not be able to get her freak on with him because he does not have a wolf to let go with. I cut the mind-link in mid-conversation when I feel he is placing me back down to my feet. He places two fingers in my mouth insisting on me demonstrating my ability to make my gag reflux disappear. He lets out a small moan as he grabs my ass pulling me into his rock-hard accomplice. I could not help but think that this man is teasing me.

"Just to let you know, I do not do safe words," Kaleb said sounding like a sex slave master.

I lick my lips in suspense. "I have no intentions to use one, Daddy."

We play tongue wars with our kisses and they intensify. He carries me out aset me on the sink as I wrestle with his belt never losing eye contact with him. This man's tongue was hypnotizing!

"Did I give you permission to touch me?" he said clenching his jaw.
"No," I pout.

"That means I need to punish you, you have been a very bad girl," he says dropping his pants grabbing me by my waist toward him.

He inserts two of his fingers inside me just far enough to gently caress my G-spot. His teasing is infuriating. I can feel myself losing control as my legs begin to shake and my knees tighten around his waist. Just as I prepare to release, he sees this and pulls his fingers free from me sticking one of them in his mouth to rate my juices.

"It should be a crime to taste this sweet, bad girl," he says sticking the untasted finger in my mouth.

He let out a brief moan as I rolled and sucked around it. This must have sent him into overdrive because he crashed into me so hard, I heard my cervix scream! Over and over, he plunged deep inside me. His grip on my waist was released by one hand as he placed it under my ass. I knew he was up to something but before I could process why was happening his finger was in my asshole. He buried his head in my neck biting and sucking my flesh. I had to calm my wolf down because I damn near marked this man because I swear this man made me see legit stars.

"Cover your mouth, little one, I am not done with you yet," he said with a sexy-ass smirk.

I cover my mouth, but I could not contain my moans or the feeling of wanting to release. I dig holes in his arm, back and one point his face. He denied me of my orgasm over and over and it was infuriating! Like a bad girl, I challenged him and failed. He slid out of me as he flipped me over and begin ramming me from behind. Kaleb grabbed my hair and forced me to look at US. I could not be mad; this man was OWNING my body. The vibration of his muscles and the look in his eye sent me over the edge, but he did not stop.

"Keep creaming all over this dick, baby," he said continuing to crash into me over and over again while spread my cheeks like he was parting the Red Sea.

This man may be Moses reincarnated! My wobbly legs were giving out, but his body plunged up against mine held me in position. Until I felt him shoot his warm sensation within me, filling me up like a glass. He held his posture spectacularly well through our entire ordeal. When slowly slid out of me, then gave me a smack on the ass. He grabs a wet paper towel and clean my juices off his manhood.

"You should sit on the porcelain throne for a while, make sure you push my hard," he says grabbing his boxers.

He stood there watching me as I made my way to dump his little swimmers in the toilet. I go to stand up, but he shoves me back down looking down at me saying, "That cannot be all of it. I cannot have little

Kalebs running around that I do not know about from a onetime fuck I just had with a complete stranger," he says sarcastically.

With this, he makes his exit not even looking back at me. I felt played, I felt so played and REJECTED! This cannot be happening, he does not get to reject me, no one rejects me. I cried out so loud I felt my diaphragm contract. My heart was physically breaking behind a HUMAN that I planned to reject but he rejected me first. I will end him; I swear I will END him!

I exit the bathroom to find him snuggled up next to Malibu Barbie!

"KILL them both!" I hear Isabelle growl.

"I have something better in mind," I say mischievously.

Kaleb did not flinch when I walked up to his table while he was probably lying to her about his bubble guts. I stood eyeing him right in front of who I am guessing is his girlfriend. I place my elbow on the tall table putting the backside of my hand under my chin and leaning in to say, "Thanks for the fuck, gorgeous," and turned to make my exit when I heard," Anytime, sweetie! Next time you should let me join. I heard that shit was HOT!" I hear the blonde bitch Julia say through giggles.

I stormed out the once cozy coffee spot to head back to the Bugatti. I was ugly crying at this point, but I would not give them the satisfaction of witnessing it. I head back to Opal Moon pack grounds. When I make it, Neko dumb ass and Malik are pissed at me. They were afraid I was snatched during an apparent rogue attack that happened last night.

"My phone died, UGH!" I said storming off to wash off the embarrassment I just experienced. I thought it was exactly what I needed, but I got played like a fiddle! That did not go as planned.

After seeing my supposedly dead sister walking around still breathing had me a little screwed up. I admit I was relieved, but quickly understood what this meant. I hated her, yes, but I did not want her dead for our plan to work. I cannot believe our own brother and his idiot friend Neko was responsible. Now that Nova was alive, I was prepared for her to expose them, but they should be thanking the goddess that she cannot remember anything just yet, but their days are numbered. The thought of her and Kylo being mates once more infuriates me. Why can't she have stayed dead? Yeah, I know what I said earlier, but I cannot have her hypnotizing Kylo again. I just hope I am not too late.

NEKO's POV

"Mel, we been looking all over for you. We were afraid you got snatched by a nasty rogue last night. You really had us worried!" As I am saying this to Melody, she has this blank stare on her face. Her usually beautiful face was covered in dried mascara and her eyes were puffy and she smelled like sex.

"My phone died, UGH!" she said storming off unsuccessfully shutting the door because I stuck my foot out.

"What is really going on?" I ask her to sit on the edge of the bed.

"None of your got damn business, Neko!" she said before launching a pillow at my head.

"Well, I am not leaving until you talk to me.," I hiss at her.

She knows I am not leaving until she talks to me and given our past, Mel knows not to deny me. I was her first kiss, first DOM, and the first person to fill her core with hard Steele. Malik and Kylo are unaware of this, but she and I know what it is. After her diabolical mother came up with the sick plan to have Melody mate with Kylo upon his return, she and I chilled out. I have not found my mate yet, but it was probably wise that I backed off of a Melody before I gave her a pup. The girl believes in raw dogging and I had no issues in participating.

"I am not ready to talk about it, Neko," she says with her voice cracking.

This made my wolf Torin rise up in my chest. "WHO HURT YOU, I WILL FUCKING REMOVE THEIR BONES FROM UNDER THEIR SKIN!" Torin growls causing Malik to burst in the room already in attack mode with his glowing golden pupils.

"Someone hurt Mel and she will not tell me who did it.," I say now standing with my arms folded.

"Who hurt you, Mel?" Malik demands to know.

"No one hurt me, really, I was just worried about mother because I have been trying to contact her for hours," Mel says looking down in her lap.

"She's lying!" Neko said angrily.

Malik rushes and grabs her hands and chin forcing her to look at him. "Sis, Mother is fine. She is with Kylo and Alpha Kade," he says trying to calm a now balling Melody.

He will knock her block off only if she puts her hands on him first and straighten her up quick when she is out of line, but will physically rip a wolf's heart out of his chest if it wrongs his sister Melody. I have witnessed this, and it is not pretty. I have never seen her like this before, though, like NEVER. Something else was wrong, but I could tell if I continue to push, it will break her. Now is not the time, we need her strong for what is to come.

CHAPTER 30: LEANING IN

KYLO's POV

Man, it has been a crazy few days. We still have not found Jacob. We see Italia slipping further and further away each day. Because she is Jacob's mate, she feels about twenty-five percent of everything they are doing to him. Our stand-in pack doctor Cecilia recommended placing her in a medically induced coma. She feared the worst, and this made Nova and Chloe does not want to leave her side. Xavier and hundreds of their warriors did the heavy lifting so they could be here with their friend.

Alpha Azrael and Luna Hannah filled us in on how Jacob came to be a part of this pack. He betrayed his father because he was angry his father murdered his mother in cold blood when he was just a pup. He let Alpha Azrael's border patrol know the location, date, and time his father had planned to have his rogue army attack. This led to the slaughter of many, with the exception of his father. Over the years, Jacob's father Robert has been assessing the strength of this pack, noting its weaknesses, shift changes, and ceremonies. Alpha Azrael decided to never have any of these remain consistent because of the threat. There is reason to believe that there is a spy among us, but no proof.

With everything going on, I have had little to no time with Nova. With all the stressful situations going on, Xavier assures me that Nova could use a day in the sun and I just needed to ask. I decided to pick out a secluded spot of the pack's premises near a huge rock looking out at the beautiful waterfall. It was within driving distance. I figured a late-evening picnic would be nice for both of us. I coordinated with Opal Moon's head Omega Chef, Mr. Walker, he was instructed to prepare us some goodies for what I had planned. He learned all her favorites in a matter of weeks of her being here. All I had to do was get her to leave Italia's side for air.

NOVA-STAR's POV

"Star, what are you still doing here?" Chloe says walking in Italia's room.

"Where else would I be?" I asked looking away from her gaze and focusing back on Italia's peaceful face.

"Um, with that ridiculously hot sex GOD!" she says with an attitude.

"It is too many comedians on this earth, and you chose to be one," I say laughing at the annoyance planted on her face.

"Star, talk to me, what is this really about?" Chloe asks staring at me with worry in her eyes.

I sit up straight to let her know that I feel confused.

Kylo is mine and I am not denying that, but I am nervous around him all over again.

"Why are you so confused?" Chloe asks.

"Because I feel a little guilty that our friend is lying in a hospital bed fighting for her life and we still cannot find her mate. Every time I am around Kylo I want to climb him like a tree! I have done everything in my power to shield my arousal from him, but that damn JAX! Amethyst has unconsciously walked me to his door trying to get her fix more times than I can count! Eventually grabbing a hint of his scent, I am able to gain control again just to realize that I am about to knock on his door. He catches me every time because Jax smells Amethyst's hot ass!" I finished completely out of breath.

"You feel guilty because you are horny?" she says laughing at me.

"NO! I just want to do all these freaky things to a man that may not even want me anymore and it could all just be his wolf desiring mine," I say sadly.

"Okay, so let me get this straight, he keeps your panties wet, you want his body against yours, you obviously love him, and his wolf wants to fuck you off this planet?" Chloe says rudely.

"Basically," I say having to laugh at myself.

196

"Snap out of your amnesia-having-ass party and go get YOUR man!" she says pushing me out of the door.

I am met with HIS scent at that very moment I step out of the hospital room and it sends chills down my spine. He looked down at me like I was the last of his favorite snack. What I would not do for this man to suck, lick, and caress every inch of my body right here. Hell, what I would not do have him up against this wall right now. I came back to the reality of my arousal now filling hospital hallway. I heard him growl and his eyes flicker from deep ocean blue to dark gray. It was Jax and Kylo wrestling for control, clearly arguing with each other. If I were not so turned on at watching this, I would have walked away, but it was just too SEXY! And here Amethyst goes reminding me that she and Jax planned to have an all-nighter.

"First off, miss thang, you need my body to agree to allow you and Jax to have a little fun tonight. Let me remind you that I am much too young to carry a pup because of you and Jax freaky asses, okay?" I say lecturing Amethyst.

"Don't worry, doll, we plan to let you guys watch. You shouldn't be such a prude," Amethyst purrs cutting off our link.

Since when does a wolf purr, clearly one in heat. I come back to reality and turned to say my goodbyes to Chloe. I shyly give Kylo a smile and head to the dining hall with him in tow.

"I could never get tired of honey and vanilla, it will always be my favorite," I hear him say making it clear that he wanted me to hear.

"Hey, where are you going?" he asked.

"I am absolutely starving! I can eat a whole deer," I say rubbing my hand over my belly making him burst out in laughter because of my extra dramatics.

"Good thing we are having a picnic," he says with a huge smile on his face.

"WE? The pack?" I question.

"No, silly, just you and I under the moonlight," as he points at the picnic basket, he has been carrying the entire time.

How did I not notice it?

"Before you say no, think about how this man has rescued you only to grieve you, only to find you and still desire you once more," Amethyst interrupts.

"Trust me, honey, I had absolutely no intentions on saying no. I just have something else in mind for him to eat," I said coming back to reality as I listen to him continue naming all my favorites he had in the basket. "Mr. Walker knows me all too well!" I say heading into the cottage where Victoria and I used to reside.

Wish I knew she was my Aunt then. My mother never spoke about her siblings. Apparently, she has a brother that is an Alpha named Antonio. She did mention him as she bragged about his title, but I heard he wants nothing to do with her or their mother. No one ever told us why and we knew she would not.

Since Victoria's ordeal with my mother and the elders finding out everything that brought it about, they thought it would be best to give her a new start in a neighboring pack with her Uncle Ron. They were all too excited about her arrival to Cannon Lakes Pack. She did not kill my mother, but she did do a number on her. She is still breathing but has yet to regain consciousness. My father Malachi does not want her to return, but wolf law states that with no evidence there is no way to prosecute her, unfortunately. It would be more hear say. She is still his wife regardless of the suspected way he became hers. I am still becoming used to having two fathers and another brother, a twin at that. They have both taught me so much since being here.

After Kylo sent Melody, Malik, and Neko home a day or two later it has been peaceful given the circumstances. Malik and Neko would speak in passing before they left but would not say very much other than that. Something was definitely up with those two. Melody was weird, but standoffish. It was clear that she was battling something within. The one time I saw her on the grounds, it looked as if she was up all-night crying or sick! Those are probably her demons coming back to bite her in the ass. What was even weirder is she sent me a text saying, "I get it now." I wanted to know how she got my number. I did not respond. I remember a lot of what she had done to me, what the three of them had me endure. I could remember all that, but I could not for the life of me explain what happened to me the day I was pronounced dead. Gamma Emit let me in on what happened the day I disappeared. He said he feared that Naomi would shift and kill me because I insinuated that she was a whore. Turns out, I was not far off from the truth. Maybe I was close to it and that is what nearly sent her off the edge.

Any who, where were we?

"Where are you going?" Kylo asked.

"Oh, can I have about fifteen minutes to change?" I ask as he nods his head and lets me know he is bringing the truck around.

I pull my clothes off so fast and grab a fresh razor head and begin to shave my lady parts bare. Cannot have him choking on the goods tonight! I grab my Dove Purely Pampering Shea Butter Bar soap and proceed to wash every nook and cranny from head to toe. I hop out of the shower and proceed to brush my teeth. The shower was scolding hot how I liked it, which caused the mirrors to fog. I was struggling to see my own reflection. My already wet and conditioned hair had curled up into it is a beautiful natural state. I did not want to be annoyed by my dripping hair, so I took my t-shirt and squeezed enough of the remaining water out of my hair. At least enough of it that so it does not completely soak my top. I moisturize my entire body with my favorite vanilla body butter and rubbed it in until it soaked within my skin. I run over to grab my royal blue lace bra and panty set and slipped on a light yellow maxi dress and gently pulled it over my curves. It stopped right above my ankles to display my golden ankle bracelet with a cute little star dangling from it and slid on my golden-colored thong sandals. I left my golden moon pendent and studs on because it seemed to match. I blindly apply my mascara and snatch my lip gloss from the drawer, grabbed my bag and headed out in record time or so I thought.

"That was longer than fifteen minutes, but I am not mad at the outcome," Kylo says smiling as I approach.

He hops out and grabs the door of the truck to allow me to enter.

"It only took me whole twenty-two minutes to look this fly," I said using hand gestures pointing at my body.

We both laugh until tears fall from our face until Kylo stops. "You really are amazing, you know that?"

I blush at his comment and deflect. "Duhhhh, took you that long to figure it out."

"No, not at all! I just needed you to realize that," Kylo says while subtly interlocking our fingers.

Once we made it to the spot he chose, it took my breath away.

"It is absolutely gorgeous!" I said hypnotized by its beauty.

"And yet, still doesn't hold a candle to you," Kylo says as he begins to pull me in the direction of the opening, he chose on top of one of the biggest rocks I have ever seen in real life.

It almost looked like the one from the movie *Lion King*, *Pride Rock*. It gives you a front-row to the waterfall and all of the riches that surround it. Bathing in its beauty irritates me bit with the thought of this not being my home instead of Shadow Moon as I was growing up. I could have avoided a lot of abuse, but then I never would have met Kylo the way I did, or maybe I would have. Mates always find each other, it may not be right away, but it happens eventually. I am brought to my senses when a text message from Willow flashes on my screen...

> *"I miss you so much, girl! I want to visit you. I understand that you are not ready to come home yet so take your time. I am heading back to Redstone to spend some time with my now neglected mate Zion as he puts it. While I am making it right with my mate, I pray to the Moon Goddess that you are too! He is a good one, No-No. Or is it Star now? Lol we will talk about your new alias in due time lol. Just make sure when you have Kylo scream your name he knows which one you chose. Ha-ha, love you, girl!*
>
> *Take care of yourself, my dear friend.*
> *XOXO*
> *-Willow"*

I smile at the thought of my friend's happiness and her wanting it for me. I really do miss her. I feel a couple of tears fall from my eyes and immediately wiped dry by Kylo.

"I miss her so much!" I say sobbing. "Why did this happen to me?" I ask rhetorically, but he answered anyway.

"Babe, the Moon Goddess had to reveal your twin and father to you and maybe she felt that this was the only way. Naomi kept you locked away from the outside world. She stifled your gifts that were always within you, but what the Moon Goddess gives, there's not a she-devil in hell that can take it away from you," he says wiping the remainder of my tears from my face.

We spend the next hour or so laughing, joking, and catching each other up on all that had happened since we have been apart.

"It smells like rain," I say sniffing the air around me.

"We should get going anyway, you have nearly eaten all the food from me," Kylo said as he began to pick up our blankets and repack the food.

"I told you I was hungry," I pout.

"I would feed you ten buffets if you wanted it, lover," he says furrowing his eyebrows in a super-goofy way, causing me to spit my Apple Snapple out of my mouth and onto his shirt.

"Oh, crap, I am so sorry!" I say before he says it is okay and proceeds to remove his shirt. "Why are you taking your shirt off? Put it back on!" I say hiding my now glowing purple eyes.

"Wait, are you blushing, young lady?" Kylo says making his enormous pecks twitch.

"No, I just do not want you to catch a cold since it is about to rain, that is all," I said knowing that it was a terrible lie.

I telepathically slap myself for that one. We are almost back at the truck when the rain begins to beat against our skin. Kylo hits the lock on the keys and we continue running. He opens the door for me to slide in and then runs to the other side. I look around to grab a beach towel that is conveniently laying on the back seat and begin drying myself, handing it over to Kylo hoping he will follow suit. Instead, "You can help me dry off, my hands seem to not want to work," he says mischievously.

I cannot resist those eyes or those lips. After I was done playing mommy to this grown man, we sat there enjoying each other's company. I reach and grab some kiwi from the picnic basket and begin eating it.

"Are you sharing?" Kylo asked while staring at the juices running down my forearm.

"I do not share my food, mister," I respond playfully.

I start to run my tongue around to catch it all from traveling further. The growl that escaped his chest sent an explosion through my body.

"Please, Nova, stop teasing me, I am begging you," he says as his eyes fill with lust, flashing from blue to dark gray.

"Fighting Jax again, huh?" I ask now staring at him seductively.

"Your first time being intimate with me again will NOT be in a car," Kylo says actually trying to convince himself that he was above taking me right here, right now.

He would not even allow me to touch him anymore. Kylo started the truck and begin heading toward the mansion. I will be damned if he denies me of what I want, better yet, what I NEED. I got something for his all of a sudden stingy ass. I begin to slide out of panties placing them under the seat. He was about to drown in my vanilla and caramel-scented arousal. It is not like he could let down the windows to mask my scent with the fresh smell of the trees. He pulled over so fast that we nearly flipped over. It did not register that he could have killed us!

Before I realized what was happening, I was already straddling him. He buried his head in my neck and begin licking around the spot where he marked me. I let out a moan when he sunk his canines in that very spot, marking me a second time. He picks up the remainder of my kiwi and rolls it around my hot spot as if he were soaking it up to save for later. He pulls it up and takes a bite of it until he has fully devoured it. This makes me dance around in his lap. He inserts two fingers within me still gently massaging my clit. This man has away with just about anything on his body and I was ready to feel it ALL. He is gripping as ass cheek so tight in hand as I allow him to play the strings of sweet cello. I try to undo his pants before hearing him say, "You are not ready for this pinned-up aggression, I promise you."

That does not stop me, it makes me want every inch of him in my stomach NOW! He is a smooth wolf I give him that. I look down and "JR" looking back at me as if he were ready for formation! Let me get my ass in line! Kylo gently lifts me in preparation to take all of him. I reach to let the seat back a little further to give me a vantage point. I got something for him trying to tease me. I dance around on the tip of "JR" until I had him begging me to take him in, ALL of him. It was driving him crazy and this was electrifying. Kylo took my hips and slammed me down on his lap so hard I thought he knocked my bladder out of place. It was sinful yet satisfying. I rode him until my spine hurt and his back bled from the constant digging of nails. I am sure at one point my claws were out. We carefully moved to the back seat not allowing ourselves to disconnect.

"I am going to make love to you all night, Nova Arabella Ryan," Kylo whispered in my ear while proceeding to grind his hips against mine.

I hitched up my hips to meet his and followed his rhythm to make a greater impact. He grabbed both my ass cheeks and lifted them toward him as I called his name in both pain and pleasure.

He quickly switched positions on me. Both my legs were on his shoulders allowing him to plunge deeper and deeper into my soul. He came for why felt like twenty minutes, filling me with our possible future Alpha. Tears involuntarily left my eyes. It felt so damn good with a combination of the thought of me living without him for so long. I hated whoever was responsible for it at this very moment. As much as he spilled over in me, I may be having quintuplets.

We worshipped each other's bodies for hours followed by climaxing and starting all over again.

It was not until Gamma Wyatt caught us in the act and told us it was getting late and we should not be out here alone with the threat still being so imminent. He turned the color of a tomato when he saw Kylo's naked ass hovering over my naked body. It was hilarious and embarrassing!

I look over to see Kylo leaning into me.

"I love you so much. I will kill everybody and anything if they try to take you away from me again."

CHAPTER 31: CHAMELEON

NOVA-STAR's POV

After getting caught by Gamma Wyatt, Kylo and I threw on our clothes and began our second attempt at the mansion. We must have laughed the whole way back as we reimagined Wyatt's beet-red face of embarrassment. Once we pulled up my cottage, Kylo took upon himself to let me know he was spending the night. I had no objections, none whatsoever. I ran to the bathroom and started to run a hot bath. I threw in my vanilla cupcake bath bombs and some Epsom salt in hopes that it would help soothe every muscle in my body, including my vagina that was now swollen. If Kylo tried something tonight I would break his neck. I smile at the fact that I also knew that he would. He just could not tame Jax! It was getting harder and harder to keep Amethyst locked away too. We hop in the warm filled bath and immediately are overwhelmed with bubbles. Kylo pulled me into his chest and buried his head in my neck.

"Do not even think about it, mister," I say accusingly.

"What are you going on about, STAR?" he responds sarcastically trying to act all innocent.

"Star, huh?" I repeat smiling at him.

"Yeah, I love that name for you. Honestly, I get confused sometimes about the name you prefer.," Kylo finishes shrugging his shoulders.

"Well, I like them both and I haven't really decided which one I will stick with if I am being completely honest," I say turning around to face him.

He pulls me into his lap so that I now straddling him in this oversized tub of bubbles. You can hear the sound of the water overflowing to the floor, but we pay it no mind.

"Nova-Star, you know I have to leave soon. I am only here to spend time with you. I have not minded helping Alpha Azrael and Xavier look for Jacob, but I am the future Alpha of Shadow Moon and I must make my presence known there," Kylo says gazing deeply within my soul.

"I completely understand, and I agree. I have enjoyed our time together here so much and wish that I could bottle it up to look upon forever. When will you leave?" I said but not before I notice the sadness in his eyes.

"Are you not coming with me? Do you not want to be my Luna? My wife?" Kylo asks me without taking a breath. "I understand that you just found out that you have a twin brother and Beta Malachi is not your father but Alpha Azrael is, but you can come to visit however often you like I promise. If you are not ready, I also understand, and I am prepared to stay until you are. I cannot part ways with you again, please," Kylo says pleading with me with a single tear running from his eye and looking away trying to hide it.

I grab his chin and turn him to face me and kiss his tear away and said, "You are MINE, and I would be a damn fool to send you back into the lioness den without me there to protect you. I would rather die for real this time than to be without you being by my side as my mate, my king, and my husband," I finish to see Kylo with a huge Cheshire cat grin on his face.

"So, are you asking me to marry you, sweetheart?" Kylo asks lifting his eyebrows up and down with a smirk on his face.

"NO, I am a lady and deserve to be wooed and swept off my feet if and when you choose to ask me to be your wife. You have been around those thots much too long, my dear Kylo," I say barely holding back my laughter.

"I know, babe, you deserve all the bells and whistles and I would not have it any other way," he says, then placed a long passionate kiss on me why he sneakily inserts himself in me. It is going to be yet another long night.

KYLO's POV

Once Nova and I finished drying ourselves after our bath, we headed to the bed and just lay there naked. She threatened to break my neck if I tried to make a move on her swollen peach. I plan to respect her wishes. Besides, I needed her to be able to walk tomorrow so we could notify Alpha Azrael and Xavier that she would be departing with me in the next day or so. I mind linked my dad of my plan to return. I would usually let Malik know but I feel I cannot trust him. He has contacted me on several occasions, and I have been cordial, and it is taking everything out of me to do this knowing that he knows more than he is leading on. I have a plan B when it comes to selecting a Beta. My Gamma Xander will move to be my Beta and his brother Zachariah will become my Gamma. I plan to make the announcement shortly after I return.

"Kylo, can Amethyst speak to Jax for a second, I kind of promised her," Nova says pouting.

"Are you sure about this? I am not to be held responsible for his actions," I say to her with wide eyes.

"Amethyst is a big girl, I am sure she could take whatever he had to offer," she said cockily.

"We should go outside then.," I say directing her to grab my hand so we can head out.

I watch as her eyes glow that beautiful Amethyst purple color before we exit the cottage well. I begin to shift to reveal Jax and turn around already staring in an obviously in heat Amethyst. Nova and I take a subconscious seat and allowed our wolves to take full control and enjoy each other's company. Some things I really wish I could unsee and I could feel Nova thinking the same. It was not until we realize that they are tied together. Nova seemed a little confused.

"Babe, I think Jax is trying to get Amethyst pregnant this first time around," I say completely shocked.

"The hell, you mean get US pregnant!" she says trying to get through to Amethyst.

So, when wolves mate, the penis expands and the vulva contracts which is causing Jax and Amethyst to get stuck also called a tie. Jax is undoubtedly trying to ensure the impregnation of Amethyst is completed.

"How long does this last, Kylo?" Nova asks now freaking out.

"Well, the tie is known to last up to half an hour or longer."

"I need you to squat, Amethyst," I hear Nova plead with Amethyst until we heard snapping of twigs nearing us. "Oh, shit! How in the hell are we supposed to fight standing here looking like a sausage link?" Nova says through our mind link.

It was not until about eight rogues jump from the trees and attack us. Out of instinct, Amethyst tried to free herself causing Jax to let out an excruciating howl.

"Jax, buddy, are you okay?" I ask him.

"I WILL FUCKING KILL THEM ALL!" Jax says charging for three rogues at once. "You hurt, MATE!" Jax growls ripping the throat out of one of the rogues. He looks over to see an enraged Amethyst hold her own.

Four more rogues charge at Jax who has taken out three of them. The last rogue took a cheap shot and locked his teeth into Jax's side losing the opportunity to make it any further before Amethyst shot over completely destroying its torso. Jax stands up and looks his mate over ignoring his wounds. Amethyst steps forward to begin healing him but he steps back. She pleads with him to please let her help her mate. He still is stepping away because he knows it will drain her. It must have pissed her off.

"MINE!" she exclaimed tackling Jax forcing him to allow her to heal him.

After the healing process was complete, Amethyst falls to the ground in exhaustion shifting into a now back into a now naked Nova. I run to her side and carry her bridal style through the woods in all our glory. After the forest animals witnessed what happened, I was more than sure they would not be making an appearance.

"Jax, are you sure you are okay?" I ask through our link.

"Besides the fact that I almost got my dick ripped off, I think I will be okay," he says cutting off our link.

He has pissed the filthy rogues screwed with him popping a pup in Amethyst. Honestly, I probably already put about three pups in Nova after today. Once we made it back to the beautiful white cottage home with the wrap-around porch, I carried her inside. Her wounds were healing themselves and she seemed to be off deep in dreamland. I had to pack my things, but I did not want to leave Nova. I decided to wait and rest because, after the day I had, I was exhausted. We have not discussed how or when we would disclose to her newfound friends and family of her departure. It had to be soon because our pack needs us. After they received the news of Nova being alive, they were surprisingly happy and supportive of her return. We left the part about her being their next Luna out.

We led our pack to believe that I am away discussing our international business relations for one of the companies we run. Truth is, Gamma Xander has been holding it down for me in my absence. I gave Malik a few tasks so that he would not get suspicious of my dealings with Xander. Malik was smart as a whip! He is majoring in Business Management as we speak. He has a natural gift for underhanded business, which keeps me suspicious of him. Our pack is built on loyalty, trust, and duty. We do not believe in doing illegal or underhanded business. Crap like that comes back around to bite you in the ass.

I am woken up out of my sleep with a now burning-hot Nova. She was shivering as if she was in pain.

"SHIFT, NOW!" I yell at her.

She would heal faster in her wolf form. She falls to the floor and you hear the sound of bones cracking combined with her screams. Jax snapped at me as well for me making Nova shift.

"We must help MATE!" he growls but neither of us have taken our eyes off her or moved an inch.

It is like we are paralyzed at the moment when a huge fluffy white wolf with Amethyst purple eyes appeared to us from the floor.

"Like a Phoenix, I shall rise from the ashes," she says like her transforming into this big-ass white wolf is no biggie.

Clearly, I am the only one a little taken back by this once I realized Jax is doing his happy dance repeating, "I am the luckiest wolf alive and I am stuck with this idiot who does not know how to appreciate our mate's true beauty," he says annoyed with me.

I cut our link because it was just too much going on for me to argue with him tonight. I place my hand on her oversized head causing her to scurry up against my neck as I continued caressing her. I did this long enough to feel her relax enough to shift back into my beautiful Nova-Star. I kind of liked the sound of that.

"We should call the elders!" she said jumping up throwing on silk black robe that accentuated every curve on her body.

"Right!" I respond as I stared at her butt.

"Seriously! Are you ever without a hard-on?" she asked visibly not disappointed at my reaction to her.

"It's your fault!" I yell shamefully.

"Come on, Kylo! We need to know what the hell just happened to me," she said in a more serious manner.

I know she was right, but my mind was elsewhere as she could visibly tell.

"Hello, Elder Christopher?" I say on the phone.

"Kylo, is everything okay?" he asks probably searching for his light, given the ruckus of things falling over from his nightstand in the background.

"Yeah, things are great, but we have a question about Nova-Star's wolf," I say unsure yet excited.

"Kylo, we already discussed why her eyes shift from orange to purple and vice versa," Elder Christopher says now annoyed.

I roll my eyes and hold back the feeling of wanting to set him straight.

"No, that is not what it is about. She shifted into a huge pure white wolf!" I exclaim.

"Well, congratulations, son! You two have finished the mating ritual!" he says laughing in the phone.

"What are you talking about?" we ask in unison feeling confused.

"You two obviously have mated in your human form, a rather lot from what I heard today," he says making Nova blush. "You two mated in your wolf form tonight, did you not?" he asked almost accusingly.

"Uh, yeah, we did, our wolves would not let it go until we let them spend time together," I finish.

"Your wolf is a part of you, and you are a part of your wolf, but there are gifts bestowed on your wolf that allows them to receive direct guidance from the Moon Goddess herself. When Nova is with you, she is destined to be a white wolf, but when she is with Xavier, she is overruled and will return back to her natural state as a midnight Gemini twin. She is sort of like a chameleon wolf only when provoked by the two people she loves most in her life," he said pausing for a second.

"Trust your wolves, Kylo and Nova. They know what is good for you even if you do not. You are now further bonded for life. Take care young, Alpha and Luna. This old wolf is tired.," he says sounding exhausted.

"We will, thank you, Elder Christopher," we say in unison before hanging up.

"I am beyond-this-world tired," I hear Nova say.

"Me too, babe, I love you past the moon, goodnight," I say placing a gentle kiss on her forehead.

"I love you too, babe," she says snuggling into me.

I would give my last breath to have this moment forever and a day, but right now, I am about to pass out. Selfishly, I do not want to think about Jacob's kidnapping, Naomi's betrayal, Malik and Neko's lying, or any other wolf problem while I am here with my future Luna.

CHAPTER 32: A SECOND CHANCE

JACOB's POV

As I sit here tied up to a huge oak tree in the middle of nowhere it seems, I reflect back on the times I spent within my father's custody. He was an evil man and I vowed that I would take him down for all me and my mother endured in his care. This has all been so unreal. Honestly, after my father's many failed attempts to have me within his grasp, this is the first time he has succeeded. I have not thought much about my wounds not healing as quickly due to the silver chains holding me captive that tend to weaken werewolves. All I picture while I am out of it is how much this must hurt Italia. I would end it all if I knew it would not harm her too. I just want her to be okay. I have been burned, beaten, starved, and almost drowned. I have tried with everything in me to escape and each time the punishment is far worse. I have to break free and warn the pack of the traitors in their midst.

"Hey, son," I hear my despicable father say.

"You stopped being my father the night you killed my mother," I say spitting in his face.

"I was ready to play nice with you, son. I will let you live if you just give me the information I need. You are strong, I give you that, but once I am done with you, you will beg for death, it is your choice...," he says walking away laughing and wiping his face with his sleeve. He then turns, "I killed your mother along with my pup she carried that night," he says looking disgusted.

"My mother was not pregnant! That is why you killed her! She did not want to carry another seed for you because you are the devil!" I yell with all the energy I have left.

"Is that what you think happened? That is a form of the story, yes, but not the whole story. Your mom was out there whoring herself around, leaving me in excruciating pain. When she found out she was pregnant, she quickly said it was mine because she actually thought I did not know what she was out doing," he says throwing his head back laughing making me angrier.

"How could a mate be proud that he ended the life of his pregnant wife? If I remember correctly, you were not so innocent either. I remember mom bending over the bathroom tub with her body on fire as you pounded only the Moon Goddess knows. If this is true that you say, then maybe she did it to finally get back at you.," I say giving him his queue to leave.

He stands up and says, "You are really naïve. It was not until after the fact that I found out from our onsite doctor that the pup she was carrying was mine," he said.

"Did you also mention to him that you were responsible for her death?" I asked.

"NOPE, I left that part out. It really didn't seem that important," he responds laughing while pivoting toward what looked like an outhouse.

I cannot believe I used to live like this. I am a complete idiot. I need to preserve my energy and harness my anger because I have been unsuccessful with mind linking anyone other than Italia who seems to be lost right now. She cannot bring herself to wake up from the state she is in. My mate is a fighter and I know she will let the others know that I am still breathing. Every day I am giving her details of my whereabouts. They have not doused me with wolfsbane in about two days, which had allowed me to gain enough strength to continue to mind link her. She is the only one I can partially reach because of our mate bond. It takes everything out of me too. I will soon find my way back and I will not stop until my sperm donor is DEAD.

JOY's POV

I have missed the packhouse being loud every day. I missed my mate, Malik. When he informed me that Nova's lives, I was shocked beyond measure! I had mixed emotions about it all. She has a twin and a different father. Not to mention, she is in some divine twin situation. It was too much to process. I honestly wanted to check on Nova to be nosey. I received her number from Melody and shot her a text.

> *Hi, I just wanted to check on you and see how you are handling everything...*
> *-Joy*

Nova never texted me back. Maybe Melody gave me the wrong number, or I mistyped. I am certain she would not ignore me she just was not that type.

I heard my brother Kylo will be heading home and Nova will not be accompanying him. I do not feel she would be a great Luna. She has been weak for far too long and nearly got herself killed on countless occasions. Who wants a Luna they have to babysit? Operation Melody and Kylo is still a go!

"Malik, you made it!" I say placing my hands behind his neck to pull him in for a kiss.

"It has been some stressful few days, to say the least," he says with worry in his eyes. "You remember Jacob, right?" he said and then stopping when he heard my heart skip a beat.

"Yeah, his dad was the pack's arsonist, right?" I ask as if I did not remember.

"Well, apparently his father has had it out for him since he exposed their intentions to Alpha Azrael's pack some years ago. Jacob claimed he did it because his father abused him and his mother, and get this, his father murdered his mother in front of him when he was just a pup. His father has kidnapped him, and we believe that he may barely be hanging on," Malik finishes making it sound like a horror movie.

I feel the tightening of my chest.

"Why would you all assume he was dead?' I say afraid to hear the answer.

"Babe, because his mate is laying in Opal Moon's pack hospital right now fighting for her life. They are hoping that the medically induced will ease her transition into the afterlife if we cannot locate Jacob in time and I fear it is too late," Malik says turning around to lay back on the bed.

"You all cannot assume the worst if you are unsure of his whereabouts!" I yell completely startling Malik.

"Why are you losing it right now?" he asked.

"He was my friend, Malik. I cannot imagine if something had happened to him," I said to him before letting tears fall from my eyes.

"You have not seen him since his family was banished, I am honestly surprised you remember his name," Malik said as he looks me dead in my eyes.

"You are right, but he was still one of my closest friends I had as a child. Have you all searched his father's old hideout? Are we going to help with the search? About the old hideout, remember when we were small and Nova discovered it and led the rogues here?" I asked lying through my teeth.

Malik shakes his head as to indicate no.

"Well, why do we not start there tonight?" I ask grabbing my sneakers.

"Babe, as much as it turns me on to see you all worked up about something, there is nothing more I would love if you redirected it to your mate," Malik says hoping to get me to help me relieve some stress.

"Malik, you are thinking about sex in the middle of a crisis?" I asked him while standing with my hands on my hip.

"You aren't? I have been gone for a few days, found out my dead sister is living, and she is some freaky twin with a different father. Not to mention she is Kylo's mate and she fully intends on returning by the way and possibly exposing us all. Oh, and to add to that, I have been in the woods on another pack's territory searching for a wolf I care nothing about!" Malik yells before storming out of the room.

"Get back here! Let us finish this, Malik!" I demand.

"Joy, go find your boyfriend by yourself! You think I do not remember you and Nova's secret adventures into the woods when we were kids after Jacob's family was banished? Yeah, pick your lip up off the ground. I never told anyone your story about Nova causing all of this was a bunch of bullshit! Now if you will excuse me, I am going to sleep now away from YOU!" he yells through our mind link completely shutting me out.

Malik knew I lied on Nova all these years. Why had he not said anything to me at least? I had so many questions! Did he know I was the one that ordered the rogue attack on Nova? He could not have, at least I had hoped not. Did he have something to do with Jacob's disappearance? He would not do that, would he? It has been years, so I refuse to believe that he would hold a grudge for four years. I have seen what Malik does to those he dislikes, and it scares me more than anything. I needed to get this done alone because he did not plan to help me. Jacob and I deserve a second chance at our friendship. I cannot allow Jacob to suffer. I ghosted him in the past to cover my own ass. The very least I could do is check our old meet up location. I used to see the other rogues when I would visit. They had some warlock to cloak their camp, but it could become visible only if one of them desires you to see it if I remember correctly.

I planned to leave within the hour. I needed to make one stop to grab a vial of Meyonna's spray. I am unsure of the contents, but I know it will hide your scent from even an Alpha.

"Where are you creeping to, miss thang?" she asked in her accusing tone perching her lips up to her nose.

"Nowhere special, I assure you," I dryly responded.

"Can I come?" Meyonna asks.

"You want to go on an unknown mission in the middle of the night with me?" I had to ask while laughing at her childish antics.

"Joy, come on! I have to take my mind off wanting to murder Melody for going after my man!" she states seriously.

"Who is your man, girl?" I ask.

"KYLO! Do not act brand new with me. You know he and I are meant to be!" she says.

"And what about the now living and breathing Nova?" I asked hoping to get a reaction out of her.

"He will get bored with that prude! She is weak and could never serve as our Luna and you and I both know that. He will be rid of her by springtime," Meyonna says while shrugging her shoulders to finish.

"Whatever, Mey, you may be right, though," I smile giving her a reassuring pat on the back.

We head to the back of the pack's mansion and begin to strip down near the wood line so that we will not be seen. We tie them to our ankles in preparation to shift. Once we were set, it was not long before we were racing to the heart of the forest. I prepared Meyonna for the long journey and she was all for it. Anything for her to see some new wolf meat, rogue, or not, she would always get excited at the thought of testosterone. She must have been born with a libido that remained in overdrive!

As we close in on the last remembered location, we both crouched down and observed. Something was not right with this. How are we able to see their hideout? Jacob's father Robert would never be this careless. It looks as if it was a ceremony of ascension. This only happens when an Alpha was assuming his new place of duty. But they are rogues so that would not make much sense. Whatever it was it had to be serious because Meyonna and I spotted Jacob's angry father ripping into some fellow rogue's ass about something not being in a place while pointing at a now limp Jacob tied to a huge oak tree. We need a diversion and we needed it quick! Just as we were about to grab a closer view, we heard something or someone nearing our position. This cannot be good. We slowly turn in unison prepared to fight off whatever, but it was not all that we expected it to be.

"It is a got damn BEAR!" I hear Meyonna yell.

"Looks like we found our diversion," I say lunging at its throat as Meyonna struck at its hind legs causing him to lose its balance.

Just as the bear began to stand to its feet, I look at Meyonna and shout, "RUN!"

"Why are we running? The two of us could kill this thing with no problem," she says through our individual mind link.

"Trust me, I am aware of the damage we could have done, but I am not interested in sending our pack to war with the bear clan if I can avoid it. Besides, we need that bear to run directly into the rogue's camp long enough for us to free Jacob," I said running directly into the camp pretending to be a rogue in distress.

"You are a fucking genius!" Meyonna says giggling.

It was so much chaos transpiring that no one even noticed we did not belong. We stop directly in front of a nearly dead Jacob. He slowly lifted his head only to quickly have it fall once more. This made my heart hurt to see him this way. First things first...

"We need to find something to release these silver chains," I say looking around for anything that would aid us and setting him free.

"Joy! The ax!" Meyonna yelled turning in its direction.

Because we are in our wolf form it was quite difficult to lift the ax planted within the tree stalk. Without another thought, I shifted into my human form and grabbed the ax proceeding to set him free. When he realizes who set him free, he looked disgusted mixed with relief.

"You may want to put some clothes on," he says indicating that I am still butt-ass naked standing with my crotch in his face. "As sweet as this reunion is, we need to get the fuck out of dodge, Capisce?" Meyonna says sounding like she was straight out of a *Sopranos* episode.

I quickly shift as Jacob grabbed on tight to my fur as we proceeded to run deep into the forest, but not before being seen by what looked like Jacob's exasperated father. It felt as if we were running forever. I was exhausted from carrying an extra load. Meyonna mind linked nearly the entire pack making them aware of our situation and whereabouts. I could feel Jacob's grip loosening until he fell from my back causing me to stop in my tracks. I tried grabbing him back on. I look up to find Jacob's father preparing to lock in on my neck when another ferocious huge gray wolf took him down where he stood. Once I got a whiff of its scent, I immediately knew it was Malik. He saw me trying to lift Jacob with Meyonna stepping in to help. Malik shook his head and proceeded to kill everything in sight alongside at least a hundred of our pack warriors. Jacob's father was yet another disappearing act. How is this guy pulling this off?

Once I made it back to our pack grounds, I mind link our pack doctor for help. She and the rest of the care physicians were outside in no time. I immediately link Kylo with the news. He freaked out knowing I took it upon myself to rescue Jacob on my own. I tuned out his lecture and redirected my attention to a now hospitalized Jacob.

"Is he going to be okay?" I asked our pack doctor.

"He has had large doses of wolfsbane injected within his system and the silver chains draped over his body drained him a lot," our pack doctor Olivia says not sounding very hopeful.

"Do all that you can for him. Save his life!" I demand.

"What do you care?" I hear Jacob respond weakening.

"I have never stopped caring about you, Jacob! I just could not risk everyone finding out what really happened that day your father attacked us," I explain to him.

"You are still as selfish as I remember. For your information, I was locked in a dungeon for a week with little water or food because I tried to stop that attack. Nova was my friend and regardless of my love for you, I would have never let rogues harm her because of a stupid vendetta they had against a man that had no knowledge of being her father," he said grimacing at me with chords spewing out of him.

"Well, she was a threat. I saw how you looked at her and I could not have that. Could you really blame me? I loved you!" I yelled pacing close to him.

"You know what, you are sick in the head, Joy, and that is never going to change," Jacob said finally allowing the doctors to lay him back.

The doctors leave us to set up a more suitable space for Jacob.

"Maybe I should pay a little visit to your dying mate and let her know about the things we used to do and how you provoked a rogue attack on my best friend. I wonder how she would feel knowing that. I am curious to know how both of our packs would feel knowing this," I threatened him.

"So, let me get this straight, you rescued me only to pin your heinous crimes on me yet again and blackmail me by dragging my mate in here with your lies? Do what you see fits. Thank the Moon Goddess I have a witness this time that they all will believe. GET THE FUCK OUT OF HERE!" he says furiously.

I turn back to see my mother with anger pierced over her face followed by wide glowing eyes. Before I could allow one word to leave my lips, I saw darkness.

CHAPTER 33: WELCOME HOME, LUNA - PART 1

KYLO's POV

When Joy linked me about finding Jacob, I was happy the hunt was over until she told me she took it upon herself to save him. I could kill Malik for allowing her to do this alone, but evidently, he was unaware too. He was equally pissed. I could hear it in the shakiness in his voice of the fear of almost losing his mate to Jacob's father Robert. He reenacted the scene in his head a thousand times, which only made him angrier.

"Nova, they found Jacob and we need to let Alpha Azrael know as soon as possible. Can you link him?" I ask.

"They found Jacob. I have to get to Italia! Wait, is he alive? Please tell me that is alive. I cannot lose one of my best friends and my friend on the same day," she says finishing now pacing the floor.

She heads to run out of the door to check on Italia.

"About linking Alpha Azrael...," I remind her.

"Oh, I did that before I went on my tirade. He is making arrangements to accompany us back to Opal Moon now," she says smiling and waving goodbye. "Oh, I almost forgot, he needs to see you. It sounded really important. Okay, bye!" she says running back to give me a kiss and then back out of the door again.

I wonder what Alpha Azrael wants to discuss at this hour. Maybe it is about Nova and I breaking the news to him of her departure over the phone instead of in person. I throw on my black sweats, a plain white t-shirt, and my white Nikes and head out of the door to head to Alpha Azrael's office.

"Alpha Azrael, is it a good time?" I ask as I knock and enter into his office.

"Of course, Kylo, please sit, son. I know you are probably wondering why I called you here today," he says sitting back in his chair.

"Yes, Alpha, I am. Is this about Nova and I leaving so soon?" I said to him sitting up straight in my chair.

"Hold your horses, young Alpha, there is no threat here. Just by your actions, I know that you are willing to anything and everything you can to protect her, but what I do not understand is where you were the day she was attacked?" he asked leaning forward on his desk intertwining his fingers. and furrowing one eyebrow.

"All due respect, Alpha, you do not know neither me or Nova very well, so do not ever insinuate that I had anything to do with her disappearance. I would never hurt her. I love her more than my next breath. I have done nothing but grieve in her absence, even after our mate bond was hidden form each of us by a witch!" I yell at him now standing at my feet.

He laughs at my anger while letting out a growl, "Young Alpha, must I remind you of your place? Kylo, I was just testing you. Judging by your reaction and the tears that are now falling from your eyes, it confirms what I already knew, you love her more than life itself. I am desperate for answers at this point, Kylo. When you two broke the news of your quickly approaching departure, it set my wolf off. I just found out that I have a daughter and forgive me for not being comfortable with sending her back in the lion's den.," he says turning his back to me to look out at his pack grounds.

"I get it, Alpha Azrael, I really do, but what choice do I have? Nova was born to be my fated mate and the future Luna of Shadow Moon. I cannot hide her forever. Now that I know she has you all, she will have twice the protection and that makes me even more confident that she will be safe. I believe I am close to uncovering something that is about to shake my entire pack," I say hoping to reassure him.

"What do you suspect, exactly? Gamma Emit filled me in on what happened the day he instructed her to run. I expected her mother was the one behind her disappearance, but he mentioned that she did not follow behind her that day. Instead, the two of them got into a yelling match of her treatment of Nova. He was fed up with her very existence. So that rules her out unless she conspired," he says with placing a hand on his chin falling in deep thought.

"I am almost certain her mother was behind this with some help from her brother, sister, and my cousin Neko. I cannot confirm it, and this makes things difficult. I have had them watched them closely these past few weeks. This has been so hard for me. The day my mate disappeared I was in my father's office discussing business when the overwhelming sensation of suffocation filled my lungs. I was left paralyzed even when I heard her distress call over our mate mind link. She told me Emit instructed her to run and I would know where to find her, but the next thing I know is I am fighting to breathe, and then everything had gone dark," I confessed to him sitting down with my head buried in my hands.

I was embarrassed that I could not protect my mate. The one I loved, then one I was born to protect. There is no way possible that we can move forward knowing the threat that continues to lay ahead for Nova.

"Our pups will not be safe in our pack until we get rid of them all," Jax interrupts as usual.

"Wait, you suspect her brother and your best friend are complicit in all of this? Is he not your chosen Beta?" he asks anxiously awaiting my answer.

"I cannot confirm or deny his involvement, but I see that it is revealing itself. The more Nova remembers about that day the better," I finish.

"I will be fucking KILL him!" I hear a voice say that did not sound like either of us.

It was her twin Xavier. He heard the whole conversation.

"Whoa, superhero! I will gladly take that off your plate for he is my problem once I confirm it. It would be my pleasure," I say getting angry at the thought of having to kill my best friend for hurting my mate.

"Unless your best friend can give you some pussy and bare our pups, he is a non-factor to us at this point," Jax interjects like his rude self, but he was right!

"Well, you know where we will be once you get to the bottom of it. We have something that would help you," Xavier finishes.

"What would that be?" I ask curiously but honestly desperate to have the help I can get.

"We will be sending a few of our best warrior to imbed with your pack as spies. Wolves talk and I know it will not be hard for these three to fit in with the she-wolves. They are interchangeable if you want to call it that," Xavier adds.

"Interchangeable?" I ask anticipating the reveal.

I watch as he links someone to meet us in his father's office. I notice Alpha Azrael's silence and may I day it is scarier to have him quiet than handing you your ass. He is contemplating something, but I cannot read him. My thoughts are cut short when we hear a knock at the door.

"ENTER!" Xavier shouts.

There they were, triplets!

"Key, meet Apollo, Artemis, and Zeus. Yes, they are all named after Greek Gods and they are more than happy to assist. It was their idea, in fact," Xavier says shrugging his shoulders.

"I cannot thank you enough, bro," I said shaking his hand.

Xavier was not lying; you really could not tell them apart from other than their choice in a haircut. I could also see why he would say they would be popular among the she-wolves. They are unmated seventeen years old, six feet tall, muscular, deep caramel-skinned, gray-eyed, chiseled jaw line, black hair, earthly Gods. I shake my head at the thought of the reactions I know my unmated she-wolves will have. This is going to be really interesting. I am knocked out of my thoughts by a panicking Nova.

"SHE IS GONE! My mother is gone!" she kept repeating.

"What do you mean Naomi is gone?" I ask to have her repeat it to ensure I was hearing her correctly.

I felt my whole body heat up at the anger that was beginning to build within me. I let out a boisterous growl before filling a now full room of staring eyes of what Nova just told me over our link. Before I had the opportunity, Alpha Azrael and Xavier were already headed out of the door behind me, followed by the triplets.

CHAPTER 34: WELCOME HOME, LUNA - PART 2

NOVA-STAR's POV

SHE IS GONE! I cannot believe she stabbed Doctor Cecelia to get away. I am glad that Cecelia is healing, but if I would not have found her with the amount of blood she was losing, she may not have been able to heal quickly enough. Cecelia said that she felt bad because she suspected Naomi had been pretending to be sedated even after her wounds were basically healed. She went on to tell us that she feared Naomi would track Victoria down and hurt her because of the irreversible scars to her face Victoria gave her with the silver infused scalpel she used. Silver can kill a werewolf and cause permanent danger with the right dose and exposure.

"She was afraid that you all were planning to kill her," Cecelia said while changing her bandages.

"I have already dispersed our warriors to get hot on her trail," Alpha Azrael says turning to head out of the room in a rage. "FIND HER!" he yelled.

"Babe, I am ready to go home. Italia will be traveling with us to Shadow Moon. We all tried to convince her that she is far too weak, but she feels that being near her mate will help strengthen them both and I think she may be right," I tell Kylo before he can object.

"Okay, babe, whatever you need me to do," he says without hesitation.

"I am packed and ready to go. Chloe and I are heading to grab Italia a few things for her stay at Shadow Moon," I say heading out of the door followed by Chloe.

"Word on the street is you and Kylo were caught getting nasty by Gamma Wyatt in the RAIN!" Chloe says placing emphasis on RAIN.

"Really, how does everybody know about this?" I asked curious to know how even my father and brother know of my dealings with my mate.

"Girl, please, do not be embarrassed. That shit sounds sexy as hell, but you have to be careful not to get caught in the moment like that!" she says lustfully.

"Do not get me started on you and Xavier! I did not realize that it was possible for someone to have you ready to screw Jesus Christ. How many times have I walked on you plastered against the wall, AFTER you tell me to enter?" I ask her freaky ass.

"It is just something about getting caught, I guess. Do as I say not as I say, young lady," she says shrugging her shoulders and rolling her eyes.

I cannot help but laugh at her.

"So, how was it?" she asks anticipating my response.

"Which time?" I respond with a smirk on my face. "That is my girl! Don't mess around and end up with a pup before me," she finishes as we enter Italia's home.

We are packed and ready to return to the place I once called home. Kylo and I decided that he should make the announcement about my Luna status tomorrow morning right after breakfast and everyone is rested. Once the three blacked-out Denalis pulled up, we were more than ready to go. I said my goodbyes to both Xavier and Chloe promising that I would visit once my life has become somewhat back to normal. We were accompanied by the triplets running in their wolf form on our entire journey home. A tired Italia leaned on my shoulder for most of the car ride to Shadow Moon. Once we were back on our pack grounds, I was quickly reminded of its beauty. We were greeted by hundreds of our pack members. It felt good to be home until I laid eyes on Neko. I could not shake the feeling I had of not trusting him. He immediately disappeared within the crowd. I had an extremely uncomfortable feeling come over me when I caught Neko's deep gaze locked on me. I shook it off and decided to head in and take a warm bath to prepare myself for Kylo's abrupt decision to announce me as his Luna tonight over a formal dinner.

I could not get upset with his level of excitement to finally let the entire pack know that their Luna has been found. Many have suspicions of me being Kylo's fated mate, but they could never confirm it. After he marked me, someone tried to kill me and failed at it. Kylo and I both agreed that waiting a little longer to publicize the Gamma as the new Beta had to wait until we confirm our own suspicions of Malik. Our current Beta and his father Malachi have expressed his concern with appointing Malik as Beta. Is not that he is not capable, but untrustworthy.

"Babe, I am heading to take a bath," I say to Kylo through our link attempting to make it pass the cheering crowd.

"Can I join you?" he asks lustfully.

"I am pretty sure the pack would like to know that their Luna can walk," I say smiling and waving him off.

"What do you mean, I did not say I was going to carry you. That would totally ruin the big reveal," Kylo says giving me a weird look.

"That went completely over your head, my love. I just know the punishment you bring when you drill into me. As much as I enjoy you getting lost in my field of roses, I would like to be able to walk tonight," I tell him through our link as I open the door to my old room. "It is empty," I say before heading to turn around and close the door. I am hit with his intoxicating scent.

"I had your things moved to OUR room already," he says grabbing me tightly in a bear hug.

"OUR room? You sure your mother will be okay with me moving into your room this soon?" I ask searching his eyes for the truth.

"My mother actually gave me the idea because I figured they would say it too soon. I am fairly sure she is ready for us to give her some grand-pups!" he said as his arousal has become evident to me as I felt his bulge through his pants.

"Kylo, I need to focus, and this, mister, is a distraction, a BIG DISTRACTION!" I say pleading to him to fix himself.

"You know you can have me anytime you want. It is just something about you, Nova. I just cannot get enough of you," he says burying his head in my neck, licking, and sucking around the place he marked me as we enter OUR room.

"I promise I will make it up to you after the ceremony, babe, I do not even have a thing to wear," I say to a now undressing Kylo.

"That has already been taken care of. So do not worry your pretty little head. The only thing that requires your attention at this moment is screaming to jump out of my pants. Do you think you could help me with this?" he says in the sexiest tone, making me flood a river between my thighs and all over his bed sheets. "Oh, baby, I could never get tired of the smell of your arousal. I can help you out with that," he says inching closer toward me.

"Oh, yeah, how are you going to do that, exactly?" I ask teasing him as I lay back on my elbows.

"Do you need a demonstration?" he asks already knowing the answer.

"Only if you promise to make me scream, Daddy," I add now letting him gently removed my black lace panties that are easily exposed from under my navy blue sleeveless sundress.

"I cannot make promises that I will not have to carry you tonight," he says sneakily.

"Why is that, Mr. Kylo Gabriel Stone?" I ask getting turned on at the known response.

"Because I am about to fuck you onto another planet," he says roughly grabbing my thighs to pull me toward him allowing him to slip his tongue within my sweet flower.

Kylo begins to gently use his fingers to slide up, down, and forth across my clitoris and my clitoral hood. I found myself grinding my pelvis within the air. He used his first two fingers to create a peace sign around it and begin to gently tug up and down while touching my labia in the process and sliding two fingers from his free hand within me. I swear I was about to orbit this planet like he indicated. What was he doing to me? He continued this using very minimal movement. Right before I could release, he gently pinches my clitoris causing me to explode all over his hand he was still using to massage my insides. Kylo buried his face and tasted all of me as my legs begin to tremble. He came up for air and begin sucking and massaging my free breast making me moan uncontrollably. He reached up to plant a long passionate kiss on me. His kissing taste so good that I devoured his entire mouth. I was overcome with arousal. I yanked him closer to me as I swung my leg around his right side allowing me to straddle him.

"You're holding back on me, baby," I say to him indicating that I wanted the dick and I am not willing to wait.

"You must be patient, I am not done teasing you yet," he whispers in my ear.

He yanks me from his lap and pushes me onto the bed on my stomach. The feeling of his tongue buried between my ass cheeks sent a sensation of curiosity mixed with pleasure filled me from top to bottom.

"Stop playing and give it to me NOW!" I beg him.

"Not yet, baby," he says lifting his head up for air.

This was my only change to get him. I flipped over and wrapped my legs around his now naked waist and jolted him toward me.

"NOW!" I demand.

"Calm down, love, your eyes are glowing and shit. Do not sick Amethyst on me or I will be forced to release Jax and we all know what his intentions are," he says puling my thigh toward him preparing to insert himself.

"Oh, you feel so damn good, baby," I heard Kylo whisper in my ear.

He took long deep slow strokes in and out of me as he massaged around my exit of my ass. I felt Amethyst surfacing.

"Calm down, girl, this is just too damn good to share. I will let you out to play with Jax tonight, I promise," I said through our personal link.

She seemed happy with my reasoning, so she decided to let me enjoy OUR mate as she took a backseat like I had once before for her.

Kylo rolled me over so that I was straddling him once again and I was ready. I became more aroused at the feeling of him filling me with his girth and length touching my cervix shooting pain and pleasure throughout my entire body. I begin to rock my hips back and forth in a grinding motion until I felt I had gotten everything I could out of him in the position. Hearing his moans motivated me to go into overdrive, now sliding up and down on my man candy quickly switching into my reverse cowgirl position dancing around the tip of his dick and followed by slamming down on his shaft allowing him to watch the brutal slaps my ass delivered to his abdomen. Kylo grabbed my hips so tight I could see the bruises becoming visible. This encouraging. I can feel him swelling within me as I am just finding my rhythm. I reach down and gently massage his balls as I cup my left breast in my hand. I feel his build up on the rise. Before I made him explode, he flipped me damn near on my neck with my naked ass in the air as he rammed me from the back releasing his soul into my body. We both collapse after what just happened.

This man did not have me moaning, he had me screaming, screaming his name that is! I am not so sure we did not just reveal ourselves to the pack. Kylo reassured me that his walls were soundproof.

We lay there for a while and end up falling asleep only to end up being woken up by Gamma Xander.

"You all are going to be late for your own dinner! I have Nova's dress that has been hanging outside of your door for about three hours!" he yells laughing through the door.

I grab the sheets to cover myself in preparation of Kylo opening the door to grab my dress. He opens the door to a smiling Xander.

"What are you smiling at, guy?" Kylo asks.

"Ky, if you would have saw the look on that young omega's face when she ran down saying,' I think they are busy trying to make pups,' it was hilarious!" Xander says while leaning over barely catching his breath in between laughs. "Sorry, Luna, for my rudeness, welcome home!" he waves.

"MINE!" I hear Jax growl.

Xander throws his hands up in surrender and backs away still laughing as he replays the young omega's embarrassment. I could tell he and I would be great friends because he was super goofy!

I think I may have underestimated just how fancy this dinner was going to be. After I see my dress, I know I had to do something special with my hair. As I stare into the mirror, I find Kylo mind linking someone, probably Xander goofy behind again. After we hopped in the shower and cleaned ourselves up, Kylo gifted me with the most beautiful white gold moon pendant and darted out of the room to greet the pack. Before I could ask if he was returning to escort me, he was already halfway out of the door.

"That is already taken care of, babe!"

I let it go and trusted that he had thought of everything, almost everything. What on earth am I supposed to do to my hair that could actually complement this gorgeous white gold sequence form-fitting ballgown? I was absolutely with the deep gold trim around the mid-section just enough to make it pop. He even had the right show size. My golden three-inch heels gave the dress just the right amount of POP! It revealed my bare chest while cuffing my breast enough to support them.

"I can help with that," I hear her sweet voice say.

"WILLOW! What are you doing here?" I ask jumping up tackling her in a bone-crushing hug.

"You think I would miss my best friend's big announcement? I am so happy the Moon Goddess has blessed you with life, Nova," Willow said while her tears freely rummage her face.

"Please let us not cry but enjoy the time we have left on this earth to spend with each other," I smile trying to lighten the mood.

"Since when are you the wise one, you are usually the ball of tears?" she says wiping her eyes giggling.

"Honestly, I am not too sure how many tears I have left to cry. I am so happy with Kylo, but I have this uneasy feeling being back here," I tell her hoping she could offer me some advice.

"No-No, that is normal. A lot of bad things happened to you here that made you feel unsafe and unprotected, but Kylo and Jax would NEVER allow anyone to hurt you again."

"I miss you so much, Willow! By the way, I go by Star now," I joke with her.

"I love that name, but you will always be my No-No!" she said pulling me into her embrace.

We heard a knock at the door and discovered it was Willow's mom Elena on the other side. She nearly crushed me she hugged me so tight. I was so happy to see two of the people that had always looked after me and convinced me to seek help for my bad cutting habits. If it were not for them, I would have never began training to channel my anger. I owe them my life!

"Now let us get started on this hair and make-up. We do not have much time," Elena says beginning to brush through my long locks.

They already both dressed in their beautiful dinner gowns and hair and make-up was flawless. I listen to them giggle about some of the silly things that I have missed.

"Meyonna was prepared to strangle Melody because she was convinced that her and Kylo were now mated," Willow said.

"Your eyes are glowing!" Elena says staring at me.

"Sorry, I guess Amethyst and I both are territorial when it comes to our mate," I say unaffected.

We all laugh and prepare to leave. Elena hooked me up. I had a natural make-upbeat and my hair was pinned up to expose my mark and my tasteful tattoo. She let two spiral curls fall to each side of my face. They both snapped to at the same time and in unison said, "They are ready for you."

I felt out of place does not begin escorted by Kylo, but I was happy that I had these two lovely ladies on my side.

As I enter the formal dining room, I hear Kylo announce, "And there she is, my perfect princess that will one day be your queen."

Every wolf in the room flashes me a small smile followed by bowing of their heads. I am led to the stage where eyes are all on me and then followed by a lot of applause. You could hear "She is so beautiful," "Star is badass," and a lot of other compliments that had me filled with butterflies. Kylo pulled me into a long passionate kiss causing the crowd to Aww out loud, make cat calls, and whistle at us.

"I will never forget this night, babe!" I say once we released each other for air.

"I love you too, Star!" he says with a huge smile on his face.

"Why is everyone referring to me as Star?" I ask.

"Because I know this place represent a lot of pain for you along with everyone dismissing the girl named 'NOVA' even without knowing her. Star represents a time where you were happy, and you discovered parts of you that were a mystery. You found home with your newly found family. I could not bring them here permanently, but I can gift you with a piece of the home you left behind," he finishes handing me an envelope.

"How did you do this?" I ask.

"Let's just say, I know a guy," Kylo says right as I pulled him in and before I realized what was happening, I felt Amethyst locked in on his neck marking him in front of the entire crowd.

Kylo's eyes immediately filled with lust followed by the huge bulge in his pants I had to cover with my clutch. It was Jax trying to reach his mate Amethyst.

"Hold on, slugger! I do not need all these horny she-wolves checking out my man's junk. I am not in a murdering mood tonight, okay?" I whisper in his ear causing his eyes to revert back deep ocean blue.

The rest of the evening was filled with conversations and drinks. I did notice I did not run into my sister Melody. I was told she had been in a lot of pain and not feeling well after she returned to Shadow Moon. At least I can keep her at bay until I figured out how to expose Malik and Neko. I did get whiff of the pack slut Meyonna before she came in my view.

"You know he when he is done with you, he will come crawling back to me!" she hisses at me.

"Meyonna, I am your future Luna. Therefore, I have absolutely no patience or time to deal with dick hungry whores that are trying to claw their way to the top. I was BORN fated to him and you were just a sexual placeholder until I came of age," I snap at her.

"Call it what you want, I experienced his gifts first and I have tasted every bit of him. He is too good for you and he will soon come to his senses and run back to this good pussy. I have no desire to be his wifey, but his Luna is something special," Meyonna whispers in my ear.

"Are you proud that you are fiending behind a man and wolf that will never love you back? You say you have no desire to be his wifey, as if you ever had the option. The way them titties sag milk done gone bad, sweetie, I promise you he is not copping. The whole pack knows that you are free game! I really do not care about who he has had sex with. You may belong to everybody, but I am who the hell that sex God belongs to. So, let me make some shit clear, you come near my mate again, I will fucking DESTROY you!" I say bumping into her causing her nasty ass to bellow over.

As I walk toward me and KYLO's seat at the head table, a swollen-eyed Melody blocks my path.

CHAPTER 35: WELL PLAYED

NEKO's POV

As I hype myself up for tonight, I throw on my all-black athletic cut Armani suit with my clean-ass black Stacey Adams. I am more than ready to end the night with a bang, literally! Thanks to Naomi, Melody and I could get our guy and our gal. Naomi assures us that this was a foolproof plan. We shall see tonight. The plan was sudden, given the fact that Naomi escaped from Opal Moon's pack hospital a day ago and no one heard from her since. She is blocked all attempts of others' mind linking her except me and Melody. She did not trust that Malik would not turn on her behind his mate and his friendship with Kylo. We helped her hideout at the Four Seasons Hotel downtown. Melody and I were able to gather some of her things to help her settle in until she can return.

Naomi expresses her need to tie up loose ends. We already knew she was referring to both Victoria and Malachi. She planned to kill Victoria and attempt to mend her marriage with Beta Malachi so she could once more assume the position of Beta Female. With Victoria out of the way, she would not be challenged for it. Word on the street is Victoria lawfully challenged Naomi for her rightful mate. Werewolf law states you must honor this if you and your mate are mismatched. Beta Malachi did not object. He has made it clear that he no longer desires Naomi as his mate, but she is dead set on it. Either he will come around or she will END him too.

When we laid eyes on the noticeable scars Victoria left on Naomi from the attack in the hospital with her silver infused scalpel, it made Melody break down. Wolves are most times permanently damaged from silver and Victoria being the pack doctor for Opal Moon, she knew this better than any of us.

Melody wasted no time to help set her mother's plan into motion when she asked for our assistance.

Melody could use the distraction because lately she looks worn down. Something was definitely up, but she was not ready to discuss it and I did not push. I suspect it has something to do with Kylo and Nova, Star, whatever the hell her name is today. That bitch was going to pay for embarrassing me. I am going to finish what I started all those years ago when her brother sold her virginity to me, but she did not follow through. She was a slave to me and the one thing I wanted from her, she denied me. I tried countless times, but the last time she kneed me in the balls and ran to Alpha Kade and Luna Leah's suite in a panic. She never told them what happened, but I figure I was too close to get caught this time. When I found out my favorite cousin Kylo laid claim to what was mine to begin with, that was the day he became my enemy. I am going to take him out after I fuck his mate into next week. Then I am going to make him watch me beat down her walls as I make her scream my name.

"Neko, do you really think this is going to work?" Melody asks.

"It better or that is her ass," I say referring to Naomi.

"You could not kill her even if you wanted to. Everyone knows what she is capable of," she says shrugging her shoulders.

"Let's get one thing straight, I am not afraid of your mother nor anyone else is this pack, you understand?" I say grabbing her chin in my hand roughly directing her attention to my face.

"You should be," is all she said before sinking her claws into the side of my cheek saying, "You ever touch me like that again, I will cut your dick off and feed it to the cats."

"My dick didn't use to offend you. As a matter of fact, you took better care of it better than most actually," I say reminding her of our time together.

"Trust me, I kick myself every day for being desperate enough to have slept with you willingly," she grimaced.

"I hear you!" I say dismissing her disrespectful comments.

I end our intense conversation there because I could seriously see myself kicking her in the throat right now.

By the time I made it downstairs and we were about an hour into the dinner, I quickly grabbed one of the young omegas that I tend to have sexual dealings with. I found out the seating arrangements of the leadership. She was able to tell me the time beverages and dinner plates would be served. A tired-looking Melody accompanied to me as we inconspicuously emptied the contents of the vial in each of their drinks. I may have given Star an extra boost. I do not want to take any chances given the special wolf she is. I watched tirelessly as she took sip after sip of her drink. I am glad I gave her an extra dose. It was not until her glass was empty did, she begin to feel the first wave of symptoms. She was agitated with my constant stares so she would shoot me a disgusted look throughout the night, but it never made me look away. All I could think about was how good it was going to feel to plunge deep within her. I planned to rummage and entangle myself with that delicious body of hers as she wrapped those long ass legs around my waist. I must have gotten a bit too excited given the fact that Melody ended up kicking me under the table darting her eyes at the bulge in my pants.

"Impressed?" I asked her to raise my eyebrows.

"Disgusted is more like it. Get your situation under control before Kylo discovers you staring at his mate and he rips you apart, LITERALLY!" she yells through our mind link.

"Agreed," I say trying to think about pigs in the mud, fat men, and a case of blue waffles in an attempt to calm my erection.

I was not crazy, Kylo would tear me apart before he even realized what he did, but the state he will be in tonight would make him vulnerable. Melody planned to have him shoot his pup in her temple tonight, even if it will be by force. It was coming together the moment I saw Star head toward the elevators trying not to look too inebriated. Always modest! She was my sweet angel that needed to be punished.

I inconspicuously slipped out using my werewolf speed up the stairs in order to catch her on the top floor. Alpha Kade, Luna Leah, Kylo, and Beta Malachi were entertaining a few of the elders so I knew I had time. When I made it to the top floor, I spot a wobbly Star barely making it down the halls. She pulled it together just enough to unlock the door and enter the room. I ran as fast as I could to catch the heavy mahogany wooden door. I hit her in the head with a hall vase and quickly grabbed her from behind and held my hand over the mouth so no one would hear her screams. Once the door shut, I hit her in the head with my bare hand and slammed her to the ground. I thought it was adorable the way she began to chant a prayer to the Moon Goddess.

"What did you do, Neko? I will END you!" she yelled through her drunken state.

"You will not, my dear, you ingested wolfsbane so mind linking or any other trick you have up your sleeve will not work," I tell her in between her attempts to reach Kylo through their mind link.

"Neko, I am not that same week as she-wolf you knew. I am warning you that if you touch me, this will be the last night you will take a clean breath," she threatened.

"This is why I have to teach you a lesson. Never will you threaten me, my little pet," I say reminding her of who has the upper hand here. "Now let's have some fun, my sweet angel," I say closing the distance between the two of us.

This is going to be fun....

NOVA's POV

As I watch Neko tower over me thinking he has won. I cannot help but to think of all the ways I want to watch him die.

BINGO! I smile internally while externally pretending to be helpless. Little does he know that the poor omega Olivia he tried to implicate to poison our drinks warned us both. She came to Kylo and I crying and afraid we would not believe her of what she needed to tell us. We assured her that we would conduct our due diligence based on whatever information she had for us. It was then she explained and showed us the vial Neko had given her the earlier part of the evening. This when we knew the time had come to punish Neko and Melody for their treacherous crimes. Olivia demonstrated no hesitation to play along. She was the one that led Neko to believe that he was successful. Right after our drinks were doused, Olivia swapped them out and replaced their now filled cups with the tampered ones. It was smooth that she was even able to pull it off. Unbeknownst to us, Neko had raped her along with a few other omegas whenever he felt like it. They never said anything because they hold the lowest rank within our pack and truly felt like no one would believe them. When she disclosed this to us, I declared my first act as future Luna would be to have both an open-door rule and support group for anyone that experiences abuse of any sort. I refuse for my pack's culture to be defined by such heinous crimes. I would later decide the punishment for those that caused their pain and those that planned to. I knew what it felt like to not have anyone believe anything you said and only to be victimized all over again.

"This behavior will never be tolerated in our pack!" Kylo yelled in his Alpha tone making Olivia take several steps backwards until she fell over.

"Olivia, Kylo is not upset with you. We want to thank you very much for saving our lives tonight and being brave enough to come forward. We want unity among our pack. We will not thrive off of hatred, evil deeds, and anyone suffering in silence," I say rubbing her back attempting to calm her.

Olivia pulls me into a quick hug and hung on for dear life as she sobbed in my shoulder. Kylo stepped forward to help pry her hands from me, but I give him the side-eye and wave him off.

"This is what she needs right now, my love. I wish someone would have given me hugs in my times of need. It was not until Willow and her family found me losing pools of blood near the forest that I knew what real love was if expressed properly," I express to him through our mate link.

I noticed the way his eyes filled with tears. I know it was his guilt from all those years ago standing by letting me be tortured. He was not present for most and I have no intention of sharing the grimy details with him either. It would only cause him to spiral and I know he would kill all that were complicit. He is my mate and I forgave him. He was forgiven before I knew he was my mate, but I would never forget. If I want to continue moving forward, Neko has got to suffer!

I hate him with everything in me. My nightmares are always filled with his sneaky smiling and looking at me as I sit through his episodes of torture. There are not enough ways of revenge that would repay him for all that he has done, but I will start with tonight as I witness his now unstable state.

KYLO's POV

As I allow Melody to guide me to her room as she assumes, I am inebriated, I cannot help but laugh to myself. I made sure to unlock the door as I allowed her to toss me on to the bed and begin to straddle me. Something was seriously wrong with this girl. For days she is in aching pain all over and the next she looks like a zombie. There can only be one reason, she has found her mate and he rejected her. It is the only thing that could explain her night terrors and her constant state of emptiness. She was emotionally dying inside. "Who was he?" I wondered to myself. That is not important right now. Just as Melody began to remove the sleeves from her dress to expose her breast, an angry Willow, and Italia lunge at her with so much power it shocked me.

"Right on time, ladies! I almost thought I would have had to pretend to enjoy the peep show over here," I say sounding disgusted, because I was. "The thought makes me want to vomit," I say as I watched them beat Melody senseless.

Before Willow and Italia snatched her body off of me, the look that flashed upon Melody's face when she discovered I was toying with her was priceless. I could tell the first wave of dizziness began setting in. She was unaware of Olivia's success at swapping her and Neko's glass to the tampered ones.

"We got it from here, Alpha! Go help Star!" they yelled as I was already sprinting out of the door alerting Star of my location.

I knew Star could handle herself and she has consistently communicating with me, Xavier, Xander, Wyatt, and the triplets through our mind link letting us know she was okay, but I was not about to take any more chances. After I felt a pain in the back of my head, I knew he struck her. It took all my willpower not to just say "Fuck this plan" and rip Melody apart in front of the entire pack and head to rescue my mate.

"You are an absolute idiot for allowing that son of a bitch around our mate," Jax interrupts per his usual self.

"First of all, you witnessed the way she begged me to let her have her revenge. I pleaded to let her know that I could not and would not risk losing her or him hurting her any further," I snap at him. "What? No words, Mr. Big Bad Wolf?" I say taunting Jax.

"You are a complete dumb ass, Kylo," Jax growls shutting the link between us.

I knew he was not entirely cut off because he could never risk not being there when I enter the room where Neko and Star were. Unfortunately, it had to be this way. We could not risk our pack knowing that we killed two pack members, even if it was to secure the life of their future Alpha and Luna. Olivia was scared shitless! She would not utter a word about this, and we knew that to be true.

I barge in the room only to find I was too late...

CHAPTER 36: HE IN MINE!

LEAH's POV

I cannot believe as I live and breathe that my daughter would be the cause of not just my heartache, but many others. Hell, a damn life! Gamma Nathan lost his life the day of the attack and she was completely fine with allowing Star, her supposed best friend at the time be blamed for what she conspired to make happen. She smelled me first, but the moment my daughter turned to see me as I listened to this revelation of her being the mastermind behind the attack that started the abuse to occur in my pack I was heated. My first reaction was to knock her the fuck out. I was not only hurt; I was afraid for my only daughter. Joy has no clue how the pack will ridicule and beg for her death. I cannot stand the thought of losing a child, my only daughter to top it off.

I step over Joy's limp body to get a closer position toward a now rambling and angry Jacob. He looked to have been all over the place in his mind. Jacob was all too willing to give me all the grimy details of what happened all those years ago.

"Joy was behind the attack on your pack four years ago. We used to meet up in a secluded wooded area in the forest. That is how she knew where to find me. When she revealed Nova's importance to Alpha Azrael, we did not know she was his daughter. Joy was hoping that I would get the rogues to abduct her, but I refused. She took it upon herself to fill in my father who had gotten rather close to the rogue king who was once a member of Alpha Azrael's pack before he was banished for treason. When I found out what they were planning, it was too late. I was locked in rogue king's main house dungeon. By the time I was released weeks later, I did all that I could to contact Joy and I never heard from her again. It broke my heart because I thought we loved each other, but in the end, she betrayed me," Jacob said finishing while looking over at my unconscious daughter.

"Star," I say to Jacob.

"Star?" he asked quizzically.

"Nova's name was legally changed to Star," I say to him before I head to lift Joy in a chair in the corner of the room. I shook her awake until her eyes popped wide open in shock. "What the hell were you thinking? She was your best friend. I certainly did not raise you to be a murderer or a traitor!" I yell at her causing her eyes to widen beyond what I thought they could.

"Wait, what?" she asked pretending to not understand what I am insinuating.

"Let me break this down for you, Gamma Nathan died that day. I almost lost your little brother Jake whom of which I was carrying in the womb, you and Star nearly died, and for what?" I asked searching her face for any sort of remorse.

"Um...," Joy said at a loss for words.

"Does Malik know?" I asked.

"No, Mother, I do not believe he knows everything, but today confirmed that he has had his suspicions," she finished.

"That son of a bitch!" Jacob growled.

"What the hell is wrong with you, Jacob?" I growl back causing him to submit to him because of my position as Luna.

"Malik! He set me up! For whatever reason, he believes that Joy and I are a thing. We were pups and I found my mate so I am unsure of why he would assume that. This whole time I assumed Jennifer and Amber acted alone. They must have conspired with Malik," Jacob said with an intense look on his face as if he had just discovered this huge mystery.

"Where's Italia now?" I asked.

"I will tell you once she is out of hearing distance," he says hinting toward Joy needing to exit the room.

"FINE! I feel like I am suffocating in here anyway," Joy says storming out.

"Do not take your trifling ass far. We are not done here. Do not say a word to anyone about what just happened," I say through our mind link.

"I know, I know," she replies.

"Italia said she had something really important to help No... Star, Willow, and the gang with," he says sounding suspicious.

"Get some rest, Jacob. Alpha Azrael wants you to be prepared to head back with him tomorrow night. I assume he has a lot of questions for you," I say walking out.

"Yes, Luna," I hear him say before lying back down to rest.

This day cannot get any worse, I think to myself. But I guess it could after being approached by Gamma Female Elena filling me in on what Kylo and Star were planning. This cannot possibly end well for those involved, but I have no plans to intervene.

MALIK's POV

When I saw Jacob back at Opal Moon pack, I was angry. I know that he will always hold a special place within Joy's heart. She was always mentioning him even after all these years. It did not take me long to spot these two freshly bleached-blonde Malibu Barbies that undoubtedly had to be siblings. I learned their names to be Jennifer and Amber. They looked like walking gossiper vending machines. I approached the two of them and pretended to be interested in having a conversation. I smelled their arousal before I let one word leave my lips. "This is going to be easy," I thought to myself. They told me all I needed to know about Jacob, his father Robert, and his new mate Italia. I was relieved he was mated to another, but that was not enough. As long as he was breathing, I would not rest well at night knowing the way MY mate felt about him. Once the attack happened, I ensured to lead Jacob right to his captives unbeknownst to him. As they piled upon him, I turned to head back to the pack grounds as if I had not witnessed Jacob's abduction. What can I say, I am possessive of what is MINE?

When Joy expressed her desire to find Jacob, I could not maintain my anger and in the end, I had to save her life. I am her fated mate and yet she acts as if he is in my mind. Everything backfired on me resulting in Joy not speaking to me. My life is in complete shambles and I have tried to clean my act up. I even tried to talk Neko out of his obsession with Star, but he was unmoved. I threatened him earlier and promised that I would end his life if he lays one finger on her. He keeps going on about how I sold her virginity to him. First off, that is sick! I said it as a joke because I would never violate ANY female in that way. I was a stupid kid that said and did dumb things, but that most certainly was not one of them. He clearly wanted me selling her virginity to him to be one of them, but as I said I would never.

Now that I know she is Kylo's fated mate I have no intention of nearing her not only as my Luna, my best friend's mate, but because she is my little sister. It will be a part of my duty to protect this pack's Luna. Not to mention I should have protected her through the years. Instead, I stood by and allowed Neko and others to torture her. I allowed others to tease her and ignore her very existence. My mother convinced me that it will make her stronger, but she was wrong. It slowly broke her emotionally over the years. She lost Joy as her best friend, blamed for a horrific accident that MY mate caused, and Melody was never at her disposal as her older sister. I know we messed up and I am not so sure if our relationship is even salvageable. The one thing I have to look forward to is my Beta induction ceremony that has yet to be announced. I have a bad feeling that plans may have changed. My father is so disappointed with me too, so honestly, I am not sure if he would be willing to pass anything over to me. I just have to tackle one thing at a time starting with my mate.

"Joy, how long are you going to ignore me?" I asked her through our mate link.

"Malik, I will ignore you long enough to get you to trust me," she says with an attitude.

"I have to speak to you on the way. We need to make it right with No... Star," I expressed to her.

"Oh, you suddenly grew a conscience after all these years. You must be afraid of what Kylo will do to you when he finds out all you have done to his mate," she says with no remorse.

"You would like me out of the way so you and Jacob can run off and raise my pup. Does that sound about right?" I ask her not really requiring an answer.

"Well, that is an idea, isn't it?" she says through a giggle.

"Do not fucking toy with me! You of all people should know what I would do behind my family. My pup will make into this world, but you will not survive birth if you betray me," I tell her sternly.

"I cannot believe you just threatened my life, Malik! I... I have no words. I will NEVER forgive you!" she says uncontrollably sobbing.

"FINE! You know where to find me when you realize I should be the one upset," I say cutting off the mate link between us.

I feel my heart physically breaking. My mate was afraid of me and wanted no dealings with my existence. I would never hurt her and never have I ever wanted to. She knew this but wanted no part of hearing me out. This cannot be happening. Joy was being overly dramatic if you ask me. I saved her life after she took dangerous matters into her own hands without warning to save an ex-boyfriend. How are we supposed to parent our now growing pup? She placed our pup in danger going after an old fling. We have not even told anyone the news yet. I love my mate, but I need her to consider the precious cargo she is carrying. I am at capacity with the bullshit. I was in no mood for dinner parties. I shot Kylo a text giving him an abbreviated version of what happened, and he enthusiastically encouraged me to not come and keep Joy locked in my room until she forgave me. It was almost creepy how happy he was I would not be in attendance, but he was right. I needed to make things right with Joy. I would speak with Kylo later.

ALPHA KADE's POV

"Mal, what are you going to do about this Victoria and Naomi situation? This is some complicated shit like a soap opera," I asked.

"Kade, I don't know, man. Victoria is my fated mate and Naomi has birthed my pups. How can I choose? I admittedly have always felt a strange pull towards Victoria, Naomi would always catch me in a daze staring at her when she would visit. Naomi made her cease her monthly visits by making up some lie I am sure. This was the first time in years I laid eyes on Victoria. I am torn because I feel she deserves a man who has not been tarnished by another woman. What would you do in my situation?" Malachi asked hoping he could offer some Alpha wisdom.

"I think you should give Victoria a chance when she wins the challenge against Naomi," I say without hesitation.

"What makes you so sure she will win?" Malachi asked him.

"Think about it, Mal, it will be a she-wolf fighting for HER mate that has been denied to her for nearly twenty years because of her sister having black magic at her disposal. She WILL win," I say confidently.

"You might be on to something, brother," Mal said as I made my way to the door.

"Oh, by the way, we found the remains of who we believe to be the witch, Kaza who caused all of this. Looks as if she was ripped apart by an angry, she-wolf," I said raising an eyebrow before he redirected his attention to reviewing our international business assets.

"Have a good night, Kade!" Mal said hinting at wanting no parts of it for tonight.

I had to focus on ensuring we had everything in place for the moves the kids were planning to make to catch Neko and his followers in the days to come.

"Do you think they are going to pull it off when the times come?" Malachi asked.

"I am more than positive that they will when the time is right," I answered continuing to turn page after page without even looking up.

I bid him farewell and proceed to my suite to clear my head from all the craziness that has transpired before the Luna announcement tonight. I am proud of the young woman Star has become and cannot wait time to watch the Luna she will be in the next few months.

VICTORIA's POV

It has been a few days since I approached the elders about formally challenging Naomi for my mate. After she was told of my request, apparently, she fled the pack hospital.

"Elder John, how can I fight for my rightful mate if my opponent is a deserter?" I ask.

"Vicky, this will be made right, I assure you," he says.

"It is pathetic that I have to even go through this. He is MINE!" I growl.

"I agree with you more than you know and if I had it my way, I would consult Beta Malachi and have him welcome you home. It is overdue that she has laid claim to the Beta Female role," says Elder Athena.

"Unfortunately, Malachi married Naomi, black magic or not. This complicates things for us because we must follow wolf law and that calls for a formal challenge request or both parties' agreement to denounce their marriage," says Elder John.

"Have you spoken to Beta Malachi, Vicky?" asked Elder Christopher as he enters the room.

"Yes, I have actually, and all of our conversations have been pleasant. He is torn in between two women and it is taking a toll on him. I can easily tell that he wants to be rid of Naomi, but their fake mate bond was taking his heart through so much turmoil," I finished noticing that all eyes were on me.

"We have eyes everywhere and our best bounty hunters are searching high and low for Naomi. We will find her," Elder Athena added.

It was not looking of feeling sorry for me but looks of hope. I knew having the Elders on my side would be to my benefit.

My wolf Celine was stirring in my head the entire day. She wanted our mate and she was willing to kill my sister in the process. We were both upset that we were unsuccessful during our first attempt. Since Naomi's disappearance, I have been looking over my shoulder. I have a feeling that she will not fight me fair and she could strike at any time. I am with my Uncle Ron's pack and they have been terrific! In the meantime, I volunteer at their pack's hospital. It could either be temporary or permanent, but we will not know until the outcome of my challenge with Naomi if she should ever resurface. I fully intend to end her miserable fucking life!

CHAPTER 37: CRIME AND PUNISHMENT

STAR's POV

Neko's dizziness started to kick in, but it did not stop him from pulling out his dick to flash me before he lunged toward me with it out fully intending to force it down my throat. The devil is a liar! I slid back just enough to give myself some space as he began to wrestle with the pullover shirt he wore underneath his suit.

"You ready for me ba...by?" he turned to say barely finishing his words when he realized that he was now sharing a room with a full-grown snow white she-wolf.

The look on his face was pure fear and then flashed to a smirk. I felt my blood boil as I wanted him dead NOW! Instead of him high tailing, he began to taunt me

"Oh, baby, don't be mad. Daddy just wanted to finish what we started all those years ago," Neko says smiling moving closer to our position.

Amethyst let out a growl. Neko really did believe that this was a game of cat and mouse. Well, I am a big-ass cat that is about to have her next filthy rat snack.

"You mean the night you snuck in my room and tried to rape me. You ripped my panties off and kept them as a souvenir just so you could hand them to me in the common area so everyone would believe I was your whore? Is that what you are referring to? Or the other four instances you tried and failed to have your away with me?" I ask sarcastically through mind link.

"Who's keeping track?" Neko says more like a statement as he inches closer and closer to us.

All I am thinking is that he is such an idiot and I plan to make him pay in the worst way. Today will be the beginning of his torture. Before he could say another word, Amethyst had his throat shaking him uncontrollably in her mouth. Kylo burst into the room with a look of shock plastered on his face.

"Do not kill him yet, Star! I have a certain type of punishment set aside for him. He hurt my mate, family or not, he will beg for death. Dying this fast would only be doing him a favor," Kylo finishes keeping his eye locked in on Neko.

Amethyst slams him into the wall and we hear countless bones break. I quickly shift back and grab some shorts and a t-shirt.

"I had no intention of killing him yet, babe. Death is too good for him," I say watching Neko's limp but now healing body lying against the wall.

"Agreed," Kylo finishes.

I watch and listen as Kylo communicates through the pack link. Within minutes, Willow, Italia, Xander, Wyatt, and the triplets barge through the door. I see a pretty savagely beaten Melody lift her bloodied head from their grasp only to see Neko lying unconscious across the room. I quickly close the distance between Melody and me.

"LOOK AT ME! I was your younger sister, yes, WAS! Instead of being there for me, you let me down. You may not have joined in on the physical abuse, but you sure as hell did not stop it! You are a pathetic excuse for a werewolf and you, and mother deserve each other. Malachi would rather die than to accept either of you after what you have done," I say right as place my hand on her heart.

"Wh…what are you doing?" Melody spits.

"Sweetie, I could rip your heart from your chest and not even give it a second thought, but I have a better idea. You see, I had the triplets do some digging to confirm what I already knew, my dear. I know about you finding your HUMAN mate and his rejection for you. You are slowly dying inside, and I feel it, right in there," I say pointing at her heart causing her to break down.

"I do not know what you are talking about!" she shouts.

"Let me be clear, you and this piece of shit are going to die by my hand," I growl in her face dousing it with every piece of saliva that left my mouth.

"You do not scare me! I hope Neko fucking raped the shit out of you. You will die! Mother will be sure to make that happen either way, you cheap whore! You will never be good enough for anyone because you are an abomination. Why do you not just fight me fairly? You are destined to lose against me every time. No matter what you change your name to, you will always be that same weak excuse for a she-wolf," she says throwing her head back laughing.

"Let her go," I tell the girls.

They obliged and threw Melody to the floor. I gave her an opportunity to stand up. I hear Kylo's growl and desperate desire to kill her. I raise my hand to him and smile. He nods back because he understands that this is my fight.

"You want to fight me?" I asked knowing she would attack.

"I should have killed you the day Gamma Nathan died. It should have been you!" she says lunging at me only to stop in her footsteps.

Before I realize what I had done, I was holding her beating heart in my hand through her ribcage. I look around at everyone is look of shock. I just stand there speechless for a second. Kylo makes his way over to pry my sister's heart from my hand as I watch her fall to the floor.

"I did not rip her heart out, but I did reach out and touch it. She will heal and I will kill her two times over. Right now, I need her to suffer behind silver bars and ache every time her fated mate makes love to someone else. When it seems their bond is weakening, I will bring the two of them together only to rip them apart again and start the vicious cycle all over again," I finish heading toward a fully alert Neko.

Given his current state of shock, I would say he witnessed the whole thing. Before I could close in on him, an angry Kylo nearly broke his neck after roundhouse kicking him in the head. He turns around eyeing us as he was starting to fume.

"I want them dead NOW!" he says.

"I know that is you, Jax, but remember they will suffer at our hand, okay?" I say to Jax in hopes of calming him from his abrupt actions.

253

"I promised this asshole Neko that tonight will be his last day of breathing and I intend to keep that promise," I say extending my claws over Neko's face as I receive pleasure from his screams.

"What did you have in mind, my love?" Kylo asks.

Over the next hour, I requested a particular audience to meet us in a secluded opening in the forest for what they believed to be a bonfire. Wood and brush were collected and stacked with a thick log perched in the middle. I needed something that would hold Neko's weight. As the triplets and Xander tied Neko to the stake, Kylo, the girls, and I awaited the presence of our expected audience consisting of Malik, Joy, Sloan, Melody, Olivia, and a few of my torturers. I needed them to witness what was about to transpire. When they all made it to where we were in the forest, you could hear a cricket piss of how quiet it was. They looked upon a savagely beaten Neko tied to the perched stake in horror. Kylo could not help himself from profusely beating Neko nearly to death. I pleaded to allow him to heal just enough to feel the wrath we had planned for him. We directed them all to move closer. As we confess Neko's sins they are all surprised at what they felt they were about to witness. No one said anything because no one and I mean no one wanted to experience a now shifted future Alpha Kylo's wrath. We explain to each and every one of them as to why they are here tonight. Pure fear is plastered on their face.

"We brought you all here to draw your attention to this worthless piece of shit tied to the stake," Zeus, one of the triplets says. "You will watch him burn in hell here on earth for his transgressions against your future Luna and her subordinates."

As I move toward the brush, I had sudden a feeling of release. I leaned down to light the flames and was taken back by how fast it grew. I could smell Neko's flesh burning as his screams filled the forest. Kylo gave the signal to one of the triplets, Artemis to cut Neko free from the stake. The others watched as we did this and could not wrap their minds around the events that just took place.

"We will not kill him. If we do, we are no better than any of you! He will be punished and live to tell the tale. Now he will be forced to wear his torched sins for as long as he shall live and he will not utter a word of this to anyone," I say pointing at Neko's melting skin.

The triplets prepare a gurney in preparation to carry Neko to the pack hospital where he will be castrated. Meaning, he will not be able to father any children so that no child shall carry the shame of Neko being their father nor shall any female be subjected to his volatile sexual behavior. In three days' time, he will be publicly banished and therefore declared a rogue. He is undeserving to serve in any position in a pack.

"JUST KILL ME, GOT DAMNIT!" Neko shouts to us all.

"I will not give you the satisfaction of killing you," I whisper in his ear.

"Oh, cousin, you should be thanking Star for sparing your life because I much rather rip off your dick and make you eat it," Kylo growls.

"You want to kill me; you are going to have to kill that motherfucker too! ," he yells barely raising a finger to point in the direction of Malik.

"And why would we kill Malik? He is my sister's mate and my Luna's eldest brother," Kylo says luring him into confession while exposing Malik in the process.

"Because we both tried to drown No... Star the day of her disappearance. It was all his fault! He was upset that she called their mother a whore. We caught her off guard and held her head underwater until she blacked out," Neko exclaims as he is on the verge of passing out.

"You are a lying sack of shit! I never tried to murder my own sister. I was just trying to scare her, but Neko took it upon himself to hold her head under the water. It was not until I was able to pull him away from her lifeless body that I realized what he had done. I was torn up about it, but I could not tell a soul because I would look guilty. I went back to grab her and escort her to the pack hospital, but she had vanished without a trace. I assumed the worst! I told my mother and it led to her killing that witch Kaza out of fear that people would begin to come closer to her secret of what she did to her younger sister Victoria and what she had done to your two's mate bond," Malik finishes right before Kylo attacks him.

I was frozen in place as I was witnessing my mate about to murder his best friend, my eldest brother, and his sister's mate. I hear Joy's faint screams trying to reason with her brother, but I knew it would not be enough to stop him. Her screams fell upon deaf ears.

"I am pregnant with his pup! Please do not kill my mate!" Joy says sobbing and falling to the ground.

Sadly, this does not stop Kylo from sinking his fangs into Malik's side. He fights back and as a born Beta he is stronger than most, but not a future Alpha. I feel my breathing increase, it was as if the Moon Goddess herself was telling me to stop it and there is another way. I tried calling out to Kylo through our mate link, but he blocked me. This was no longer Kylo, it was Jax! Right as he began to gouge Malik's eyes from their sockets I acted desperately.

"Amethyst, I need you!" I call to her as I shift into my midnight black wolf with blood orange eyes.

I did not realize that I was not my usual white wolf until I had gotten through to Kylo. I needed all the power I had while tapping into my Gemini Twin power. I would apologize to my brother Xavier later for tapping into our power without warning. I caused the earth to shake through my elemental power, which caused Jax to expose Kylo's beautiful blue eyes for a moment. He was again able to gain control of Jax and back away from Malik's bloodied body, but I fear we may have been too late. I watch as Joy falls to her knees grieving over her lost mate. I peer over to Kylo to check in on his mental state. I could see that he did not realize what he had done to his best friend and he is still processing it. This will eat away at him over time, even if it was all to avenge his mate. What had I done to him? He was against unnecessary violence, but I know he would go to the ends of the earth for those he cared about and I feel I took full advantage. I have to do this for him. I run over to Malik's savagely beaten body. I watch the slow rise and fall of his chest. I place my hands over his heart and channeled the energy from all around me as a small glow left my palms upon his chest. Once I felt depleted of my energy, Malik took a huge gasp and I collapsed at his side.

DARKNESS...

CHAPTER 38: SINS OF THE MOTHER AND FATHER – PART 1

KYLO's POV

I had an impulsive reaction after listening to Malik expose the reason behind Star's disappearance. She told me about the abuse the night of the ball. Maybe a combination of my already pent-up aggression and his confession of things I only suspected sent my temper into overdrive. Jax forced me to take a back seat into our subconscious as I soaked into an abyss. I was dragged from the pits of an oblivion by my frightened mate desperate to reach me. Whatever she did seized me and brought me back to her, but it was then I realized that I had already nearly killed Malik. He may not be either my best friend or Beta, but I would prefer a different punishment for him other than death at my hand.

"You killed him, your sick bastard!" Joy yells running over to her Malik's body.

I look over to see Star shifting back into human form grabbing a t-shirt to throw over her naked body. She quickly closed the distance between us and grabbed my face searching for a reaction and to verify Jax's obedience to stay put. She sensed my state of shock as I glanced down at what I had done. If the pack finds out what happened here tonight, that I killed who they suspect to be their Beta, I will most likely lose their trust and loyalty. This is the exact opposite of what I want my pack to represent. I am internally battling with myself before I realize my mate has thrown herself over Malik's body as she perfectly placed her hands over his heart and began to heal him. When Malik let out a loud gasp, I felt my heart pick up its natural rhythm. I was relieved for a second until I see my precious mate's body limp next to Malik's body.

"Star, babe, wake up! WAKE UP!" I loudly growl.

No response. I quickly lift her ice-cold body bridal style and took the quickest route to the pack's hospital. I realize the rest of the small audience was in tow behind me with Malik and a sobbing Joy. If she is not okay, I will finish what I started and face the consequences later.

NAOMI's POV

As I sit in the wood line just beyond our border masking my scent, I witnessed my son betray me as I knew he would. There is not one thing he would not do for both Joy and Kylo. He often times acted as if they are his biological family even before finding out Joy was his mate. He was drawn to them like a moth to a flame. I search the small audience until I saw my badly abused daughter with her arms shackled behind her back as she rested on her knees being forced to watch as they torture Neko. I heard when she called Malik a traitor and swore to his death by her hand. I listened to Nova, or should I say Star's little speech about not wanting to be any better than her supposed torturers. I was impressed until little speech. Her and Kylo do not want anyone to know what transpired here tonight but I plan to make sure the whole pack was aware of what the goodie two shoes and their future Alpha had done.

"Hey, dumbass, how did you get caught? It was a fool-proof plan!" I say through the mind link to Neko as he lay on the gurney.

"Somehow they found out what we had done. Judging by this boney-ass omega Olivia witnessing my near-death experience, she ratted us out. The bitch is DEAD on sight!" he exclaims.

"Quit making excuses and get the shit done and stop cowering behind your inability to perform simple tasks," I hiss at him because I am quickly getting annoyed with this conversation.

"It is easy for the bitch who gets to lounge in the background while others do all the work. Who is really the coward here, Naomi? This all started with your INABILITY to keep your fucking legs closed, may I remind you," he says boldly.

"Neko, I know I do not have to remind you who the hell you are dealing with, so I won't. Let us not forget your sick as infatuation with my daughters, yes, DAUGHTERS! And because one would not give it up, you decided to take it by force. You think I was not filled in about your little tantrums you directed toward her, huh? To think that you really believe I was oblivious to the whole thing truly shows me how much of a DING-DONG you really are! I have gotten back at you in more ways than one and you still do not know it yet," I say to him who is now barely hanging on.

"What the fuck are you talking about. Naomi?" Neko asks.

"Oh, that little omega that ran and told of your scheme, where do you think she got that advice from. huh? She did not know it was me, I made it seem like more of a whisper. I scare her shitless too! Her only option was to run her mouth. I needed to teach you a lesson."

"You nearly got your daughter killed with your childish-ass games," he growls at me.

"Melody was an innocent bystander and it is unfortunate that she is in this position," I say almost laughing.

"Why would you sabotage the only two people who have helped you?" he asks.

"I have loyalty to no one, just like you! Now that I have your attention, do you want my help or not?" I ask him already irritated.

"Why should I trust that you will get me out of this hell hole? I do not want to be a rogue!" he says almost sounding remorseful.

"Are you kidding me or are you really that fucking stupid? YOU ARE ALREADY A ROGUE! In three days' time they are public information banishing you while announcing your castration to the entire pack and you scream in pain shackled in silver shackles! It is already too late for you, ass hat!" I yell at him.

"How do I get out of this mess?" he asked.

"If you really want to blow it up, expose Malik for being complicit in Star's disappearance. That will rock the boat for sure," I say to him knowing this would cause a reaction out of the one of the two people he loves most in the world.

I listened as Neko followed my directions like the good pet he his. He may come in handy one of these days. Neko cut off our link as I watch pass out and him being carried to the pack hospital. I hate that he missed the show of Kylo killing Malik! Too bad, I really loved that kid, but he was getting in the way of my plan. They all were going to pay! I will start with Victoria. She will never see me coming....

JOY's POV

I cannot wrap my mind around the crazy events that took place tonight. I watched as my brother nearly murdered my mate who I love most in the world. To top of off, his sister and my ex-best friend watched as it happened. No one intervened in their tussle and that makes me angrier! Yeah, I messed up all those years ago, but I would not change a thing! It was better me than her.

"Joy, you are further complicating things for this family! How could you do this?" my mother asks.

"I guess I did not think all of this through. Now I am pregnant, and I do not know the fate Malik and I face," I respond breaking down into tears.

"Do not give me those crocodile tears, young lady. First off, why did you not tell me you were pregnant? Second, you are selfish and spoiled. You show absolutely no remorse for your actions and that makes this situation worse. My dear daughter, I love you, but I cannot help you if you are not willing to help yourself. I will speak with your father and ask him to consider leniency for you both for the child's sake because it would be unfortunate for him or her to have to pay for sins of its mother and father," my mother says reaching out to touch my cheek.

"Thanks so much, Mother! I will do better for you, Father, Malik, and our child! You will not regret it, I swear!" I say pulling my mother into my embrace.

CHAPTER 39: SINS OF THE MOTHER AND FATHER – PART 2

STAR's POV

I wake to the sound of the doctor telling everyone that I just need some rest along with plenty of fluid. I then realize that I have an IV flowing through my veins. It is refreshing to say the least.

"How are you feeling, babe?" Kylo asks as he runs his huge baby soft hands across my face.

"Better now that I see your face," I say smiling up at him.

"The doctor says that your healing power took a lot out of you, but you ultimately just require a bit of rest and you will fine," he says.

"That is great! We have so much to sort out. How are we going to keep them all quiet about what happened tonight?" I asked him.

"Do not worry, my father, mother, Beta Malachi, and Gamma Emit is taking care of that. They were all too happy to assist. They were really happy that we did not kill either of our pack members too," Kylo says looking down at his hands, obviously a bit ashamed of his actions.

"Hey, you were protecting what is yours. Anyone would have reacted the way you did, if not worse," I tell him in hopes he shakes his guilt.

"I am not ashamed of my actions, Star, I assure you," he says confidently.

"Then what is it?" I ask desperately awaiting his answer.

"I was frightened that I could not contain Jax! As I ready myself to become Alpha, I must learn to be patient, fair, and discerning. My wolf was out of line, but I know and respect why he did it. We are one in the same, but I am ready to move past it because we have a whole life ahead of us," he says as he shrugs his shoulders nonchalantly.

"That is right, my love, sometimes we have to experience conflicts in order to gain the wisdom that will come from them. Fall seven times and get up eight, right?" I asked him with a smirk planted on my face.

"You are absolutely right and now that I have my sexy-ass mate along my side, I would fall down a hundreds time just to get up a hundred and one times if it meant you would still be by my side," he says leaning over to give me a kiss.

"Forever, baby!" I say to him causing him to hop in my hospital stretcher just to snuggle up against me and dismissing everyone else.

I watched as he waved them out. They all said their goodbyes followed by a few giggles from the girls.

"So, Joy and Malik are expecting?" I asked Kylo.

"Apparently so," he says flipping over to look at the sky.

"What is your dad planning to do for both their punishments? I know it will not be a decision he can take lightly," I say pulling myself to rest my chin on Kylo's monstrous chest.

"I know! He has decided to consult the elders on this matter. No man should have to dictate a punishment for his pregnant daughter. I am scared for her, Star. I know what she did was all the way fucked up, but do not want them to kill her," he says sounding worried.

"I am certain neither of them will die but I cannot promise that they will not receive a punishment that is fitting for the crime," I say to him dryly.

"I guess we will just have to wait it out. In the meantime, Joy, Neko, Melody, and Malik will be placed on twenty-four-seven surveillance. While Joy sits in a cell, she will be provided with the appropriate prenatal care. Enough about them! I think you would agree that we have other things that are more important to discuss," Kylo says lifting his eyebrows.

"Oh, yeah, Mr. Stone? What would that be?" I ask.

"Well, your mate has some needs that you are just spectacular at fulfilling, but that is not exactly what I was referring to," he says realizing that he has already aroused me.

"Okay, then what?" I ask unsure.

"Your Luna ceremony! My mother cannot wait to get started with the planning, so I have to let you get your rest," he says teasing my clit under my gown with his fingers.

"I thought you said I needed my rest, Mr. Stone?" I ask raising one furrowed eyebrow.

"I did and you will. You can rest when you are dead, Mio Amore. Do not worry, I will do all the work," he says sliding down to engulf my sweet nectar in his mouth.

I tried to stop him; I really did. We were in the hospital, for goodness' sake! I am thinking this release of pleasure may just speed up my healing process. Do not judge me!

MALACHI's POV
There she was in all her glory sitting in the back seat of my smokey-grey Jeep parked in the pack's mansion garage. How did I not catch her scent before I entered the vehicle?

"Where have you been, Naomi, and how did you get in here unseen?" I ask her.

"What? Are you not happy to see me?" she asks poking her lip out like a child.

"Naomi, please put some clothes on and let's talk like adults," I tell her.

I felt a sting in my neck right before she hopped her naked ass across the seat and into my lap and began grinding her hips.

"What are you doing?" I ask her.

"I am taking what is mine," she says greedily.

"I cannot move, what did you stick me with Naomi? Why could I not catch your scent?" I ask plunging her with questions.

"Shhh, let take care of you. You are asking way too many questions. Mal, you should know more than anyone that when I am in the mood I am not for much talking," she responds sliding off my lap to undo my pants.

"Please, Naomi, do not do this," I plead with her.

"Oh, Mal, you know you want me to and judging by Mr. Stallion's current position, it tells me all I need to know," she says excitedly shoving my dick down her throat.

She had me speechless! My limbs were paralyzed except my manhood where she took long slow strokes up and down as she

263

massages my testicles. I felt her jaw muscles begin to contract around my shaft. When I began to tense, she slides her tongue around the tip of my penis to take in my pre-cum before she abruptly took my testicles in her mouth moving them around in her mouth.

"What is your point, Naomi? Do you think this will change anything? I cannot trust you and you lending me a head job will not change that," I plead with her again.

"You sure about that, Daddy?" she asks in between gulps of my shaft down her throat.

I give her one thing; she was always talented in this arena but her demonic ways overshadowed it all.

"Just stop demeaning yourself any further, Naomi. Even this is low for you," I say to her hoping to get her to finish.

"So, you do not want me, Mal? It is my weak little sister you desire, is it not? I promise that you will be mine when it is all said and done!" she yells at me completely stopping exercising her head power.

"Why do you not accept Victoria's challenge and let that decide the outcome of the whole ordeal?" I ask trying to get he me to turn herself in.

"I cannot accept the challenge of a she-wolf that will be dead by sundown, now can I?" she rhetorically asks.

"Naomi, NO! You should not hurt her. She has done nothing to deserve death," I say to her in hopes to have her change her mind.

"I actually have something better in mind," she says thrusting down on my dick and began to grind on me once more.

She tied a blindfold around the rims of my mouth. I did everything in my power to move my limbs when I was once more doused with, I am assuming is wolfsbane. It weakens the mind link and your ability to reach your wolf. I tried focusing on everything but was transpiring because I knew her end game.

"How about we make one of our famous home videos?" she asked leaning over to pull out her cell phone simultaneously hitting record.

"Yes, Daddy! Put a baby in me as you promised!" she yelled as she pleasured herself off my still erect penis.

I was helpless and she knew it. When I shot my warm sperm babies into her womb, I figured it would be the end. Naomi left my lap to lean back and prop her legs up in the passenger seat for about 30 minutes. I listened to her ramble on about how I was meant to be hers and the Moon Goddess made a mistake when she paired me with Victoria. I tuned half of it out as I was too busy trying to figure out how in the hell no one has come in the garage yet. This woman straddled me again and again for hours as she readjusted my seat to switch it up to make it seem real by whomever she decided to share these videos with. Naomi even had me butt fuck her a couple times. This crazy bitch was desperate! By the time she was through with me I must have had a healthy dose of wolfsbane and Viagra in my system. Before she left, she removed my mouth tie and shoved her toughest down my throat. I but down and locked on her lip until a tasted blood splatter into my mouth. It was not until she dug her claws in my chest over my heart that I released her. She slapped the piss out of me and began to throw her clothes back on. There was no need to mask her scent any longer because I had wallowed in her all afternoon and evening. She would smell like...ME. I could not move, and she left me with my dick out and splatters if dry cum on my thighs. I yelled as loud as I could for Kade and Emit knowing with their highly intensified wolf hearing they would hear me. Within forty seconds I was face to face with both Alpha Kade and Gamma Emit who had curious but disgusted looks on their face.

"Mal, you called us out here because your arm got tired from jacking off?" Kade said laughing.

"Yeah, man, this shit is not cool," Emit says turning his back.

"Na... Naomi," I say fatigued.

"Naomi? What, you were picturing her while you messily jacked off over your legs, man?" Kade says grimacing.

"You should have at least thought of Victoria while you did its man. I am out of here," Emit says.

"NO! Naomi was here! She was waiting for me in the truck. That fucking traitorous bitch assaulted me for hours and your assholes did not even notice I was missing for hours," I say angrily.

"She what?" Kade asks.

"Mal, man, I am sorry. I would not think she would stoop so low as to rape you in your own backyard," Emit says sincerely concerned.

"Man, can we not call it that?" I ask.

"Wow! I cannot believe what I am hearing or what I am seeing. How in the hell did she get past our patrols?" Kade wonders out loud.

"Kade, your best friend of over 23 years was just raped...I mean assaulted and that is what you are concerned about?" Emit asks with all seriousness.

"You are right, it just does not happen every day that a man is raped by his wife. Forgive me, old friend," Kade says rubbing his hands to the back of his head.

"So, do you plan to press charges?" they ask in unison before letting out a chuckle.

"Man, fuck you all. This is no laughing matter and I am not joking! She is trying to get pregnant and carry another one of my seeds. I cannot have her corrupt another soul that is undeserving of that. I just cannot!" I yell causing them to see the seriousness behind it.

"We have your back, this I promise," Kade says sternly.

"On my honor," Emit growls.

"Let us get you out of here and cleaned up, man," Kade says.

"Okay, that sounds good. This shirt is embarrassing! You two are to not mention this to anyone, including your mates," I say staring into their eyes searching for one once of betrayal.

"On our honor, no one else needs to know about this," they say in unison.

Kade dispersed some of his best trackers to see if they could get a lead on Naomi. There is nothing left to do but wait, but I could not help but to think how she did all of that for nothing.

"Does she know that you got a vasectomy fifteen to sixteen years ago?" Kade asked.

"No, she does not. It is crazy because she was the one who asked me to get one. I got it while she way away visiting her brother Alpha Antonio. Now that I think of it, he hates her, so she was most likely lying about that too. The timeline adds up around the time Star was conceived. Makes perfect sense!" I exclaim reaching a revelation.

"Yeah, oddly it really does!" Emit says.

"Why did you not tell her that before she took you on a six-hour sex-capade?" Kade asks.

"It did not dawn on me what her intentions were as far as trying to get impregnated until she said it aloud. I tried telling her fast ass that before she mounted me, but she placed a tie in my mouth," I say shrugging my shoulders.

After they carried me to the hospital, Kade had a few omegas prepare some dinner for us as we set around listing the many dilemmas we are faced with. We called on the elders to provide us wisdom with a few, especially the ones dealing with our children. To think, this all began over Naomi's transgressions. If she would not have had an affair there would not have been an outside child to take her anger out on, Joy would not have set her best friend up to be taken by rogues, and so much more could have been avoided. I thank the Moon Goddess for Star's existence, I really do. I just cannot get over Naomi's desperate actions to lock me down and secure her spot as Beta female of the me pack. I pray to the Moon Goddess for wisdom when handling this situation. This is such a delicate matter.

CHAPTER 40: BECOMING LUNA

KYLO's POV

A few months have passed since the Elders Counsel and parents along with a few of their constituents came to an agreement about Malik, Joy, Neko, Naomi, and Neko.

Neko was publicly declared a rogue after he was castrated. His looks to be an abomination given his current state. He is nearly unrecognizable. No one asked questions about his appearance. Before he left, the young Omega Olivia told us Neko threatened her life. By the time she made this evident, he was already gone in the wind and it was suspected he had help. My father told the patrol to kill him on sight because he would not be satisfied until he was no longer breathing. Neko's parents would be so disappointed if they were still living. It was hard for my parents because he was like their child and he was like a younger sibling to me. I would have thought he would be fed up with the schemes by now. We will not stand for threats against our pack members regardless of their titles.

As for Joy and Malik, because they are the son and daughter of the Alpha and Beta of the pack and expecting their only grandchild their punishments were carefully decided. They both were issued 50 lashes of wolfsbane-coated hits. Not many survive this. Joy's punishment was delayed due to her pregnancy, but it is written in wolf law that she will receive it three days after giving birth. Both were stripped of their titles and forced to move out of the pack's mansion and spend three months locked in a cell. They will earn their keep just like the rest of the pack. Because of the sins of the mother and father, their offspring shall not regain a title unless an heir is needed for either Alpha or Beta if one cannot he produced by the current Luna and Beta female. Their pup has Alpha and Beta blood running through its veins but still will not rightfully carry the title unless what is mentioned above. Malik thought this was fair, but Joy had a mental breakdown. They both were locked in a cell for three months. They were recently released in order to prepare everything before their pups' arrival. Joy was made to make a public apology to Star and the pack and explained what happened all those years ago. We watched as the crowd threw angry faces at her while others had some of pity and disbelief. Those are her burdens that she must carry. She has made attempts to speak to me, but I am just not there yet. Joy refuses to speak with Star after being humiliated in front of the pack. I remind her that this is her doing. I do not see her very often since they were kicked out of the pack mansion but heard they were all settled into their home. Malik has apologized to us every day but neither me nor Star are ready to engage with him. I pray to the Moon Goddess that we will one day because we would hate to harvest this much anger and it is passed to our pups. My parents are excited for their first grandchild to make into this world. They have gone overboard with baby gift purchases!

In other news, the mention of Naomi's name has Beta Malachi on the edge. Maybe the idea of two incredibly beautiful she-wolves is starting to get to him. Even with Naomi's permanent scars, she was still beautiful. Not my type! I like my women sweet with a touch of sassy, not flat-out power grabbing evil seductress. Because she failed to accept Victoria's challenge within two weeks of it being issued, the decision has been left completely up to Beta Malachi. It is clear that he desires Victoria even with their mate bond being broken by black magic thanks to Naomi. The Elders said if the two of them were around each other for some time, the bond could possibly be rebuilt naturally. Victoria moved to our pack's mansion after a few weeks of negotiating with Malachi. He has tried to convince her to move on because she deserves so much better than him. He feels she should never play second to her sister. That did not stop her from landing a room right next door to Malachi's room thanks to my parents. They just want him to be happy.

Victoria's life is still in danger because of Naomi but the patrols are on high alert and Victoria does not leave the premises. She is to be escorted everywhere until the time bring. Everyone already considers her our Beta female. They love her! She is obviously wearing Beta Malachi down because I heard him say that he was considering visiting the doctor to have his vasectomy reversed. They are slowly trying to figure it out, especially after the setback of Naomi's video of the two of them leaked to Victoria, of course.

Naomi tried her absolute best to inform the pack of what happened that night, but it backfired on her. The two pack members she engaged dragged her from her hiding place kicking and screaming before Neko jumped out and attacked the two of them along with Jacob's father Robert in tow. It is suspected that the three of them have dark magic within their grasp, masking their identity from the rest of the world. The order to kill all three on sight has been issued.

As for Melody, a threat to cypher her wolf from her existence is still in discussion. She will be forced to live her life as a human for as long as she shall live. We are waiting the final outcome of that decision to come in from the elders. It is an extremely dangerous ritual but the sincerely believe that this will give her a chance at a normal life. She will also be publicly banished in front of the pack. Her first punishment was also going to be 50 lashes of wolfsbane dipped hits but the Elders fear if they break her body down this way, the ritual to cypher her wolf would not work. She is to live among the humans and permanently banished from the pack premises l. If she is to return, she will be killed in sight.

This is just beginning of weeding out the bad eggs. The others that were in attendance to Neko's situation in the woods have been monitored closely by the triplets, who decided to join our pack permanently. We have Joey Alpha Azrael and Zavier updated with all happenings since they have a vested interest for Star's safety. Things are really looking up!

STAR's POV
It has been a few months now that all those complicit in wanting to cause me and other pack members' harm.

"Babe, have you seen my gold hoop earrings from the dresser?" I asked Kylo.

"No, I have not. Maybe you set them in your actual jewelry box," he says sarcastically.

"Oh, yeah, you are correct," I say grabbing them from their rightful place.

I throw on some jean shorts with my light-yellow tank, with some beautiful light-yellow sandals that have a golden feather that run vertically on each foot. I complemented it with my golden locket that Kylo gifted me when we were visiting Opal Moon pack about a week ago when we were escorting Jacob and Italia's home. I straightened my hair bone straight and flipped it over my shoulders to give myself one more looks over before we headed downstairs for breakfast. We were starving after the last three days!

"Why are you so nervous, my love?" Kylo asks burying his head in my neck.

"Because this is a big deal, Mr. Stone," I say to him pouting.

"Everyone knew you were in heat. It is normal among she-wolves. Why are you embarrassed? It was inevitable that this would happen," he says shrugging his shoulders.

"We do not even know for sure yet if everyone knew I was in heat. I was acting like a raging maniac. Maybe we should wait until we are certain that everyone was aware that my erotic behavior was caused by the heat, okay?" I ask hoping he would give in.

"We are going to be late. Are you done yet, woman?" Kylo screamed.

"Almost! I forgot to moisturize my feet! You do not want your mate out here with ashy planks, do you? Did not think so!" I respond to him.

"My breakfast better not be cold," Kylo says playfully but I know it had ninety-nine-percent truth behind it.

This man hated cold eggs, I swear! I swore by the microwave, but he calls it a crime to reheat eggs. I love this man! We made it downstairs as we see the first batch of eggs being served to Xander. Kylo runs over and snatches his untouched plate.

"Hey, man, I am starving!" Xander says angrily.

"Xan, have you been up for the last three days trying to trying to cool a horny she-wolf of her heat, were you?" Kylo asks looking him dead in the eye causing me to blush from embarrassment.

"Oh, man, I am sorry, I heard that shit was brutal but enjoyable for a male wolf," Xander says as he stands up to grab another plate.

"See, no one knew!" I yell at Kylo smacking his arm.

"Well, I am just glad you two have been working on me another grandbaby," Leah says with happy Alpha Kade standing next to her agreeing.

"Apparently everyone knew from what I hear!" Willow says as she headed toward the counter to grab a dish.

"WILLOW! You came back!" I yell running to greet her with a hug.

"Of course I did! Why would I miss...?" she says pausing in mid-sentence after being interrupted by one of the triplets Apollo.

"Why don't you two finish eating, and we will be out on the deck waiting for you once you are done?" Apollo says.

"Yes, what he said!" Willow says grabbing her food and scurrying out of the massive patio doors.

I look over to see Kylo linking someone as we sat in silence. All you heard was the clinking of our forms hit the plate. We felt severely dehydrated and malnourished after the last few days of satisfying my heat. I mean it got so bad that I would wake from a deep sleep on fire! I would harass Kylo during his work hours, wonder out on the training fields, and sneak in his vehicle all just to get my fix. I just could not get enough. After we would finish one sex round, it soothed me just long enough for me take a fifteen-minute nap then we had to start all over again. I held Kylo hostage in our room for the last three days. I know he was tired, and I wanted to give him a break, but he could not stand to see me suffer so he did the only thing he could and rock my whole world! It was both painful and pleasurable.

"I wonder what Willow was up to?" I rhetorically asked.

"What do you mean?" Kylo asks suspiciously.

"You guys are up to something, I can tell," I say peering into his soul.

"Babe, I have been pinned up by a horny maniac for the last three days. I have been depleted of all my electrolytes and any and all food. When would I have time to conspire with these people? Your heat has you seriously paranoid, woman," he says turning back to his food.

"Whatever! I am rarely ever wrong," I say angrily.

Kylo was silent for the rest of breakfast. He had kind of hurt my feelings a bit, but I did not have time to soak in my feelings. Luna Leah could not wait to discuss my future duties with me in detail. We are to take over our Alpha and Luna duties within a matter of months. Things have been so great! My inner circle has become more like my family. I feel so grateful to have Xander, the triplets, and Olivia! I just hate that Willow, Chloe, and Italia are not here with me. I was super excited to know that Willow and Italia bonded during their time here and are really great friends also. Chloe just loves everybody so when we all chat, it just feels right! I smile internally at the thought of this. I snap back to reality and notice a scary nervous Kylo.

"Babe, what is wrong with you? Are you okay?" I ask barely granted him an opportunity to answers.

"Yeah, I am fine. I was just thinking about grabbing another bagel and the hurt it could put on my eight-pack," he says running his massive hand over his abs.

"You are so conceited!" I yell out slapping his arm.

"Come on, let us go for a walk around the garden. It is such a beautiful day and we should not waste it," he says pulling me from the table pulling me up so that I am tiptoeing to lock his lips with mine.

"That would be great! Your mother wanted to meet in the garden later anyway. Two birds with one stone," I say ending our kiss.

We made our way out of the same patio doors the gang exited earlier. When I stepped to turn the corner, I saw a lot of familiar faces staring back at me. I turn toward Kylo to find out why was going on because they said nothing! I turned and almost jumped out of my body.

"Star Arabella Ryan, would you do me the honor of becoming my wife?" Kylo asked as tears filled his eyes.

"Are you crazy?" I asked as I watched him remain on his knee in shock.

"What do you mean? Is that a n...no?" he said stuttering.

"No, you are crazy to think that you would even have to ask! Of course, I will marry you! Can we do it tonight? Can we do it right now?" I asked incredibly excited.

"HELL YEAH!" Kylo said hopping up from his knee to place the ring on my finger and embrace me in what felt like a forever kiss that I never wanted to end.

Just as he placed me down on my feet, I launched about two pounds of vomit at the freshly bloomed yellow roses.

"We knew it!" I heard Leah and Elena say in unison.

"Sorry, guys, guess I ate much more than I should have, and the combination of nervousness did not help," I say partially embarrassed.

"I am willing to bet my life that you are pregnant, my dear," Leah says to me.

"Yeah, we have suspected for weeks now!" Elena says excitedly.

"But Star just came out of heat yesterday," Kylo says and it is pleasurably brutal.

"Exactly! Her hormones are going crazy because of the pregnancy. It multiplies the heat experience times three!" Leah says.

"There is no way I could be pre...," I say unable to finish my sentence as chunks of pineapple exit my mouth and nose.

We decide to take a visit to the pack hospital. Victoria was among the audience to witness my engagement and she assured me that I was pregnant but wanted to do a blood and urine test to confirm. Within a matter of moments my result confined my pregnancy. Apparently, I was three months along and I did not know because I assumed, I was skipping monthly visitor because of all the stress I was undergoing. I suspected but did not know if I wanted it to be true. Everyone was so excited to find out I was carrying a boy until the realized I was carrying two! Leah and Elena have already began planning both my baby shower, wedding, and Luna ceremony. How would I have ever guessed that "Becoming Luna" would feel this wonderful? I guess it is time for me to walk into my purpose with my head held high and my right-hand man by my side.

We understood that we would face many enemies, and we more than certain they would be brought to justice. We had no intentions on showing any mercy to either of them. I am happy beyond measure and I refuse to let anyone steal my joy. We shall stand to fight another day here in the Shadow Moon Pack and may the Moon Goddess bless my delivery.